Nella pulled ber  **pocket and** **an urge to inv** **and ensure ev** **there. But she**

After all, she was a cop. A cop on alert.

Still, when he insisted on preceding her inside, she felt a lot better. He locked the door behind them, then walked around, examining each room, even each closet and under the bed.

"Looks okay," he finally told her in the apartment's living room, near the door. Though she'd been checking, too, she let out a sigh of relief. "I'll head to my place now, but call me when you wake up in the morning."

So he could protect her again tomorrow, she figured.

She appreciated it.

She appreciated him.

And so, after assuring him she'd call, she walked up to him and put her arms around him, planning to give him a brief good-night kiss.

Only...it didn't turn out so brief. The feel of his hard body against hers. The relief that she remained safe and alive, at least for now.

* * *

If you're on Twitter, tell us what you think of Harlequin Romantic Suspense! #harlequinromsuspense

Dear Reader,

Her Undercover Refuge is the first in my Shelter of Secrets series, a spin-off from my K-9 Ranch Rescue series for Harlequin Romantic Suspense. It, too, takes place in the town of Chance, California. And it, too, involves—what else?—dogs. And also people.

In it, the new Chance Animal Shelter provides a second chance for the many animals its management and staff save from their prior difficult lives. But even more critical, it also provides the potential of a new life for many of those staff members. The shelter's undercover, primary purpose is to provide new identities and protective custody for people threatened with domestic abuse, kidnapping or worse.

In *Her Undercover Refuge*, after a particularly stressful operation, former police officer Nella Bresdall also needs a new direction for her life. Helping vulnerable people and pets sounds ideal to her. And the fact that Scott Sherridan, the special shelter's officer in charge, is handsome, sexy and dedicated to helping people and animals may be irrelevant, but it certainly doesn't hurt her inclination to work there forever.

Until she starts receiving threats...

I hope you enjoy *Her Undercover Refuge*. Please come visit me at my website, lindaojohnston.com, and at my weekly blog, killerhobbies.blogspot.com. And, yes, I'm on Facebook and Writerspace, too.

Linda O. Johnston

HER UNDERCOVER REFUGE

Linda O. Johnston

If you purchased this book without a cover you should be aware
that this book is stolen property. It was reported as "unsold and
destroyed" to the publisher, and neither the author nor the
publisher has received any payment for this "stripped book."

HARLEQUIN®
ROMANTIC SUSPENSE™

Recycling programs
for this product may
not exist in your area.

ISBN-13: 978-1-335-75936-8

Her Undercover Refuge

Copyright © 2021 by Linda O. Johnston

All rights reserved. No part of this book may be used or reproduced in
any manner whatsoever without written permission except in the case of
brief quotations embodied in critical articles and reviews.

This is a work of fiction. Names, characters, places and incidents
are either the product of the author's imagination or are used fictitiously.
Any resemblance to actual persons, living or dead, businesses,
companies, events or locales is entirely coincidental.

This edition published by arrangement with Harlequin Books S.A.

For questions and comments about the quality of this book,
please contact us at CustomerService@Harlequin.com.

Harlequin Enterprises ULC
22 Adelaide St. West, 40th Floor
Toronto, Ontario M5H 4E3, Canada
www.Harlequin.com

Printed in U.S.A.

Linda O. Johnston loves to write. While honing her writing skills, she worked in advertising and public relations, then became a lawyer...and enjoyed writing contracts. Linda's first published fiction appeared in *Ellery Queen's Mystery Magazine* and won a Robert L. Fish Memorial Award for Best First Mystery Short Story of the Year. Linda now spends most of her time creating memorable tales of paranormal romance, romantic suspense and mystery. Visit her on the web at www.lindaojohnston.com.

Books by Linda O. Johnston

Harlequin Romantic Suspense

Shelter of Secrets
Her Undercover Refuge

The Coltons of Mustang Valley
Colton First Responder

Colton 911
Colton 911: Caught in the Crossfire

K-9 Ranch Rescue
Second Chance Soldier
Trained to Protect

Undercover Soldier
Covert Attraction

Visit the Author Profile page at Harlequin.com for more titles.

As always, many thanks to my wonderful editor, Allison Lyons, and my fantastic agent, Paige Wheeler.

Chapter 1

Sitting in the chair she had chosen along the wall near the front door, Nella Bresdall looked around the otherwise empty reception room of the Chance Animal Shelter. Then she sat still, listening for dog barks.

No dogs, but she thought she heard a muted human voice from beyond the door across the room that was, unsurprisingly, closed and locked. She had checked.

In fact, there was nothing open about this place except that the front door hadn't been locked. Maybe she shouldn't have come early after all.

But this did give her mind a chance to imagine the realities of this very special shelter, and how she would do here.

If she got the job.

Nella hadn't been on a job interview for—how many years? Nearly ten. And the last job she had taken on, as an officer of the Los Angeles Police Department, had

had a huge and complicated hiring procedure. She'd had to undergo a many-step process, including everything from writing an essay to taking physical fitness tests, polygraphs, and medical and psychological exams.

Here? Well, since she was hoping to take on the role of a shelter manager, she figured the process could be simpler.

Or not, since most important was the underlying basis of the job...

She wished she had someone to talk to about it right now, but her reason for coming early had been to look around, observe the place and think about it while alone.

And try to convince her stressed mind and body to relax and ultimately indulge in the interview process as if she enjoyed it, had no qualms about it, was doing it for fun.

And not as a result of wanting to leave her former emotionally devastating and sadly dangerous job behind.

Feeling her pulse rate speed up as her thoughts once more landed, as they did so often, on what had happened during her last major assignment, she inhaled deeply to relax.

Predictably, this room contained an underlying odor of—what else?—dog. But not much. In any case, instead of it causing Nella to run out of there, she found it surprisingly inviting.

Or not so surprisingly.

Looking down at herself, she wondered if she had dressed up enough for this interview. For most noncop jobs, she would have put on a professional-looking suit with a dark skirt and matching jacket, and a white shirt with conservative jewelry.

But now? She had donned a suit, yes, but one with nice slacks rather than a skirt. No jewelry.

It was probably still dressier than she would want to wear while working with untrained shelter pets who needed new homes, and the other portion of the job would mean working with people who probably couldn't care less about her clothing—only about how caring she was and how she helped them.

And protected them.

She reached up to push her long dark brown hair behind her ears. On the job as a cop, she wore it in a bun to keep it out of her way. Here, since she thought she appeared as professional yet less cop-like with her hair down, she hadn't rolled it up.

But how much longer did she need to wait? She pulled her phone out of her pocket and looked at the time.

Her interview with the Chance Shelter Director, Scott Sherridan, still wasn't for another fifteen minutes. She'd called him when she arrived inside this reception area but only got his voice mail. The building's front door was unlocked, and when she came inside and pushed the doorbell button beside the locked inner door, she was soon greeted by a thirtysomething woman, maybe a few years older than Nella, in a bright green Chance Animal Shelter T-shirt with the word Manager on the pocket, and jeans. She'd introduced herself as Telma Andelsen.

"You're a little early," Telma had said. "Scott's always prompt, so please wait here and he'll be with you soon." She'd left Nella alone in the room with a smile and a wish for good luck—that would have seemed more sincere if she hadn't stared at Nella with such curiosity before leaving.

Well, as Nella knew, this animal shelter was a whole lot more than it appeared to be.

Which was undoubtedly why she'd seen Telma open the inside door with a keycard, then heard the lock click on the door after Telma disappeared through it.

Nella sat back in her chair and looked around again. She saw some magazines on a squat plastic table between two of the wooden chairs matching hers around the perimeter of the moderate-sized room. She stood to grab one. The magazines were all about pet rescues and care, mostly published by national animal protection organizations. She picked up the one that looked most interesting.

It undoubtedly contained information she would soon need to know—if all went well.

She sat back down on her chair's seat, a blue vinyl unlikely to be damaged or destroyed by any animals brought in to meet prospective adopters, she assumed.

Along the far wall was the door through which Telma had entered and left this room. Did she have an office there?

Did Director Sherridan? Most likely.

And the animals—she presumed the shelter area extended far beyond that, although the whole site was enclosed and not visible through the outer fence to anyone driving or walking around it.

For good reason.

Would she at least get to see the shelter animals, even if she didn't get the job? She hoped so. She liked pets, particularly dogs and cats, and also liked the idea of helping to rehome them, along with other duties here. If she got the job.

Damn. She was getting tired of thinking. Speculating. She wanted to see a person. Scott Sherridan.

Knowing she wouldn't absorb anything from the magazine, she stood and began pacing. The floor's tile surface seemed appropriate for cleaning if any rescued animals wound up in here and weren't particularly housebroken.

But the people. The other people. Who were they? Where were they? Behind the fencing with pets? Upstairs, possibly, since the upper floors, with the exterior visible when she looked up from outside the entry door, seemed fairly large. Which was logical, since the site had once been a major apartment complex before it had been turned into a pet shelter.

She assumed that, like this downstairs reception area and the shelter outside that she'd yet to see, the apartments had been renovated.

If all went as she hoped, she would soon get a tour—and meet their current residents.

She glanced at her phone again. Twelve more minutes to go. And Telma had said Scott was prompt.

She hoped so.

She sat again after pulling the magazine off her chair. The cover featured an article on cat intelligence. And another about a new method for dog training. Both sounded potentially interesting, although she doubted she could concentrate right now.

She forced herself not to look at the time on her phone again.

And then the front door she had come through opened, slamming against the wall.

Nella gasped as she turned to look that way. A woman ran in and shut the door hard behind her.

She appeared middle-aged, dressed in jeans and a yellow shirt that looked too large for her. She stood there, leaning against the door as if to hold it shut, breathing almost frantically.

"Hello?" Nella said tentatively. "Can I help you?" Of course she didn't work here, not yet and maybe never. But she suspected this shelter existed for women like this.

"This is that Chance Animal Shelter, isn't it?" The woman's voice was raspy, since she was crying. Her eyes were huge, her face pale, and she appeared terrified.

"Yes, it is." Nella knew better than to reveal the real character of the place, even to this woman, who might already know it. "Are you looking for an animal to adopt?" That might sound ridiculous, but Nella thought it would be best to get the woman talking, revealing as much as possible about what was in her mind.

"No!" The woman's voice was emphatic. She continued more softly, aiming a quick glance toward Nella before looking away again. "I... I mean I might like to start working here. I like animals."

"I see." Nella wondered how much word was out there regarding what this shelter really was about. The idea, she gathered, was to keep it covert. Highly covert, to the extent possible.

But some people worked here as managers, like Scott and Telma. Others became residents, as she understood it, and perhaps talked about it when they shouldn't. And they probably were referred here by someone who knew. The residents ostensibly, and maybe actually, worked here to help the animals. But they were also under the protection of the managers, because things in their lives had put them into danger, and they needed involvement in a protection program to keep them safe.

Like the Chance Animal Shelter.

Which was largely why Nella was interested in being hired here as a manager and protector, making use of her police officer background in a very different way. Helping animals, sure, but helping people even more.

Like this one?

Nella assumed the shelter managers had a protocol about how they accepted people into the human program. Someone diving through the door like this lady most likely wasn't following it.

"Am I hired?" the woman asked, her tone hopeful.

"I'm very new here," Nella told her. "I can't hire you." Or let you stay for protection.

Why did she even need protection, assuming that was really why she was here?

"Then please, please, let me talk to someone who can."

Which made the most sense to Nella, too.

"I'll see if I can contact one of the senior managers," Nella told her. She wanted to know more first, though.

What if this woman was trying to pull some kind of scam—even though she appeared genuinely distraught and possibly in need of help?

Okay, Nella realized she might be too suspicious, as well as protective of this place she wanted to work for—but was far from being hired herself, at least not yet. Still...

"Please tell me your name," Nella said, "and I'll see what I can do."

"I'm Ann," she said, and took a step closer to Nella, looking her straight in the eye. Hers were light brown and bloodshot. "I... I have a good reason for wanting to work here. Really." She hesitated. "And I really do love animals."

That *and* suggested that animals were not the only reason Ann was there, as Nella had figured.

"Okay, Ann," she said. "Just wait a minute."

Nella didn't like turning her back on Ann, despite her assumption the woman was being honest. She maneuvered so she only partly faced away from her and pressed the bell near the door Telma had come through before.

At the same time, she pulled her phone from her pocket again and pushed in Scott's number. After all, it was close to the time they were supposed to meet.

And Scott did answer. "Hello, Nella. I'm on my way to the reception area to come get you so we can talk."

"Great," Nella said. "And when you get here, I'll introduce you to Ann, who just came in through the front door. She's kind of upset—and she's looking for a job here, too."

"Really? I'll be right there."

Almost as soon as Nella touched her phone screen to end the call, the door beside her opened. She moved slightly to get out of the way of the man who stepped through the opening.

After closing the door behind himself, he glanced down at her. "Hi, Nella. Welcome." He quickly looked beyond her to where Ann now paced near the chair where Nella had sat before.

"Hello, Scott," Nella said to his back, smiling slightly in amusement at their strange meeting.

She hadn't even considered what her potential boss might look like, though she figured he would be somewhat in disguise from his real job, part of the Chance Police Department, as she understood it. But at first glance, she found him quite a good-looking guy, tall, with broad shoulders and a no-nonsense stride. He wore jeans and a blue denim work shirt with a red-and-brown Chance Animal Shelter logo on its chest pocket, complete with the outline of a dog and the word *Manager* on it, too. His face was long with angular cheeks, and Nella had noticed how blue his eyes were during the instant he had looked at her. His facial stubble matched the darkness of his crown of short hair.

His appearance was irrelevant, though, despite her finding it noteworthy.

His way of dealing with people like those Ann might represent? That was important.

"Hi," he said to Ann. The woman shrank back in obvious nervousness, but he continued, "I'm Scott Sherridan, director of this shelter. I assume you're aware of the nature of this special animal shelter, right?"

She nodded. "I like animals," her voice squeaked.

"I do, too," Scott said. "And people. But are you interested in working here to help animals?"

Ann nodded, not meeting Scott's eyes. "Yes. Please. I need... I need a job."

"And we can always use new staff members. But let's talk, okay? Come with me inside the shelter, and, Nella, you can join us. I'll interview Ann first, then come talk with you."

"Fine." Nella soon followed Scott through the door he'd unlocked to the inner part of the shelter, with Ann close behind him. He locked the door again behind them.

"I'll show you this first," Scott said. Nella grinned when he walked them down the wide hallway lined with closed doors, to its end, where, before another door, there were fenced-in enclosures containing dogs. A couple barked at them.

Whatever else it might be, this definitely was an animal shelter.

Each enclosure contained different sizes of dogs. Nearest the door were two small ones. Next was an area with three medium-sized ones, with one larger one toward the back. Nella figured this was mostly to show people coming in, since there were likely to be larger areas containing more dogs, as well as other pets, beyond that door. Of course each enclosure contained water and food bowls and dog beds, and the floors were all tiled like the waiting room, the easier for cleaning, she assumed.

Scott didn't stop to introduce either Ann or her to the dogs, though. "Thought you'd want to see this, but let's go back," he said.

He turned and they followed him nearly to where they had entered the hall.

"Here, Nella." Scott pushed open a door on the left. "As I said, Ann and I are going to have a little discussion first, but I'll come back to talk to you here soon." He gestured for Nella to go inside.

Which she did. She understood what he was up to, or believed she did, but wished she could participate in his initial inquisition of Ann to see what she really wanted, and if she was qualified to be one of the people housed here. Still, since Nella wasn't yet one of those who helped to take care of those people, and might never be, it wouldn't be appropriate for her to join them.

Even so, it hurt. But it also added to her desire to do a good job of talking to Scott later.

So for now, she entered a small conference room that had a table surrounded by chairs. She pulled one of the austere chairs out and sat on it. She extracted her phone from her purse, checked for emails and searched to see if there was any more news about the LAPD and the situation that had caused her to leave the job there.

Nothing new. So, she next looked up the Chance Animal Shelter, as she had many times recently, and read once more about the many kudos for the wonderful place up in the mountains near San Luis Obispo that helped to save so many needy animals.

And let her mind wander around to how it also, covertly, apparently saved a lot of needy people.

Scott couldn't help feeling a bit perturbed that his interview with Nella had been delayed by the appearance of this clearly distressed woman, Ann. He had been looking forward to talking to the former LAPD officer who had sent in an application for a managerial job at his shelter.

Her credentials looked good. Real good. And he had checked her references, which were excellent, most from other cops he knew of and respected.

The delay wouldn't affect his impression of her background. But his initial thoughts remained on Nella as he led Ann into another of the interview rooms on the first floor of the Chance Animal Shelter reception building.

He supposed he could add Nella's response to the wait to the list of things he needed to consider before offering her a job.

"So, here we are," he said to Ann, gesturing to the obviously stressed woman to sit on a chair at the table in the middle of the compact and stark room. It was a good place to interview potential pet adopters while bringing in the dogs, cats or whatever they'd expressed interest in and watching their mutual reactions. It worked even better for interviewing potential "staff" members— those people who came here not only to be hired to help with the animals, but also to acquire new, safer identities and hide from people who tormented them in their real lives.

Was that the situation with Ann?

She remained standing until he took a seat and again gestured to her to join him. Appearing quite tense, she obeyed, sitting straight in the chair and staring at him with her moist brown eyes.

"So how did you hear about this shelter?" was Scott's first question, as it often was.

"I… I have a new friend who lived—worked—here for a while. She just moved to near where I live, and—"

"Which is where?" Scott interrupted. He wondered who she was talking about but assumed she would say.

"Santa Maria. And the friend is Edna Short. I figured you'd want to know that."

"Yes, I do. Thank you." Scott recalled that Edna Short was the name they had given to Babs Morgan, who had been at the shelter for about a month right after it opened. She'd chosen to leave after her abusive stepfather was arrested in Arizona for assault and battery on another woman, but wanted to stay as far as possible from the guy's radar as she could for the rest of her life. Hence, the new, retained identity.

Scott would reserve judgment whether to be angry with Edna, and perhaps contact her to warn her not to mention the place ever again, until he had heard Ann's story and determined whether Edna had merely done an endangered friend a favor by telling her about it.

"Edna," Ann continued, "well, we met where I worked at a coffee shop. She became a server, too, and was there when my stepson came in a few times and—" her eyes teared up even more "—he hit me there, in front of everyone. My husband was even with him some of the times. I'd tried to stop him, to convince my husband to help, to tell him I wasn't stealing his money. Even got the police involved, but, but…"

"But you needed more help than you were able to find. I understand. And it was good that Edna suggested us."

Maybe. But Scott would still contact Edna—carefully, of course—and confirm that Ann was who and what she claimed to be.

"We may be able to offer you a position here," he continued, choosing not to be overly encouraging until he knew more. "Right now, I'll send in one of our managers to talk with you and get additional information."

Which would give him a chance to go talk to Nella, whom he was supposed to be interviewing.

"Thank you." Ann sounded almost breathless. "And—"

"And?" he encouraged when she stopped talking.

"And—well, could I get to see some of your animals up close?"

Which made Scott smile. Ann just might be a good fit.

"We'll ask the manager who comes to see you to introduce you to some," he said, then stood to leave the room.

Chapter 2

Not a lot of time had passed since Nella had been shown into this room to wait, but she was getting antsy nevertheless.

Her mind kept circulating on questions she wanted to ask about the facility and those who lived or just worked here, even about the animals who were brought in to be cared for.

And would she enjoy talking with Scott as much as she anticipated? Not that her enjoyment of that conversation would be paramount in determining whether she would work here.

But it might help.

Scott would interview her, though her questions might suggest an interview of him, too. There was a lot she wanted to know. But he would be the person who would ultimately decide if she'd be offered a job—and what it would consist of.

Her anticipation was driving her nuts. She really wanted to get this conversation over with.

But if it didn't go well—

The door finally opened. Nella had been pacing near the chairs. Now she stared at the open door, wishing she was seated, nonchalantly studying her phone or otherwise not appearing to care too much about what was to come.

"Hi again, Nella." Scott strode into the room. He was followed by a woman who appeared to be around Nella's age, thirty-three, but instead of being dressed up, as Nella was, the other woman wore jeans and a red T-shirt with a large red-and-brown Chance Animal Shelter logo in the middle that resembled the one on Scott's work shirt.

Since Telma had been wearing a similar T-shirt in green, Nella assumed that was a standard uniform around this place, although Scott's and Telma's shirts indicated they were managers.

Wearing that kind of shirt would be fine with her if she started working here.

"Hi," Nella responded. "And hi to you, too," she said to the woman.

"Hi back." A wide grin lit her round face, revealing a gap between her front teeth. "I'm Bibi. I work here. Would you like some coffee or tea while you talk to Scott?" She leaned closer before Nella could respond. "He's a nice guy," she added softly, as if revealing a big secret.

That remains to be seen, Nella thought, but said, "I'm sure he is. And I'd love some black coffee, if that's possible."

"Yep, it's possible. See you in a minute." And Bibi left the room.

Nella laughed, sitting down and looking up at Scott. "Okay, Mr. Nice Guy. How about showing me how correct Bibi is."

"Looks like I've got a challenge ahead." Scott appeared to struggle not to smile in return. "But I'm up to it."

I'll just bet you are, Nella thought. Before he started asking questions, though, Nella had some burning ones of her own. "How's Ann?" she asked.

"She's doing fine, as far as I can tell." Scott settled down in the chair across the table from Nella as she sat, too. He regarded her with blue eyes that appeared to try to permeate her mind and determine what she was thinking.

"Good. And is she—does she want to be—one of the people who…well, helps to take care of animals? Or—"

"Yes, we're possibly going to bring her in as a staff member. That's what we call our helpers who also get our help, if that's what you're asking. They act like volunteers at other shelters but to the outside world, since they also get room and board, we claim that we're hiring some homeless people who help us—but we reveal nothing more about their backgrounds. Certainly not the truth, that they're staying here under our protection. We don't stress the homeless part, either, to avoid getting a bunch at our door. Is that what you thought?"

Nella nodded, feeling her lips curve into another small smile. "Yes. And—well, did Ann know already the kinds of services you provide to people, and not just animals?"

Scott nodded, his eyes now studying her face as she studied his. "Yes, she did."

"How?" Nella realized she'd blurted the word, but she was curious. From what she had heard, the underlying function of the shelter, and its primary reason for existing, was generally one big secret. Only those involved with running it or referring potential residents here, or those who otherwise needed to know, were told this wasn't just a sanctuary for animals or for homeless people, but mostly for people fleeing horrible situations in their lives. Of course, others probably found out about it, too, and she wondered how they were also encouraged to keep it secret.

"First," Scott said, "what do you think the Chance Animal Shelter is all about?" He leaned toward her over the table and stared once more, with his flashing blue eyes, into her face. His expression seemed chilly now, yet inquisitive. Very inquisitive.

"I assume it's okay to talk about it here, on-site, and with its director?" Nella made that a question.

Scott nodded. "Good start. It tells me you're aware of our covert nature."

"If the little I've heard is true, then yes, I am."

"Okay. So tell me, what's our real primary purpose?"

It was an amazing purpose. That was why Nella had come here to flee, not necessarily her job as a cop, but some of the unanticipated results of an assignment to help bring down a street gang.

"Saving endangered people from their horrible lives," she said. "A program that lets those people get away from what—mostly who—is hurting them, obtain new identities, stay here in protective custody for a while, then eventually go somewhere other than Chance and start all over."

Nella noticed Scott nodding throughout her description. "You got it," he said as she finished. "And you were right that it's a highly covert undertaking. Hardly anyone is encouraged to talk about it." He paused. "So how did you hear about us?" He again leaned toward her, hands clasped together in the middle of the table, and continued staring at her. The face she'd considered amazingly handsome before still looked good, but was almost scary in its intensity.

What would he do if she told him she had heard about this place in some manner he disapproved of?

He probably wouldn't offer her a job, which was bad enough. But would he allow her to leave? And if not, what would happen to her?

Okay, she was undoubtedly worrying over nothing. And how she'd heard about this place was through a channel that was permitted.

She hoped.

She forced herself to smile at him. "I think it was through an appropriate source. As you know from my résumé, I was an officer with the Los Angeles Police Department. I… After some situations that I found difficult to deal with, I rethought where I wanted to go with my career and…well, mentioned that to my superior officer, Deputy Chief Daniel Poreski." Did Scott know him? Was Dan entitled to know about this shelter? Since Scott didn't react, Nella continued. "He'd heard of the Chance Shelter, mentioned it to me with an immediate caveat not to talk about it to anyone else and gave me a brief rundown of what you're about. I tried to check it out but—well, you're good at keeping things covert. That's when I tried contacting you, asked about a job, explained—"

"Explained your background and that you hoped to work with saving animals and more. Yes, I was the one to read your introductory email."

Nella had figured that was true, since he'd been the one to respond, to tell her what a wonderful pet sanctuary this was, to say in his email that they were always looking for excellent managerial staff—as well as finding ways to bring in more *beings* who needed help.

Somehow, the implication was there that *beings*, as he used the word, included more than pets, although no absolute confirming statement was made.

After her next response asking for more information about any open positions, he had requested her résumé and some references. She had used Dan as a reference, plus a few other cops Dan suggested whom she knew well and he trusted. Apparently Scott had liked them, since this visit and interview were the result.

When they had talked to schedule her visit here, Scott had never come right out and confirmed that this place helped people in real need. But he hadn't exactly denied it, either. He'd told her to come and see for herself.

Well, here she was.

She wanted to know more, of course. See the place. Talk to people, not only animals, and—

A knock sounded on the door but it opened before anyone responded. Bibi walked in, juggling a couple of mugs that had the Chance Animal Shelter logo on them.

Apparently, promoting the place's name that described it as an animal shelter was important around here. Well, if she stayed, Nella would be glad to help.

"Here you are." Bibi placed a mug on the table in front of Nella.

As she circled the table to hand the other one to Scott, Nella took a sip. Definitely black coffee and definitely tasty. "This is good," she said. "Thanks, Bibi."

"You're welcome." She seemed to hesitate, then said, "So, since you're still here and no animals are...?" Her tone turned into a question.

"We're having a discussion now," Scott said. "And if you hope to see more of Nella, you'd better give us some time to talk."

"Sure," Bibi said, but her gaze assessed Nella. "Do I want to see more of you?"

Feeling somewhat amused despite being put on the spot, Nella responded, "I love animals, and that's not all. So, sure, we should become friends." And since Nella gathered that Bibi was a staff member under protection and not a manager, she figured she might actually help Bibi if she wound up getting hired.

"Got it. Well, I'm out of here." After sending another gap-toothed smile in Nella's direction, Bibi exited through the door.

Nella, also smiling, looked at Scott. He, too, had a grin on his good-looking face. "We do get some interesting people here," he said.

"I see that," Nella said, then, after hesitating, asked, "So why is Bibi here?"

Scott's expression chilled. "You'll learn eventually if I wind up hiring you," he said. "It's time for me to start asking the questions. Okay?"

"Definitely okay." Nella ignored the tremor of unease that slid through her.

Before beginning, Scott took a long sip of coffee, watching Nella. He hadn't expected her to be so gorgeous. She suddenly looked worried, as well she should. Yes, he intended to conduct an inquisition.

Things about her looked good, sure—and not just her lovely face. Her skin was light and smooth, her lips wide and shining in a pale pink shade that didn't appear spoiled by lipstick. Her hair was dark and shoulder-length and enhanced by her arched, matching brows over deep brown eyes.

Right now, those brows were contracted in a scowl.

Well, he should possibly be scowling, too. Was it a good thing that she was here—and knew whatever it was she knew?

The Chance Animal Shelter had been in existence for not quite a year, but word was getting out to the law enforcement community regarding what it really was about.

Scott couldn't control everyone who learned about it, but he did find appropriate contacts in different police and sheriff's departments and let them know, in case they wound up having people in their jurisdictions who needed the kind of help and protection this shelter provided. But he also made it clear that the reality of this place was highly confidential and it needed to remain that way to stay effective.

Deputy Chief Dan Poreski of the LAPD was one of the people Scott knew of who'd been told about this shelter—and one of the few people in that department Scott had authorized to know about it.

And when Dan had contacted Scott, saying he had a skilled, smart and dedicated police officer who herself needed not the kind of protection the shelter provided, but a new job away from Los Angeles, Scott had given Dan the go-ahead to tell that officer about the Chance Shelter and suggest she apply for a job here. And Scott liked Dan's referral of Nella, plus he was one of the references she had supplied. Scott had talked to him again, as well as with her other references, grilling them quite a bit about Nella's skills and trustworthiness without discussing the true nature of the shelter. She'd come out sounding really good, which was why he wanted to talk with her further. Maybe hire her.

Since Scott wanted this shelter to continue growing, that meant having additional managerial staff—people to help protect not only the pets but also the staff members who came here needing new identities and new lives.

And the way Nella had handled the appearance of Ann, who'd come looking for help, without knowing what the protocol was—well, Nella had acted pretty much as a trained member of the managerial staff would, since they, too, needed to introduce him first to any potential new residents without giving away the true mission of the shelter.

"Before I get into your credentials—which look pretty good, by the way—I want to know why you decided to leave the LAPD and find another, less official job."

He watched as she took a deep breath, but her eyes didn't leave his face. "I've always wanted to help people," she said. "As many as possible. That's why I became a cop."

"Me, too," Scott tossed out there. "I'm still part of the Chance Police Department so I get it. But I repeat, why did you decide to leave your cop job?"

"Because of a difficult experience I had there," she blurted, perhaps louder than she'd intended. He noticed her lovely brown eyes tear up, but she blinked and continued to stare at him, as if challenging him to ask how.

Which, of course, he did. "Tell me about it."

He wondered if she would go into a long tale about how she had been threatened as a cop. That, of course, happened, and it could definitely be scary.

But hers wasn't what he'd consider an ordinary tale.

"Like I said, I've always wanted to help people. That caused me to volunteer for extra duties, like taking special training within a new LAPD Special Operations division. Reporting to others more senior than me, I wound up heading an excellent task force charged with rounding up a nasty gang responsible for killing innocent, nongang civilians in a bad area of L.A. And—"

She hesitated, so he had to ask, "And what?"

"And I lost a good friend, damn it!" She stood now as she glared down at him, as if angry with him for whatever had happened—or at least for making her talk about it.

But what did she expect?

"I'm sorry," he said. "Tell me about it."

He had a sense, from that continued glare, that she might just stomp out of the room and leave the shelter, leave Chance.

But then she seemed to pull herself together.

"Well, we succeeded. We brought down that horrific gang after a standoff in which several gang members were killed. But so was...so was my partner, Sergeant Lou Praffin." She sank back into her chair, but she seemed to get hold of her emotions. "That only happened a few months ago. I was assigned a new partner and given some less dangerous tasks. And I can and would stay there. But—well, I wanted something different, in a place where I could still help people but away from where that all went down. Far away. Like here, in Chance. Although if this doesn't work out, I'll go back to my job there." Her look at him now was challenging, as if she expected him to tell her she couldn't do what would be expected of her here.

But he had a feeling she could.

More important, he felt she might be a very helpful addition to his managerial staff.

"I get it," Scott said. "And I can understand your wanting to distance yourself from such a difficult situation."

She seemed to study his face now, as if attempting to determine what he was thinking.

He figured he could tell this lovely, damaged, yet apparently skilled cop—one who'd been chosen to head that special task force—what was on his mind.

"So here's what I'm thinking," Scott continued. "I want to take you on a tour of this shelter, introduce you to some of our animals, staff and managers, not necessarily in that order. And then, if you get along with them the way I like, and you also think this could be a good choice for you, we'll sit down and discuss a job offer. Sound okay to you?"

"Sounds more than okay." Nella's tone suggested relief and maybe a touch of happiness. Plus, her smile seemed to erase all the negative and sad expressions he had seen earlier.

And Scott realized that, if she did accept a position, he might have to be very careful. He found her attractive. Too attractive.

But having any kind of relationship except a professional one with an employee—especially in a situation like this, where being fully observant and keeping others, both human and animals, safe were critical—couldn't happen. It might result in some pretty severe damage to everyone.

So, Scott would have to keep his feelings to himself. Even if his feelings for Nella strengthened over time. There was no other choice.

Chapter 3

Nella felt her shoulders slump in exhaustion. That interview, if that was what it had been, had made her think even more about Lou—her partner, her friend, her mentor—and she had been right there when he was shot by gang members attempting to flee.

Now she felt as if she'd just relived her frantic effort to keep him alive, waiting for the EMTs while she attempted CPR on his damaged body. Furious with herself for not catching those gang members as they fled—but not wanting to leave Lou alone, perhaps to die. Which, of course, was what had happened.

They hadn't been alone, naturally. Other members of their task force had been with them on this raid, including several who'd been really good backup, and some went after those gang members while Nella stayed with Lou. They'd caught quite a few, but Nella believed several were still out there, even now.

And Lou was dead.

She didn't mention any of this while Scott made some phone calls, apparently to other shelter managers. She just sat there, forcing herself to smile as she waited.

She studied his face, and not just because it was probably the best-looking face she'd ever seen on a guy.

No, she appreciated his compassion as she'd spewed her difficult tale, and he hadn't made a big deal about it. Acted professional. Treated her professionally.

Which somehow made her feel damnably attracted to him.

Well, even if she got the job and continued to feel this way, it wouldn't matter. She, too, was a professional. She had already, as a cop, worked with guys she'd found attractive, but she'd kept that to herself.

She certainly would do so with Scott, no matter what happened to her attempt to work here.

If she got the job, she would be here helping people in need of new identities. She would be helping abandoned and needy pets, too. She could focus all her attention on them and not on her past.

And certainly not on her admiration of Scott, which was inappropriate.

She would force herself to—

"Okay," Scott said, rising. "I've warned everyone in the back, so you'll get to meet some people and animals. The most important ones for you to meet as far as I'm concerned are our managers, and you've already met Telma. But it's also important for you to meet more staff members we're helping besides Bibi."

"I want to meet everyone," Nella said, meaning it. "Animals included."

She liked how he nodded approvingly as he turned and walked toward the door. She rose and followed.

The hallway was empty, as it had been before. Scott gestured toward the first door across the hall and nearest the entry and said, "In there is a larger set of rooms that I hope will soon become our own veterinary clinic. I'm still looking for the right vet to help out."

"Having a vet on the premises sounds like a great idea," Nella said.

Scott then led her down the hall in the opposite direction from the entrance. The place was quiet, although Nella did hear sounds from beyond the doorway in the direction they were going. Nella saw several closed doors on both sides. She assumed at least some led into meeting rooms like the one she'd waited in and then spoken with Scott. They soon reached the end of the hall, and some dogs in the enclosures stood and greeted them.

Scott reached into his pocket and pulled out a keycard. "All our managers have keycards that work at the front door and here and some other locations inside. If you're hired, you can feel privileged once you get your keys." He laughed slightly before turning and unlocking the large wooden door at this end of the hall.

As it opened, Nella heard more noise, mostly dogs barking, with the sound of much quieter but caring human voices possibly responding to them.

Just outside, Scott led her along a walkway between two concrete buildings that appeared three or four stories high. He pointed first to the one on the left. "That contains our eating area downstairs and residents' apartments upstairs." The other one held the managers' offices, he told her.

Beyond the walkway was an open area. The outdoor portion of the shelter had a concrete walkway down the center, with grass areas fronting additional buildings on either side. "Let's try here first." Scott led her through an unlocked doorway into one of those buildings.

Inside were two rows of kennels enclosed by chain-link fencing, all containing dogs, some of which continued to bark.

Two women and one man leaned into different kennel areas. Nella recognized one: Bibi, who saw her, too, and gestured for her to join her. Nella did so without asking Scott if that was okay.

"I'd like you to meet Honey and Shupe." Bibi pointed at the two dogs behind the fence nearest to her. One looked like a black Labrador retriever mix, and the other a Shetland sheepdog mix with lots of fur.

"Which is which?" Nella asked, "and is it okay to pet them?"

"Of course! They're both lovable and need new homes." Bibi reached in and scratched the Lab mix behind the ears. "This is Honey."

"Then this must be Shupe." Nella began patting the furry head of the other dog between his ears.

Meanwhile, Scott had gone to talk to the two other people, who also joined Nella and Bibi beside that enclosure, which looked clean and comfortable for its inhabitants, including fluffy beds, and water and food bowls on the concrete surface.

"Nella, I'd like you to meet Campbell Green." Scott gestured toward the man, who was in his twenties, shorter than Scott and with a full blond beard. "We call him Camp. He's one of our managers." Which his shirt also indicated. "Camp, this is Nella."

Since he was a manager, Nella assumed he was a law enforcement officer, too, or a former one.

"Hi, Camp." Nella reached out to shake Camp's hand.

His grip was strong. "Welcome. And—well, is this a permanent welcome?"

"We'll see," Scott said, then gestured toward the other woman who'd joined them. "Nella, this is Darleen, one of our longest-term staff members."

In other words, she had been given a new identity and had lived here for a while in protective custody, maybe since this shelter had opened almost a year ago.

"Good to meet you, Darleen," Nella said.

"You, too." Darleen's voice was soft yet curt. She didn't look Nella straight in the eye but kept her gaze through her thick glasses downward. Darleen looked middle-aged, with her graying hair cut short and her face drawn and wrinkled.

Even more than with Bibi, or even Ann, Nella wondered what had gone on in Darleen's prior life to bring her here—and also why she was still here. Because of her attitude? If so, what was that about? Nella's understanding was that the shelter's goal was for the people it helped generally to only stay for a few months while getting used to their new identities, and to receive assistance in getting over their fears. The shelter also ensured that whoever had been harming them before didn't know where they were, whether or not those perps were in police custody since they might not remain there.

She might be wrong, of course. She didn't know a whole lot about the facility or how it worked—not yet, at least.

But if she was right, she gave the place more silent applause if they treated each situation, each needy person, individually. As they apparently did, at least with Darleen.

Nella had an urge to help this sad woman. For now,

she said, "I assume, since you work here, that you're an animal lover." Which wasn't necessarily the case, although people who hated pets wouldn't last long here. "Which is your favorite?"

Darleen's face lit up, and Nella felt delighted she had done something to ease her apparent pain, even momentarily. "That's definitely Pebbles. She's a Maltipoo, we think."

A combination Maltese and poodle, Nella thought. A small dog, and probably cute. "Fun," she said. "Could you introduce me?"

"Of course. She's down here."

Darleen led Nella along the center path between the two rows of enclosures containing lots of dogs eager to be noticed, to the one at the end where several toy dogs leaped at the chain-link fencing. Although Nella liked dogs, she didn't do well at identifying most breeds, or breeds contained in mixes, though that might have to change if she started working here. She wasn't sure which was the Maltipoo, but figured Darleen would let her know.

She noticed that Bibi and Camp followed them. Where was Scott?

Had she done something to make him back off observing—and possibly hiring—her?

Or was she worrying too much?

When they reached the enclosure, Darleen unhooked the gate, then, clearly careful not to let any dogs out, edged inside and picked up a little canine—a reddish-white one with wide Maltese black eyes and curly poodle fur, if Nella was right. When Darleen returned to the gate, Nella helped her get outside again without allowing any of the excited small dogs to follow her.

"This is Pebbles." Darleen snuggled the dog closely

against her. "She's been here about a month. When she got here, she was so scrawny, and her fur was all matted. From what we gathered from neighbors, the person who'd owned her never let her inside the house, hardly ever paid attention to her—and didn't feed her much, either. Fortunately, one of those neighbors called us and—well, thanks to Scott, we were able to save her."

Although Nella was aware that Chance had an animal services department, she wondered if this shelter could take on a similar role sometimes. Maybe so. Especially if its director was able to simply go in and save an abused dog.

Or maybe it hadn't been simple at all. She hoped to learn more soon.

And she had a feeling that Darleen empathized with this little pup. Nella hoped she would also learn about the situation Darleen escaped from to move in here. At least she had seen that dogs, or at least this one, helped to lighten Darleen's mood around strangers, and maybe other people, too.

"Would you like to meet some of the other dogs?" Bibi asked.

Nella glanced toward Camp. What would this manager want to happen now?

What would she want to happen now in a similar situation if she became a manager?

"I'd always love to meet more dogs," she responded. "And I'd also like to hear your system for finding them new homes."

"We'll talk about that later." Scott's voice from behind her startled Nella. Where had he been?

Was sneaking up on conversations his norm?

But she wasn't going to ask him—especially when he gestured to her to follow him.

"Where are we going?" she asked.

"To finish your interview."

Which made Nella wave to the others, the manager, staff members and dogs, as she strode up to Scott and joined him while he left the kennel area, heading back inside the building where they had talked before.

Scott had gone into the back of one of the kennel areas where he wouldn't be particularly noticeable. He'd sat on the concrete floor petting a couple of medium-sized pups as he observed Nella briefly to see how she got along with both the people and the dogs there.

She clearly gave a damn.

He liked that. In fact, for having just met her, he realized he liked a lot about her.

He had intentionally requested that one of the staff members present be Darleen, who still had a lot of emotional issues, especially when she met a new person. Nella's asking her about her favorite dog had been a perfect way to get Darleen to focus on something other than her own fears, at least for a short while.

Nella clearly had empathy and knowledge about how to help people.

Now Scott led her back to the room they'd occupied before. "If you want more coffee, I'll ask Bibi to get it," he told Nella as he gestured for her to sit in the same seat she had occupied before.

"No, thanks. I'm fine. Or at least I will be after you tell me poor Darleen's background." Nella stared at Scott as if attempting to extract the story from his brain.

He lifted his eyebrows, hoping his amusement didn't show. "We're here to finish your interview."

"I know, but what you tell me about Darleen will help me decide if this is the kind of place I want to work."

He hadn't thought that was in question, but he figured her inquiry was her way of attempting to get him to do what she wanted.

He liked that attitude.

"Okay," he said. "Short version."

He explained quickly that Darleen's parents had passed away when she was a teen, and she had married in college, possibly to have some family in her life.

However, her husband had abused not only her, but their pets. Fortunately, they hadn't had children, or Scott assumed they'd have been abused, too. Surprisingly, their childless marriage had lasted nearly twenty years, but the last time Darleen had landed in the hospital and nearly died, one of her nurses had looked for some way to help her and had asked the right questions at the Los Angeles Police Department. Darleen's husband had disappeared before he could be arrested, so she was terrified he would come after her again.

That was when the Chance Animal Shelter was just starting up, so Darleen had been one of their first residents.

"And she's still here," Nella said. "Isn't that against your policy?"

"Yes, but each situation is different. Darleen is still nervous, especially around people, and even the therapist who visits here to work with and counsel our residents hasn't been able to help much, but as I'm sure you can tell, Darleen comes out of her shell around dogs. Since we haven't found the perfect place for her to continue her life, and we don't know where her husband is, she's still here."

"That's wonderful." Nella's warm expression was like a hug.

He wouldn't have minded hugging back. But he stayed where he was.

It was definitely time to change the subject. "I know. Now, here's where we are." Scott asked Nella several additional questions about her background, including why she had decided to go into law enforcement.

"Because a lot of people need more help than instruction, like a teacher would do, or medical, like a nurse would do, or...well, we didn't talk much about my childhood, but I grew up in Los Angeles and had quite a few friends whose backgrounds were similar, with parents who were involved with show business. Mine were both in production. They traveled a lot, so I hung out with sitters. If I'd wanted to go steal things or whatever, it'd have been easy. Not my style, but I saw other kids get into that kind of trouble—partly because, even if they had their parents around, those parents were... well, you can guess where this is going. They and their parents hurt other people, and I wanted to stop that as much as I could."

"I get it," Scott said. And he did. His background was different. He'd liked animals because his mother had been involved in rescues, but he'd gone into law enforcement because his uncle had been murdered and he wanted to do something to help prevent that happening in other families. He admired Nella for also wanting to stop crime.

"One additional question for you," Nella said then. "Does this shelter act like animal services and rescue animals in difficult or abusive situations?"

"Sometimes," he responded. He rather liked that question, too. "Not officially, although we always get an okay after the fact from the official agency. They understand what we're about, and that includes helping animals." He paused. "So, okay now, let's go over a few more things." He asked some standard questions about items on Nella's résumé, including her education. She had attended Cal State Fullerton, which had a good law enforcement program. Her first job had been with the Fullerton Police Department but she had soon applied for the Los Angeles Police Department and landed the job she was just leaving.

All sounded great, especially factoring in her references whom he'd contacted. They all liked her. Admired her. Thought she was highly intelligent and motivated and dedicated to her job.

It was time.

He shuffled through the papers he'd brought along that included her résumé. Then he looked up to see she was staring as if attempting to read his mind.

He smiled. "All right," he said. "I'm offering you the job of Manager of the Chance Animal Shelter. Here are the particulars." He went over responsibilities she would have, including working with their staff members to help them start and live their new lives here, as well as helping to care for and rehome animals who were there not only as a cover, but as part of the shelter's duties, too.

He said that he and the other managers would work with her and always be available to teach her more of what she needed to know to do her job, and every question she had would be addressed. Her main responsibility would be to work closely with those other managers, including him, to protect the residents, both human and animal, and they would work closely with her. There would be meetings and dog walks and training and research online and otherwise, to try to ensure the safety of this facility and its staff and animals. And more.

"And here is the compensation." He told her what the monthly pay would be, paid biweekly, as well as holidays and vacation. "We hope you'll stay with us for a long time, but you can resign on thirty days' notice." He paused. "Now, how long do you need to consider this?"

She scowled, which surprised him. And then she broke into a big smile. "Oh, about two seconds," she said. "I accept."

Chapter 4

She got it! Nella was thrilled.

Oh, she realized it wasn't a perfect job. No job was. She had learned that the hard way. The very hard way.

But now she could start over, sort of. Her skills in law enforcement would come in handy here, as she helped to create and carry through with new identities for the staff members under their protection.

And that protection would also benefit from the skills she had acquired as a cop.

She still had some questions, though. She looked at Scott, who had pulled a tablet computer from somewhere. Now he was studying it and typing things in, and she assumed it was a possible contract for her to sign or something else relating to her new job.

Her new job!

Working here… And with this man who might be too good-looking, too nice, too—well, sexy—but she would handle her thoughts about him in a highly professional manner. Absolutely.

As soon as he looked up from the screen, she said, "I understood from what my boss, Dan Poreski, said that some of the managers here started out in law enforcement. He told me you had, too, and you confirmed that before."

She assumed Scott had given Dan permission not only to mention the shelter but to also reveal something about its true mission. But she didn't want to get Dan in trouble with her new boss, so maybe she should have thought that through better.

But Scott didn't appear concerned as he responded. "Yes," he said. "I worked things out when I started this shelter to also remain with the Chance Police Department as, essentially, an undercover officer within a special, covert division. Part of my responsibilities are to be the director here and help protect people we take in, our staff members. We're even partially funded by the Chance PD."

"Got it." That was great, Nella thought. Having an actual police department as backup was incredibly helpful.

"In addition," Scott continued, "you should know now, since you're joining us, that our managers, when asked, are all supposed to admit that they had prior jobs in law enforcement, because that's easy enough for civilians to find out. But we also say that circumstances forced us to quit or retire and work with animals instead. And definitely don't mention how we managers all take on roles helping to protect every shelter resident, including the human ones. Plus, Telma and Camp also maintain their connections with the Chance PD. I'll introduce you there soon, and maybe they'll also add you to their personnel."

"I'd like that," Nella said. And she would. Although becoming part of this police department might make it more difficult to go back to her prior job with the LAPD.

Not that she wanted to. What she wanted was for this new life she was starting to work out well. And continue for a good long time.

A wonderment she'd been tamping down crossed her mind again. "Have there been any instances where one of the staff members has been found here by whoever they were fleeing, or otherwise threatened?"

"Unfortunately, yes," Scott said. "Although that's not surprising. Threats and dangerous prior lives are why they're here."

"Anything recently? And did it put that staff member and others in danger?"

"Yes, and yes." Scott appeared grim, his dark brows furrowed.

"How—"

"It was one of the former staffers you won't get to meet. We always confiscate our residents' phones, then dispose of them in case anyone's following the GPS. Unlike with Ann, we usually conduct an interview of potential residents before they come to this shelter thanks to the people who refer them. That way, it's less likely whoever is threatening that person will find us. But that particular new resident had a phone we didn't find and was using it to contact her ex and text him how glad she was that he wasn't in her life anymore."

"And he showed up here," Nella surmised.

"Yes, about three weeks ago—in a rage and with a gun. I called some colleagues in the Chance PD and the guy was arrested—and I unfortunately had to kick that new resident out for not following our rules."

"Did she—"

"We found her a new job at a discount store in Phoenix, where she'll hopefully not contact her ex again, especially if he doesn't serve time."

But the damage had been done here. "Did the remaining residents know about it?"

Scott nodded, still looking grim. "Yes, and I can assure you they were damn scared."

She didn't ask if the other managers were, too. She would have been, especially after her most recent issues at the LAPD.

But she, too, would have done everything necessary to protect all residents of this place.

So she wouldn't have to go through what she'd had to after Lou...

She had to ask—"Have you looked much into Ann's background yet?"

"We got her phone immediately and had it transported, while still turned on, down the mountain and to a town far away. Telma interviewed her first, then I did. I also contacted Edna, the former resident who'd told her about this place—and asked her to be more careful in the future and to contact us first. But she also confirmed Ann's story. Ann has an abusive stepson who apparently thought she was stealing his dad's money. He attacked her several times, and her husband just let it happen. We're not sure we got her phone quickly enough, but we hope we don't see either man around here. We haven't accepted her yet, but we're close."

If Ann was accepted, Nella would make sure she remained okay. Of course she would follow whatever the shelter's protocol was, but she would stay on top of it.

Now that she was a new manager.

And was aware that this shelter was definitely not immune to danger.

"So," Scott said, "are you convinced working here isn't a good idea after all?"

That was how he apparently interpreted her reaction to what he'd told her.

"Just the opposite," she said. "I may not want to have my old job any longer, but I'm definitely ready to help people around here. And animals, too."

"Then we'll give it a try." Scott handed Nella the tablet he had been working on, along with a stylus. "Take a look at this. If it's okay, I'll want you to sign it and I'll get you a printed copy and an e-copy. Plus, we'll get you some Chance Animal Shelter T-shirts later that indicate you're a manager. You've probably noticed they're essentially our uniforms here, and so's my work shirt."

"Great. And I have a few more questions. Nothing major, though, like the last ones. Just how parts of what happened here were designed to be established."

The agreement looked fairly simple, nothing different from what they'd discussed, and a minimum of legalese. Nella signed.

"Excellent," Scott said, smiling at her.

"Definitely," Nella responded, smiling back. At least, she hoped all would go well.

Scott began to stand, but Nella said, "My other questions?"

Scott sat down again and looked at her with an expression that suggested he was as pleased about her signing on as she was.

She had an odd, inappropriate urge to seal their contractual commitment with a kiss...

Forget that, she told herself. "How many staff members are being protected here now?"

"You've met two, Bibi and Darleen, and we hope to accept Ann, too. We've got another five people at the moment, in different stages of getting or keeping new identities—after our loss of the one we talked about."

"So…eight now," Nella said.

"If all works out with Ann. But as I've said, we haven't been open very long. We're here in Chance, not a big city, where strangers who could be after our residents should be at least somewhat obvious. I hope to grow the number of people we're protecting. I have both local and federal contacts who help me establish our residents' new identities and obtain new ID documentation for them. And, oh." He leaned toward Nella over the table, causing her skin to tingle as if she hoped he'd touch her.

Not going to happen, she told herself sternly. At least not in any suggestive way, though professional colleagues sometimes came into contact with one another. "Oh, what?" she pressed.

"In addition to hoping to start that vet clinic I mentioned, I intend to grow the number of animals we're protecting, too, including those we rescue ourselves. None will stay forever, but they'll each, human and not, have a place to be until their lives are favorably turned around."

"That's wonderful," she said, meaning it. "Do you hold big adoption events to try to find the animals homes?" She had been to several at Los Angeles shelters, although she was always concerned she was away from home too much to actually adopt a dog, no matter how much she wanted to.

"No, we just invite people or families to come here to check out our available pets after sending us their information to review," Scott said. "As you can probably tell, we don't want too many outsiders hanging around at any one time. Too potentially dangerous for the people we're protecting. We keep our eyes on possible adopters at all times, to make sure that's really why they're here."

"Of course. I'll need to get my mind in gear that way." Then another thing she'd thought about before came to mind—something pretty important. "I'll of course want to meet the rest of the people and animals," she said. "And—well, if you have room for more people, I'm hoping you have an empty apartment I can stay in for now, till I find someplace else to live. Is that okay?"

"It's what I figured for now, though the management staff members don't live here but in nearby homes or apartments," Scott said. "That includes me. I'll introduce you to the shelter's apartment area first, then we'll go around so you can meet the other people and animals." He stood and gestured toward the door. "Ready to check it out now? We keep all our units furnished since it's unlikely our visitors will bring much with them when they arrive."

"Sure," Nella said. "A furnished place will work out well for me. I've already canceled my lease in L.A. and put most of my belongings into storage for now." Not that she'd felt certain she'd get this job or even want to stay here. But she had been hopeful, and figured that if this didn't work out, she would probably seek something else away from L.A. despite recognizing she could return to her job there.

This apartment? She felt certain she'd be satisfied with it, no matter how small it was.

And she found herself sharing another smile with Scott as he showed her down the hallway to another door, larger than those that led to the kind of room where she'd been interviewed.

But what distinguished it most?

He pulled out his keycards. This door was locked.

Scott led Nella up the wide staircase to the second floor in one of the buildings near the front of the shelter that contained the kitchen and eating areas. There were also three more floors above it containing mostly apartments, though most weren't occupied. Not yet. But there was also a community room on the third floor so residents could get together during off-hours if they wanted to be outside their units.

There were also other stairways to the apartment levels. Their doors opened safely to the inside of the shelter's grounds. Still, no one needed to use them, for now at least.

And it was more secure keeping them locked.

Of course, because of the emphasis on safety at this shelter, there were security cameras at all entrances and in most areas outside the units, including at some locations in the animal shelter.

No sense taking any risks that anyone could get away with anything here without being observed. Not at a place like this, where the people they protected might otherwise be placed into danger.

Nella's light footsteps behind him made Scott reflect that she was definitely a physically fit woman—and not just because she was a former cop. No, although he had attempted not to stare at her, he couldn't help noticing her curves beneath the somewhat dressy outfit she wore to be interviewed. Her white shirt beneath her dark jacket didn't completely hide her attractively full bust line, and her slacks, too, suggested the shapeliness beneath.

Not that he'd ever get to see anything beneath—although the idea was a bit stimulating. He just ignored it.

And though none of the current residents had any issues with the stairs, either, it wouldn't hurt to have a manager present to help out in case a future person they were protecting needed physical help, too.

He opened the door to the first floor of apartments without using a keycard and waited in the well-lit hallway for Nella to join him. Although there were small windows at both ends, most light came from lamps hung on the wall, all with bright fluorescent bulbs. They stayed on all night, too, though dimmed. That helped the peace of mind of the people who lived here.

And also would help in an emergency. Which Scott hoped never happened.

But having someone like the lovely and apparently brave woman who now stood there looking up and down the hall as if taking it all in, to help in one of those emergencies...

That should be a good thing.

"So which one is mine?" she asked. "Oh, and I'd like for you to point out who lives in which unit, in case I need to talk to one of the residents after hours, when I assume they'd be inside."

"You assume right," Scott replied, "although they all know, and hopefully you do, too, that everyone's on call if there is any need to help our animal guests."

"Of course." He liked the way her expression turned slightly annoyed, as if she wondered why he would even ask such a thing.

And even that expression looked good on her pretty face.

"Okay, you'll be near the end," he said quickly, and

edged by her toward the far end of the hall on the right side of the stairway.

"Do I get a keycard?" Nella asked.

"You get several. Here we are." He stopped outside the next to last door along the hall and pulled two cards from his pocket. He used one to unlock the door, then handed Nella both and pushed the door open.

He watched her expression as she went inside and studied the place even more intensely than she had the hallway. He edged in front of her again and gave her a brief tour of the main living area, small kitchen, bathroom and bedroom. He couldn't help glancing at the bed, then back at Nella. She, too, seemed to be studying it.

But he felt certain that whatever she was thinking, it had nothing to do with the possibility of their sharing a bed someday.

Which, no matter how great that sounded, was entirely inappropriate.

"Does it all look okay?" he asked as he stepped back out the bedroom door.

"For now," she said, "it looks perfect."

Chapter 5

And it did look pretty perfect, Nella thought. Not that she intended to live here forever, or even for a very long time—unless it was necessary to keep the residents safe. But at least for her initial foray into working at the Chance Animal Shelter, and until she found her own place nearby, this small but appropriately located apartment would be great.

Now she sat on the sofa in the little living room. Scott had left, but she would see him later. There wasn't much else in that room except for a small television screen on the wall, a low-slung mostly glass coffee table in front of the sofa and a padded armchair in the same gray as the couch.

She realized she was smiling. It had turned out that Scott wasn't just the director and therefore head manager and a member of the Chance PD. He also was a gentleman, since he'd offered to bring up any luggage she had in her car in the shelter parking lot.

She might just take him up on it, too—later. Right now, she was taking a small break before returning downstairs to meet the other staff members.

And then—well, Scott had also asked her to join him for dinner that evening, a good thing since she obviously didn't have any food in her brand-new apartment.

She pulled her cell phone from her purse and pressed the number for her friend and former superior officer, Dan Poreski.

The LAPD deputy chief answered immediately, even though he was most likely at the station. "How did it go?" he asked, obviously seeing her identity on his cell phone.

Nella pictured him sitting in his office, leaning forward as he usually did while talking on the phone. Dan was in his late forties, with a shaved head to finalize his growing baldness. He kept in good shape, so his uniform fit well, and although there was, of course, nothing between them, Nella always appreciated the way he looked at her with his twinkling brown eyes.

"I got the job," she told him.

"Fantastic! Tell me more about it—but only what you're allowed to talk about, of course."

Nella hadn't initially known how much Dan knew about the place besides the basics and its covert nature. Now she understood better and filled him in a little bit about the two levels of employment—and that the staffers weren't just volunteers.

"Then there are all the animals we help," she continued, using *we* since that was now appropriate. "I'll meet more of them this afternoon when we're done talking."

"Glad to hear that," Dan said. "I want you to keep me fully informed about what you do there—and I promise to keep it to myself, of course. And—well, I love the concept. I've actually been pondering how to maybe start something similar here."

"Really? Wow!" Maybe Nella could eventually even return to L.A. to help out.

"I'd enjoy coming to visit sometime to see how it works." He paused for a second and went on before Nella could offer her opinion that it might be a great idea. "Jon's been asking about you. I've told him you're okay and were applying for a good but covert job now, but after the gang task force—well, he's concerned about you."

Nella sighed. Sergeant Jon Frost had also been on the gang task force with her. In fact, he'd been a great backup, which she had appreciated except for when he attempted to take over its leadership—to help her, he'd said. Plus, he'd seemed overly concerned about her for a while. She liked him as a friend but that was all, from her perspective, though she'd believed he wanted more.

"Please tell him you've talked to me," she said, "and I said hi, but I'm fine."

"Will do," Dan said. "So—I'll hope to see you there soon. And be sure to keep me informed."

"I will," Nella replied, said goodbye and hung up.

And shook her head about Jon—a nice guy but too interested in her. And too overbearing at times when they worked together. Well, she could put him in her past now with everything else.

She had work to do.

She'd been facing the window in the room that opened over the courtyard. The windows in the outer walls were decorative, but their wood-framed panes were narrow and the glass was thick—the better to keep bad guys out, she figured.

Oh, yeah, this place might have been a regular apartment building before, she thought, but it had definitely been redesigned to minimize danger. Or so it appeared.

Now Nella was eager to see the rest of the shelter, meet those people she hadn't yet and also visit the poor pets in need of a new home.

Only, they clearly weren't so poor, since they had wound up at this kill-free shelter, where their care was important to everyone.

She removed the jacket she had worn over her blouse and hung it on a hanger in the bedroom closet. Then she left her apartment, locking the door after her.

She went down the steps and was glad the door at the bottom opened from this side without using a key, although she had brought both cards Scott had given her.

In the shelter area, she saw Camp and hurried toward the dog enclosure where he stood with three people Nella hadn't met.

"Hi," she said to Camp first, then turned toward the others—a man and two women. "I'm Nella, and I'm a new manager." She was well aware that they seldom used last names around here—and that the names Camp would introduce them by would be the given names for their new identities.

The man approached first. He looked a little young to be a staffer, but of course people of all ages were subject to threats that could require them to flee and take on new identities. "Hi, I'm Leonard. Nice to meet you, Nella." His brown hair was fairly long, and something in his hazel eyes suggested pain. Nella hoped to hear his story eventually.

The other two were Kathy, a very thin senior, and Muriel, thirtysomething and lovely, with a dark complexion.

Nella would have several stories to hear—and even

more she realized when Scott appeared with two more people, Warren and Sara. Two men, then, including Leonard. All the other staffers Nella had met were women.

For the next half hour, they all strolled from one dog enclosure to the next inside a couple of buildings. In the final building was a cat sanctuary, where Nella was introduced to Meower, Kitty and Blackie, though a couple of others remained at the backs of their enclosures. A smaller back room held some other pets, including gerbils and guinea pigs.

Each enclosure, no matter what size and for which type of animal, looked clean and well maintained, often decorated with comfy-looking beds on the concrete or tile floors, or cages for the smaller animals. No bad odors permeated the space.

Nella loved how everyone seemed so centered on the animals and on each other, talking and laughing and apparently getting along great—no matter what in their pasts had brought them here.

Would she remember all their names? Maybe the people's, yes. And perhaps the cats. But not all the dogs because there were so many. Not immediately at least.

Eventually, though, Scott said, "Okay, gang. Nella and I are leaving for a while. Have a great dinner without us tonight."

That was apparently directed only toward the staffers. As they turned away, Scott told Camp to go get Telma and join them in his office in fifteen minutes.

"Sure, boss," Camp said, and headed toward another of the shelter buildings.

Instead of going to his office right away, Scott showed Nella the dining area on the ground floor of the apartment building, with a kitchen attached. He explained that the managers kept a good supply of food there so no one ever had to leave the grounds. "You'll get to go on a shelter shopping expedition soon," he told Nella, who liked the idea.

In fact, she hadn't seen anything she hadn't liked here, nor met anyone, person or pet, she didn't like.

Next, he brought her into the offices at the shelter, upstairs in the other building just beyond the entry. He showed Nella around, including the small reception office in the front, then his office, which was the largest, and next the offices belonging to Telma and Camp.

The last one he showed her was hers, and he introduced her to her new computer and how to access it, and also a few files he wanted her to get to know, mostly about the staff members and animals who lived here. Most important, though, he showed her a document that contained a detailed description of what managers were supposed to do and told her to study that carefully when she had free time. It was organized into descriptions of general but vital duties such as observation and security, then additional ones about what was expected of managers while working with residents and the shelter animals.

"We'll discuss your duties, too, of course," he told her, "but this is a good, organized way for you to learn it all in depth."

There was also a file with the shelter's goals and methods of potentially achieving them.

"You can add to that," he said, "but be sure to send a group email out to the other managers containing any changes." He also showed her how to do that, including establishing an email address for her. In addition, he showed her how to access the emails sent to the entire facility.

Before they joined the others, Scott also introduced Nella to the shelter's main phone, a cellular resting in a charger on the main desk in the reception office. "We sometimes get calls or texts at this number, so we all check each time we're nearby and handle anything accordingly."

Then he showed her a closet area off the main office where the shelter T-shirts were kept. He let her choose five from the stack that had Manager on the pocket in whatever size and color she wanted, and she brought them with her.

As they then headed to his office, Nella, impressed, said, "This place is amazing." The shelter had so many wonderful things about it, and she figured it had the magnificent possibility of saving all its residents from all their woes, as planned.

"Of course it is," he said with a laugh, gesturing for her to enter his office before him.

There, Camp and Telma were sitting on a couple of the chairs facing Scott's large desk. "Glad all my managers are here," Scott said as he sat down. "I've got some good news." He told them he'd checked further into what Telma had said regarding her interview of Ann and had done some additional checking himself besides his call to Edna. "From what I gathered, her claims of being abused by her stepson are true, and pretty nasty. So my decision is that she will now be hired as a staff member here at the shelter. Her name will be Alice from now on. And I'd like you two—Camp and Telma—to start her orientation tonight while Nella and I grab dinner. Okay?"

From the big smiles on her fellow managers' faces, Nella figured it was all definitely okay.

She looked forward to the time when she would learn

more about those orientations and be able to work with a new staff member that same way.

This wasn't a date, Scott reminded himself as they pulled into the parking lot of The Last Chance Bar. He had just been a nice guy and invited a new employee to join him for dinner.

So where did he take her? To one of the nicest places in town, which served really good food. He led Nella inside, where it was crowded as usual—but they were nevertheless shown to one of the round tables characteristic of the place, one near a wall.

"This restaurant looks pretty popular," Nella said as she sat down across from him. She was dressed up again—or at least she had put her jacket back on.

He had changed his usual Chance Shelter denim or T-shirt for a cotton shirt with a collar, so he figured he was dressed up, as well.

"Yes, it's one of the best places in town," Scott said.

"Do you...do any of the staff members at the shelter come here to eat?"

"Definitely not. Too dangerous." Scott kept his voice low, but he stared at Nella with eyes that he hoped expressed his dislike of even the idea. "We can't take the chance that someone might recognize them and defeat the whole point of the shelter. That kitchen I showed you is where all their food is cooked, and they eat in that informal dining area next to it. Plus, they're given additional supplies so they can also eat in their apartments. But we managers go buy it all." He moved slightly toward her over the table and said, "It's safer that way."

Nella nodded. "I understand. I intend to keep learning all I can and appreciate your telling me anything I should be aware of."

"Definitely."

A young female server came over, handed them menus and asked if they wanted anything to drink. This was a bar, so Scott considered getting something alcoholic, but decided against it. "Just water," he said.

He appreciated it when Nella said, "Me, too, please." He wouldn't have minded if she'd asked for a glass of wine, but staying completely unaffected was best.

When the server left, Scott looked around. He saw some familiar faces, since he'd been a resident of Chance for a while, but he saw none of his fellow cops.

Which was probably just as well.

"So I assume it's better not to talk here about…what we're up to," Nella said. Her voice was soft, but she did look around at the filled tables near them.

"Good assumption," Scott said. "There's a lot more I can tell you about it, but this isn't the time or place."

They'd gone through the basics today, and Nella had seemed to pick them up well. But one of these days it would be good to describe his vision for the shelter a bit more, and what he hoped it would ultimately become.

Not now, though.

Nor would it be a good thing for him to start talking about his career before this one, in case there were eavesdroppers. And he wouldn't attempt to get Nella talking more about her prior life, either. What they'd already talked about had seemed difficult for her, and there wasn't any need to go into it further, at least not until they knew each other better.

But she spoke first. "I called…my previous boss, while I was alone in my apartment before," she told him. "I let him know I'd landed the job here, and he sounded really happy for me. He's even thinking about starting a similar animal shelter one of these days."

It was fine to talk aloud about the animal shelter aspects of their work. To the world, that was where they were both employed—a rescue organization for pets.

"Glad he was happy about it. Is he interested in hearing more?"

"So interested that he said he might like to come for a visit one of these days."

"He's always welcome." Scott had liked Dan's attitude from the time they'd first held a conversation. And if he was truly interested in the possibility of starting a similar shelter in Los Angeles, even better.

The server came over with their water and also took their orders. Nella requested grilled salmon, and Scott chose pasta with chicken. They both asked for salads.

For the rest of the meal—a good one, as always—they discussed only acceptable topics. Nella mentioned her college degree in law enforcement, but didn't discuss it or her prior, or new career. They'd already talked about her childhood a bit.

They also didn't discuss his earlier life—or why he had started the shelter.

They instead focused on something logical—the pets they'd had while growing up. Nella's parents were always traveling for their film production jobs but allowed her to have a dog—Squishy, a Pembroke Welsh Corgi mix. She smiled a lot as she described running with her short-legged dog.

Him? Well, he'd had a dog, too—and more, which he described to Nella. His parents had owned a small hardware store in Los Angeles, and he had grown up before it became acceptable to allow pets in most retail establishments.

But his mom had also volunteered at a private animal shelter and brought a lot of foster dogs home, one at a time. They'd played with their own Doberman pinscher, Dobie, so he wouldn't feel ignored, and Scott and his brother, Mike, helped out after school by taking the foster dogs and Dobie for walks before doing homework.

Thinking about Dobie and the foster pups from his childhood forced Scott to think about why he'd decided to become a cop, although he didn't mention it. But his uncle Andy had been an employee at the hardware store and helped out with the dogs, too—until he was murdered.

Scott, fifteen at the time, admired the cops who solved the murder. The rest was his history—despite the fact he wished his uncle, who'd been killed for the sparse money in his wallet, was still around. But that murder had been his impetus for first enlisting in the military, and after his four-year commitment he'd joined the San Luis Obispo Sheriff's Department.

Chance, California, was in San Luis Obispo County.

"Are you okay?" Nella was staring at him with worried-looking eyes. Damn, but he hated when his mind went off on tangents like that.

"Fine," he said. "Just thinking a lot about Dobie and our foster dogs." And the rest of his family…

And he liked that she showed concern by asking about what was on his mind.

He was really beginning to appreciate her.

He would have to be careful.

The rest of their dinner went well. And fast.

He enjoyed Nella's enthusiasm when they talked about the animal shelter, her eagerness to hear more about how and why he'd planned the shelter.

Once they were done, and after insisting on paying the bill, he drove them both back to the shelter and parked in the back. The small park area across the street was dimly lit by electric lights, and Scott looked over there to make sure it was empty.

"Do you live here, too?" Nella asked.

"No, though not far away. I want to leave the apartments here for people who need them—including you for now."

She laughed and didn't wait for him to open the door before she got out of the car.

It was around nine o'clock. Though she now had an appropriate keycard, Scott unlocked the door to the main shelter building from the parking area to let Nella in.

He liked that she suggested they walk around the shelter area and check on the animals. It was late enough that no residents were likely to be doing so unless there were any problems.

Which there weren't. The staffers, Scott told Nella, were under direction to feed the animals before eating their own dinners and take care of any cleanups.

All looked well, and some of the dogs came to the front of their enclosures to greet these humans, who kept going.

"This is so fun," Nella said as they started walking.

Rather than heading to her unit, though, she said she wanted to go upstairs to her new office in the main building and check a few things out.

"Good idea," Scott said. "I was thinking about heading to my office, too, to look at my emails." He hadn't actually been thinking that, at this hour, since they could wait till morning, but it wouldn't hurt to remain in Nella's company as long as he could.

They entered the main building and walked up the back stairs to the office levels. Scott left Nella in the reception office when she said she wanted to take a quick initial look at the file describing her responsibilities on her computer.

"Okay," he said, appreciating the way this woman jumped in to do her job.

He left her there, sitting at that desk and reaching for the shelter phone before heading to his own computer.

He didn't get far, though, before he heard Nella gasp and call out, "Scott, you need to see this."

He hurried back to see her holding the office cell phone she'd lifted from its charger, staring at the screen.

"What's wrong?" he asked.

She said nothing, but her mouth was tight and her expression grim as she handed the phone to him.

He looked at the screen.

A text message on it said:

You have allowed someone to move to your hell pit of a shelter who is going to be killed. Soon. You should be more careful next time. If there is a next time.

Chapter 6

Nella wanted to pound something as Scott read that damn message.

It was a horrible, nasty statement, a warning, of course.

Equally important was that the primary purpose of the Chance Animal Shelter was far from as secure as intended.

At least one person knew enough about it to make threats.

One of the tormenters of a current resident of the shelter? It certainly sounded that way.

And considering the timing, was it Ann's—Alice's—stepson or someone else who'd been close to her? Someone with the same inclination, to hurt that poor woman?

Or did the threat relate to one of the other staff members at the shelter?

Did—

"What the hell?" Scott burst out. "We'd better lock

down this place even more. And I'll send the phone number behind that damn message to one of my contacts at the Chance PD to try to trace its source, but I'll bet the person used a burner phone."

"Probably," Nella shot back through clenched teeth. "Has this happened before? If so, what did you do?" She stood behind the reception desk, and Scott lowered himself into a chair across from her.

"I told you about that situation a while ago when one of our new staffers contacted her ex to brag about having gotten a new life, and he came after her. That's the only time we've had an issue, even though it's not easy to keep this place completely under wraps." He spoke evenly but looked furious, with his blue eyes almost issuing lightning bolts of anger.

"What are we going to do about this?" Nella asked. "Assuming we can't find out who sent it, which is the most likely scenario."

"Oh, we'll find them eventually." Scott sounded so positive Nella wanted to hug him.

And that wasn't the only reason she'd considered hugging him since meeting him that day. He'd hired her. He trusted her.

Now she wanted to do something to earn that trust.

"Yes," she agreed. "We will. And I want to be part of your investigation, be right there helping when you bring them down."

She was staring at him, knowing her expression was grim and hoping it appeared determined. He looked back at her. "I know you've been in law enforcement," he said. "That's one reason I hired you to be a manager. But there's no need for you to place yourself in danger like that. I'll—"

"There's a need to get this fixed," she returned. "I'm going to help. Period."

They glared at each other. And did she really want this kind of responsibility?

No, especially not after what she had gone through with that gang task force—and losing her friend and partner.

Well, she wasn't going to lose anyone under her care here. At least she had backup in Scott and the other managers. But she was going to stay involved.

Their mutual glare lasted only a little longer. Then Nella found herself smiling—sort of—at her boss.

"You want to save everyone, human and animal," she said, the emotion in her voice now no longer that of anger but of understanding—and admiration. "I get it. And if you could save the world on your own, more power to you. But reality—"

"Reality is that I need help. I realize that. It's why I've hired genuine managers here, like you. So—"

"So you'll let me help." There was no question in her voice. Not now.

"Yeah, I guess I'd better."

She stood. "So what's next?"

"Well, neither Camp nor Telma live here, though they're nearby—for the same reasons I generally don't want our managers or even myself to live here and make what's going on even more obvious. But I can have them come in tonight, and—"

"I live here now, and I have experience dealing with bad guys. I'll take care of the shelter, then we can all meet tomorrow and decide on a plan."

She watched the irritation in his expression. Was it combined with admiration, too?

"Tell you what," he said. "At least one of the apartments on the same floor as yours is also vacant. I'll stay here tonight, too. You and I will check first to make sure all the staff members are okay, then I'll patrol the halls periodically through the night, though not at any scheduled time to make it too easy for anyone who might be watching the place to figure out."

"You think they're watching and not just threatening?" That kind of unnerved Nella, despite it being logical.

"We don't know, but we can assume, and try to deal with, the worst."

"Of course."

Scott was one smart law enforcement officer—and shelter director. Nella liked that about him. In fact, she probably liked too much about him.

Too bad she had made a vow to never become involved with someone she worked with, especially in security or anything related. She hadn't had a relationship with Lou, of course, but it hurt to lose him nonetheless.

"Let me make my phone call, then we'll get started, okay?" Scott asked.

"Yeah," she said.

He pulled his phone from his pocket and pressed in some numbers, and as he did, Nella walked around the desk and out the door behind him, into the upstairs hallway outside the offices.

And listened to the rest of the shelter.

Nothing seemed out of order. She didn't even hear any dogs barking, and hopefully a few, at least, had enough watchdog in them to make some noise if anything unusual was happening.

"Okay," said Scott from behind her, startling her a little, since she'd been concentrating. "Let's go."

"Fine." She turned to look at him—and saw him staring at her again with those brilliant blue eyes.

Before she considered what she was doing, she reached out to hug him to try to reassure him—and herself. "We'll figure this out," she told him. "No one around here is going to get hurt."

"Absolutely," he said as they continued to hold each other—possibly too closely.

And, dumb as it was, Nella found herself not wanting to end that hug.

In fact, she wanted more.

And so she stood on her toes, pulled Scott's head down toward hers and kissed him.

It wasn't a simple, friendly kiss, either. Her lips searched his, as if attempting to learn their every line and angle, their every sexual suggestion. His tongue got involved then, as if he, too, were in investigative mode, learning about her, as well.

But they both stepped back after a long moment. Nella considered stepping way back, like running away. But did she really want to do that? Heck, no.

Neither did she want this to go any further. At least, it shouldn't. "Okay," she said, ignoring her own breathlessness and refusing to apologize. "Let's go see how our staff members are doing."

Our staff members. She was definitely part of this shelter. Part of what was going on.

Part of the people Scott could rely on.

That kiss? It was only a punctuation mark, a comma or a colon, suggesting that they would work together to protect the staff members and see what happened next.

That had been wrong. Very wrong.

Even so, Scott looked at Nella and smiled. He wasn't blaming her. He certainly had participated—and then some.

"Okay," he said. "Give me another minute, then we'll check on everyone."

"Great," Nella said as Scott looked at his cell phone, which he had removed from his pocket again—though he didn't yet check the sites he was after.

He needed to get his concentration back.

No matter how good that had felt or who had initiated it, it was totally inappropriate for him to kiss anyone connected with his shelter, particularly one who reported to him as an employee.

Especially the way Scott had shared that kiss with Nella.

He didn't want to give her any ideas. He didn't want to give himself any ideas.

He only wanted to help endangered people, and pets, too. He'd had relationships with women, of course. Some had felt quite good—though he didn't recall any kisses that dug inside him as deeply as this brief one.

But no relationship had been long-lasting—just as well, of course. He had goals in his life that he was on his way to achieving. And besides, one okay relationship had just ended recently. That was enough.

He needed no distractions... Like Nella.

They needed to work together. Potentially close together, to ensure everyone's safety.

But not that close together, no matter how enticing that kiss felt.

"Let's head to the apartment area," Scott said, his voice calm and firm and not suggesting any reminder of what had happened.

"Definitely," Nella responded, sounding somewhat relieved. Her expression appeared worried, though, with her furrowed brow and pursed lips.

Lips that, fortunately, did not appear to be seeking further kisses.

In moments, Nella and he left the offices and headed toward the steps leading to the apartments.

Once they were in the hallway where all the currently occupied apartments were located, Scott decided to call each resident staff member rather than startling them by knocking on the doors.

He explained that to Nella, who stood beside him looking down the hallway with obvious concern, hands on her hips, shoulders leaning forward as if she awaited an order to go dashing ahead, perhaps pounding on doors. Her posture relaxed just a little when he explained his plan.

"Good idea," she said softly.

Scott decided to call Alice first, since she was newest and potentially most vulnerable.

She had already programmed his number into her phone, apparently, as he had told her to, since when she answered she said, "Hi, Scott. Is everything okay?"

"That's what we want to know," he replied. Nella and he were right outside her door, one of the ones on the end. "How are you doing?"

"A whole lot better than before." He caught a note of possible humor in her voice—and so, apparently, did Nella, who smiled a bit since Scott had put his phone on speaker.

"Glad to hear that. And you'll let us know, won't you, if you hear or learn of anything that upsets you, right?"

"Of course. Why? Did you hear something?"

"No, we're just concerned about you."

"Good. And thank you so much again."

"You're welcome," he said, and hung up.

He looked down at Nella's face. The concern he'd

seen before was back. "We're the ones who heard something," she said, her voice low. "Or at least saw it. Since we don't know who or why, we can't assume Alice wasn't the target."

"Of course," Scott said. "But let's do some more checking."

Standing near the end of the hall, he called the other staff members one by one. All sounded happy to hear from him.

All sounded relaxed, unthreatened and eager to go help the shelter animals, if that was what he was calling about.

Looking again at Nella as he thanked each of them, he found himself enjoying her increasingly wry smile.

They found no answers, but neither did they need to call in the other shelter managers or more official assistance, either. All sounded well.

All except for that damn message the shelter had received.

"Let's go down and check on the animals," he finally said. "As I said, I'll stay in an empty apartment near yours for tonight, but I don't think we're getting any answers, assuming our shelter animals are doing as well as our shelter people."

"I certainly hope so," Nella said. "And I'll be delighted to help you check."

"Great," he said. "Let's go."

As they reached the stairway near the end of the hall, he resisted the urge to take Nella's hand.

He appreciated that she had gone through something difficult, being the first to see that texted threat, yet she still clearly intended to do her duty here alongside him.

And that kiss? An anomaly. It wouldn't happen

again. He hurried down the steps in front of Nella toward the shelter areas containing the animals.

First stop was in the reception building, where just those few dogs were kept to greet visitors. They all seemed okay, so he locked that door again quickly.

As he unlocked the next door to go outside, his phone rang. Stepping out onto the concrete surface, still holding the door for Nella, he reached into his pocket with his other hand and drew his phone out.

The name on the screen was Detective Vince Vanderhoff of the Chance Police Department, one of Scott's primary contacts there. Vince had done a lot to help screen backgrounds of the staff members at the shelter, getting help from other cops when needed, too. Scott had called to give him the phone number on the text to the shelter office.

"Yeah, Vince. Anything?" Scott pulled the door closed behind Nella and checked to make sure it automatically locked.

"Best we can tell, it's a burner phone, like you figured." Vince's tone was raspy as usual and rather grumpy. "Anything else happening? Anything else we should be doing?"

Scott's eyes met Nella's. Her gaze was highly inquisitive. But he looked away. He'd tell her what he could in a minute, after hanging up.

"Nothing since I talked to you last." Scott maneuvered to face one of the shelter buildings that contained dogs. "I'll let you know if anything comes up."

"Good. You do that. And be careful, man."

"Will do," Scott said unnecessarily as he said goodbye and hung up. Vince was a good guy and always appeared to care about his fellow cops, no matter what their level.

And at the moment, Scott wasn't exactly any of them. His current assignment kept him part of their team, yet without an official rank.

Nella immediately sidled up to Scott beneath one of the tall lights lining the path between the shelter buildings. "What was that about?" She sounded worried.

"It was one of my contacts at the PD." No sense hiding anything like that from her. She needed to know—even though there wasn't really any news.

"And?"

"And…nothing. Best they can determine, the phone number on the text you saw in the office—"

"—came from a burner phone," she finished, looking toward the ground shaking her head. "Damn. I really wanted to know—"

"We both did." Scott interrupted Nella this time. "The department is still on board, so if we have anything to report, or if we request protection, they're with us."

"Good." But Nella didn't sound particularly relieved. She pulled ahead as he headed to the nearest building, where he unlocked the door.

Some of the dogs inside remained asleep. Others lifted their heads and stared at Nella and him, and most rose and approached the chain-link fencing with heads raised and tails wagging—from the smallest to the largest.

Good dogs, Scott thought—even as Nella smiled and reached over or through the fences to pet those that seemed to request it, including a couple she'd met before. "Good dog," she said to Honey, Pebbles, Shupe and others.

She wasn't really reading his mind, Scott knew, but their thoughts were clearly in sync.

In more ways than this, Scott realized. But he could and would keep things professional between them. That was the best way they could both achieve their goals—protecting not only these great shelter pets who needed new, loving homes, but also, and more importantly, the people, the staff members who also needed new, loving homes, or at least refuge from their old homes as well as new, safe, more enjoyable lives.

Scott had no doubt Nella would work with him in all ways possible to achieve both.

Platonically and professionally—despite that mind-captivating kiss he kept thinking about.

They soon left this building and repeated pretty much the same entry and greeting with dogs in their remaining kennels in the buildings from the beginning to the end of the pathway, ending up in the building that housed cats and smaller pets.

All appeared fine. No surprise.

It hadn't been the animals in the shelter who were threatened, but one of the human residents.

Nella was clearly relieved nevertheless as they once again stepped onto the path and he locked the final door behind them. She obviously cared about all the residents.

"Anything else we should do tonight?" she asked, standing beside him and looking up into his face. The lights were relatively dim here, yet he had no problem seeing how pretty she was—and how obviously concerned.

"Let's go to bed," he said, then wished he could erase the words for their potential suggestiveness—especially when he noticed a small reaction in Nella's expression. Interested? Humorous? Both?

Neither?

He clarified, "As I said, I'm hanging out here tonight in one of the other empty apartments. Let's go back upstairs so we can both head into our respective units and hopefully get some sleep."

There. That should make it abundantly clear that he wasn't suggesting they spend the night together or anything like that.

Although the thought did make him react below, at least a little. But he would keep that completely to himself.

They finished traversing the path back to where the door led to the upstairs stairway, and he unlocked that door again.

Soon they were both on the level where the staff members lived. He walked Nella the few steps to the door of the apartment to which she was assigned.

"Which one will you be in?" she asked.

The thought of telling her where, in case she wanted to join him… *Forget that*, he told himself quickly.

"It's across the hall from yours, closer to the hall's end." He strode to where he was near that door, then gestured toward it.

"Great," she said. "And we have each other's phone numbers in case anything happens and we need to get together again."

What she said was completely accurate and unsuggestive, yet it still suggested something to Scott.

"Right," he said, with no inflection in his voice. He walked back to her unit as she pulled her keycard from her pocket and unlocked the door.

"Good night, Nella," he said.

"Good night, Scott." But instead of walking through the now open door, she turned back toward him. "This place is amazing," she said. "In so many ways. I want to talk to you more about my duties soon, not just read that file. And I intend to work with you in as many ways as possible to make sure people and pets all thrive, as they should."

"Then you're already one damned good manager," he said—and suddenly, without his planning or even anticipating it, he had Nella in his arms again.

Who'd initiated it?

He wasn't sure, but the kiss they now shared was every bit as hot as their earlier one.

"Good night," Nella said again a very long minute later. Her brown eyes were lowered and enticing as she looked back into his face, then turned and shut the door behind her.

And fortunately, Scott noted, the hall had remained empty.

Chapter 7

Nella stood at the entry of her small apartment for a minute, breathing gently, her back against the door.

The door that she had locked behind her after opening it with a keycard. And after sharing another kiss with Scott that made her entire body quiver in unwanted anticipation of something that would never, could never, happen.

Oh, she definitely enjoyed sex with the right man. But except for some short-term affairs over her thirty-three-year life, she hadn't discovered a man who was right for more than a short while. She'd been glad when a relationship of sorts lasted for a year, which had happened a couple of times.

But most of the guys she'd cared for were also cops, since other guys she met didn't seem able to get into the idea of dating a female law enforcement officer for long. And other cops? Well, she wasn't certain what they were looking for, but so far she hadn't found one she wanted to share any kind of long-term commitment with.

Okay. Enough of this. More than enough.

She realized she was thirsty. Fortunately, she had some bottled water in her car, which was still parked in the shelter's lot outside. Although Scott had offered to help bring her things in, she hadn't yet gotten him to act on it, and she hadn't yet brought in her suitcase, either. This was a good time to do that—and use the keys Scott had given her.

But just as she unlocked her door, a knock sounded on it.

Why wasn't she surprised to see Scott standing there when she opened it? "It just dawned on me that we haven't brought up the luggage from your car," he said. "Right? Let's go get it."

Once more, Nella was pleasantly surprised about their appearing to be on the same wavelength for many things, mostly wanting to protect people and animals.

Being in sync in other ways as well was an additional asset.

Too bad their relationship had to be, and would continue to be, completely professional and platonic.

"Good timing," she said. "I was just planning to head that way." Their eyes caught then, and she saw what she interpreted to be not just amusement, but a touch of pleasure in Scott's expression as if he, too, enjoyed their "kind-of" connection now and then.

"Got your car key?" Scott asked as she started into the hallway.

"Yes. I was already used to keeping my keys with me, and as long as I'm here that's clearly going to be an important part of my life as long as I include cards."

"You got it."

They continued to the stairway, still seeing none of the floor's staff residents.

After walking down the stairs and unlocking and re-locking even more doors, they were soon in the parking lot in the shadows at the rear of the shelter. Nella directed Scott to her blue Toyota hybrid, which sat not far from the black Honda SUV in which he'd driven them to the restaurant.

She'd brought one large suitcase and two smaller bags, since she'd been optimistic about getting the job. In addition, she had a backpack in which she'd stored the water bottles she'd been thinking about.

"This all your stuff?" Scott asked as she slammed the trunk closed.

"All I brought," she said. "I won't need any more now, and if this becomes long-term, as I hope, and I move into a Chance apartment, I'll have my other things in storage in L.A. brought here."

"Good move, in many ways," Scott said.

And again Nella liked his attitude.

He insisted on carrying the heaviest bags, which she thought was kind and gentlemanly. Soon, all her things were upstairs in her apartment, sitting on the floor near the door.

It was time again for Scott to go. Which was a good idea. It was getting late—and she'd need a good night's sleep to face the next day.

"Thanks," Nella said to him, then realized this was an appropriate time to ask him something that had been on her mind.

Sure, she'd ended her prior lease, but she hadn't signed anything here yet—so she had no idea about the rental amount.

"You're welcome," Scott said.

"So will I get my lease tomorrow? How much rent will I be paying?" She didn't allow herself to cringe in anticipation. She was hoping, in this small town and in these circumstances, with a small apartment in the facility where she would be on call all the time, that it wouldn't be too pricey.

She'd taken a cut in her salary to work here, after all.

But she wasn't a "volunteer" like the staff member residents.

"You'll certainly get to see the documents our staff members sign to make sure they're aware of what this place is like, and that, like our managers, they have to keep it completely confidential." Scott stood facing Nella now, arms crossed, his blue eyes narrowed as if helping to tell her how serious this was.

Which she already knew.

"Good," Nella said. "And my lease?"

"You don't need to sign anything as long as you live here as a manager. Nor do you need to pay any rent. I'm aware we don't pay as well as the LAPD, but giving you this benefit, at least for now, may help. Okay?"

His serious expression suggested she'd better say yes if she wanted to stay here. Wanted this job.

And the answer was yes to both.

"That's great!" Nella grinned. "I love it."

And so far there wasn't anything she didn't love about being here, at the Chance Animal Shelter, with its nice staff and protected animals.

With caring managers.

With Scott.

But there had been that threatening text that needed to be solved...

"Good. We'll discuss your specific duties tomorrow. Right now, I think we both need to rest."

"I agree," Nella said. "But—well, after that text message and what you said, I'm planning to wake up once or twice, too, and walk around this hall to make sure all's well."

Scott's serious expression morphed into a hint of a smile. "Well, maybe we'll run into one another then," he said.

Nella laughed. "Should we coordinate, or would it be better if we chose different times?"

"Either should work—although be sure to let me know if you see anything when you're out and about and I'm not. And don't leave your apartment if you hear anything outside. Just call me. If it's me you hear, I'll let you know."

"Likewise," Nella said.

And almost as if they'd choreographed it, they approached each other. This time, their hug was brief, their kiss short and more friendly than anything else.

But Nella couldn't help remembering those other kisses again as she locked the door behind Scott.

The first thing Scott did after leaving Nella was return to the shelter's offices. He checked to make sure there'd been no more texted threats on the main line, then went into his own office to pick up the backpack of vital things he kept there in case he needed to stay in this facility for a while—mostly pajamas and a few changes of underwear, plus a charger for his cell phone. Something he hadn't needed to get into before. His real home was close enough that he could get anything else fairly quickly, but during daylight, when other managers were around and in charge, was best.

In his temporary apartment, he sat on the small sofa for a while, checking local law enforcement sites on his phone for anything interesting, particularly reports that might be related to the threat the shelter had received, but found nothing.

It was getting pretty late, but he decided to take a walk down the hall before heading to bed. He'd received no calls or texts from Nella, so presumably she hadn't heard anything that worried her, either. He was unlikely to see her again now—which sent a brief wave of regret through him that he quickly shrugged off.

Better that she stay in her apartment and sleep through the night. He just wanted to ensure that she remained safe, and that the others living here did, too.

He rose from the small sofa, headed to his front door and unlocked it, glad that, when he'd had this building redone, he had paid to have it made as silent as possible, with its specially designed laminated floors with pads underlying them, and heavily plastered and insulated walls. The damaged staff members who lived here needed their privacy. Especially when, stressed out, they began pacing their units. Or, worse, crying. He'd seen that happen to both the women and the men.

No, this hadn't been cheap. And he wasn't wealthy.

But this shelter did have a substantial group of wealthy, quiet patrons, including one whose daughter had disappeared from his life for a while when she moved here to escape her menacing husband.

Now the ex was out of the picture, the family was reunited and the shelter had benefited from the father's gratitude. And the Chance PD had other similar, generous benefactors, including people who had adopted pets from them.

But mostly, they were funded by the police department.

Now Scott stepped outside and quietly pulled his

door closed, making sure he didn't see or hear anything to cause him to dive inside again and lock himself in.

But all he heard was silence. He locked the door behind him and started slowly down the hall.

And saw the door across from him begin to open.

Nella.

He couldn't help smiling and shaking his head. What was it about that woman? She seemed to be reading his mind somehow. Aiming for the same results around here that he intended, as far as helping people and animals. Wanting to achieve them the same way he did. Attempting to do it at times and in ways that matched his.

Unless he was reading her wrong. She had just arrived. And although he'd been happy with his current managers, he had really hoped to find an even better one with whom he could work closely.

Well, he couldn't work too closely with Nella, of course. He'd already seen that.

But it wasn't a huge surprise when she did indeed walk out into the hallway across from him, stopped and stared at him.

Shook her head so her long brown hair swished sexily over her shoulders. And immediately placed a smile on her beautiful face that gave him a sudden urge to join her across the hall and take her into his arms. Again.

Not going to happen, of course.

Except for joining her across the hall. And—well, yes, he did put an arm around her to lead her in the direction he'd intended to go. He leaned down as she turned her head up toward his.

"Fancy meeting you here," she whispered, her voice as low as he'd hoped someone speaking at this hour in the hallway would talk. Not surprising, coming from this highly cognizant and caring woman.

He merely nodded at first, then asked in a voice even quieter than hers, "Did you hear anything?"

She shook her head. "Just wanted to peek around before I went to bed."

They walked slowly from one end of the hallway, where their units were, to the far end, then back again. Scott heard nothing from any of the apartments, not even any TVs, although they were each equipped with one. But the quietness was at least partly a result of the insulation he'd had put into the walls. They also went upstairs to the meeting room, which was empty.

Soon, they were back outside their respective apartments.

"Let's both sleep well," Scott said, and waited till a nodding Nella entered her apartment and he heard her lock the door.

And was a bit miffed at his own disappointment that they hadn't shared so much as a brief hug this time as they parted.

Nella checked her phone before changing into her pajamas. Nothing there.

She checked the local news briefly on the television, with the sound turned down. Nothing particularly interesting there, either—not in Chance, or in Los Angeles.

She figured she would sleep well. It had, after all, been a long day, with plenty of ups and downs—from meeting and helping Alice, to getting hired, to that terrible threat to the shelter and to meeting Scott and feeling much too attracted to him despite all the chiding she'd given herself.

Well, tomorrow would be another day. But before going to bed, she set her phone alarm to go off in a couple of hours. She'd check the hallway again then to try to ensure its security.

That next time, she surely wouldn't see Scott. Nor would she now. She threw on her robe, unlocked her door and went back into the hallway.

The lights along the walls were dimmer now, apparently on some kind of timer. It was still light enough to see.

But Nella saw nothing new. The walls were the same, as were the doors, ceiling and floor. And no person was in the hall.

She heard nothing, either, undoubtedly a good thing. None of the staff was calling for help or arguing or making any other noise that could be heard in the hallway.

She hoped that meant they were all safe.

No matter what that horrible text had said.

Well, she was here because she'd been a cop. She still had a cop mentality. That was why she felt she hadn't done her job well enough before, or that gang task force situation would have had a better ending.

With no one on her side killed.

Did she have a minor case of PTSD? She didn't really want to look into it—but wouldn't be surprised if she did.

In any case, here, she would do everything she could to make sure nothing went wrong, that all staff members—and managers and animals, too, of course—remained safe.

She had a sense that the closer she worked with Scott, the more likely she'd have the outcome she craved.

That was the reason she missed him now, she told herself as she returned to her apartment.

The only reason.

Chapter 8

Scott woke up at his normal time of 6:30 a.m. But this wasn't a normal morning, since he was in an apartment at the shelter.

After a quick shower, he threw on a shelter T-shirt and jeans. Then he unlocked the door, after listening for any sounds in the hallway.

He heard some soft voices from down the hall, as well as a few barks from outside. Ahh. Not only were some of the dogs awake, but Nella was, too. He felt certain that one of those voices was hers.

She'd gotten up at least once last night to meander down the hall and check on things. So had he. Twice. The first time, he had just returned to this apartment before he heard her door open.

Of course he'd had an urge to join her. She might as well get used to his teaming up with her when she did her job and worked at taking care of things around here, at least when they both were in the same area. He wasn't sure how long he would remain in this apartment. Probably a while, until they figured out who'd sent that text and dealt with it. But once they did, he liked the idea of having Nella be the only manager to continue residing here, and patrolling the residential hallway would make a good duty for her to accomplish on at least some nights.

Did he trust her more than his other, longer-term managers, Telma and Camp? Of course not. If he didn't trust either one of them, he'd fire that person.

But his interactions with Nella so far had convinced him of her dedication to helping both people and animals. And she didn't have anywhere else to live at the moment. He wouldn't have any qualms about attempting to convince her to live in this building as long as she worked at the shelter.

The fact that he might wind up seeing her more often that way? Irrelevant.

He closed his apartment door behind him and strode down the hall toward those voices. Sure enough, Scott saw Nella's slender T-shirt-clad back in the open doorway as he reached the last apartment on the same side of the hall as his current residence. Bibi's unit.

Both women exited it and stood still, looking toward Scott. "Bibi was just about to head downstairs when she saw me walking down the hall," Nella said. "I asked to see her apartment, to learn how similar it is to mine." Nella's cool glance at Scott suggested she didn't want him to ask questions, which he wouldn't. Not now, at least. But he figured Nella had wanted to go into Bibi's unit for reasons other than checking its appearance.

He'd find out more from her later.

"They're all pretty similar," Scott said, "but it's a

good idea to find that out for yourself." He paused. "Does anyone else seem to be up yet?"

"Nope. Just us," Bibi said. "But I bet some of the others are already outside walking dogs. They usually are by now. I want to show Nella our kitchen and eating area, but first we plan to walk some dogs, too. I explained to her that's one of our first responsibilities each morning besides keeping the kennel areas clean— although we wind up cleaning them even when our doggy residents have been good all night."

"Exactly." Scott nodded at both of them. "That's what people who help rescue pets do. I'll come with you."

Nella seemed to study his face, as though trying to read how truthful he was being.

He figured she wasn't questioning the need to walk dogs or clean up after them—but whether it was okay to take walks this morning after that threatening message.

Was he just guessing her thoughts? Maybe, but she looked as concerned as he felt, so he figured he guessed correctly.

"Good thing we have some large areas inside our fence to walk the dogs," Scott said, responding to what he believed were Nella's unasked questions about security. "They can get their exercise and do what else they need to do better and faster than if we had to take them off our grounds."

"Sounds like fun," Nella said as she fell into step beside Bibi, and Scott trailed them a bit. "The walking part, I mean. Not the cleaning, but I'll do whatever's needed around here."

"Me, too!" Bibi sounded excited. "And I think it's cool that even our managers don't mind getting their hands dirty. So to speak."

She turned briefly and smiled at him, revealing the

gap between her front teeth as she did very often. Bibi was damned good with the animals, and with her fellow staff members.

And he knew she had a good reason to be a resident at this shelter.

They reached the end of the hall and Scott was amused when Nella was the one to reach into her pocket and pull out her keycard. Soon, they were all outside within the shelter area, heading toward the rear of the facility to go leash up a few dogs.

He allowed Bibi to pull ahead and was glad when Nella began walking at his side. "I hope this is okay." She talked so softly he had to strain to listen—which was a good thing. "I thought about trying to get up even earlier and making everyone stay in their rooms this morning—except to let me in, like Bibi did, so I could confirm everything looked all right, as it did in hers. And she seemed calm and happy and...well, unthreatened, so she appears okay—assuming whoever issued the threat would also attempt to scare the target before doing anything. But I didn't tell her anything, wasn't sure you wanted the residents to know anything. And I figured you'd have given orders to me and the other managers if you had something in particular in mind for us to do."

"That's right," he said. "And I did get in touch with Telma and Camp to tell them about the message, as well as that Chance PD contact who had the phone number checked. Our two managers are walking the outside perimeter, looking for anything out of the ordinary. And we'll have police car patrols today." He paused. "But aside from checking in Bibi's room, have you done or seen anything unusual—either this morning, or when you got up again last night?"

"How did you know I was up again last night?" Her brows furrowed as her eyes briefly met his in a glare.

"Because I think I'm beginning to know how you think," he said in a playful tone. "And because I think similarly and also got up."

Before Nella could respond, Bibi stopped walking and looked at them as they caught up with her. "What are you two whispering about?"

"I just want to know what we have for breakfast," Nella replied.

"I told her about how some of you, especially Sara, cook really good pancakes," Scott said, "and I rarely get any, since I don't generally live here."

"You stayed here last night, right? Looked like you came out of one of the apartments when Nella and I left mine."

"Good catch," Scott said. He didn't want to tell one of the residents the whole truth—but some of it wouldn't hurt, to ensure they remained particularly careful. "We've heard some rumors about information regarding this place getting out in public more than it should. I'll talk about it a bit at breakfast. Right now, I think we're okay, but I do want everyone to remain alert and careful—and I may just hang out here a little more than usual in the meantime."

Bibi's face seemed to grow even puffier than usual as the edges of her mouth drew down. "Are all of us in danger? Some of us?"

"We hope not," Nella said. "But now that I'm here, I'm glad I'll be staying in your building at night. Rumors often don't have substance, but we don't want to take any chances with our staff members. I know that Scott and the other managers really care for all of you, and I'm joining in on that."

Scott wanted to take the couple of steps between Nella and him and give her a big hug, but of course he wouldn't. Not with others around, and most likely not again when they were alone, either, not even a strictly friendly gesture.

Even so, he nodded toward her, then smiled at Bibi. "Looks like I did a good job in hiring Nella, doesn't it?"

"It sure does." Bibi was the one to draw close to Nella and hug her. "Now, as long as it's okay, I think we've got some really nice and needy doggies who need our attention."

"Let's hurry, then." Nella smiled at her new buddy, then aimed a glance at Scott that suggested she was really into this, being both a manager and a protector at this wonderful shelter of his.

Okay, Nella thought as they walked out of the apartment building and onto the concrete area inside the shelter. She understood why Scott had said what he did, telling Bibi he wanted to let everyone know to be even more careful without unnerving them with the complete truth.

She agreed.

Especially since she would remain here and help to keep all residents safe. And so, apparently, would Scott, for as long as he thought his increased presence was needed.

But how best should they do that? Clearly Scott didn't want to alarm them with the details of why they were more concerned than usual.

A lot more, she was sure.

Anyway, they remained inside the safe, covered fencing. She wanted to check to see who all was out here walking dogs and who was in the kitchen area, do a census of sorts to make sure everyone was well.

And not dead, the way that threat had gone.

Unless she could take Scott aside comfortably, though, she wouldn't announce her intention to him or anyone else.

Despite the threat, it was certainly fun to be out here. Of the eight staff members, four were out already with dogs on leashes, walking back and forth, allowing their pups to sniff the narrow grassy areas at the sides of the walkway—and stop and sniff and squat and whatever else they wanted.

The people? Nella had tried to make herself memorize who was who. But she appreciated it when Scott began reminding her.

"Since you're so new here and we've got a bunch of staff members and pups, I'll point out who's got who with them right now."

"And since most of the dogs are our medium and larger ones, I'm going to pop in here—" still standing beside them at the beginning of the path, Bibi pointed toward the shelter building nearest them "—and get myself a small dog to walk. Care to join me?" She looked toward Nella.

"Yes, in a minute." And Nella was glad when Bibi left, since none of the other people were particularly near them. "What do you think?" she then whispered to Scott, who drew up close to her. Very close. She even felt his hip against her side, a feeling that she noticed too much. And also liked too much.

But he said, "Just wanted to fill you in on more before we join the others in walking the dogs," he said. "I'm going to leave Camp, Telma and you in charge after breakfast while I visit the Chance PD and request more help. Maybe that threat meant nothing, but—"

"But we have to assume otherwise, of course, till we know for sure," Nella finished. This was important to her, and it was also important that Scott understood her dedication to his shelter.

"Right."

"In case you haven't noticed, I really give a damn."

Scott smiled and look her straight in the eyes with his sparkling blue ones. "I've noticed," he said. "Now, we need to go ahead with what I started pointing out before."

He quickly began indicating each staff member and which dogs they walked. "You probably remember Darleen's favorite pup is Pebbles, the Maltipoo," he began, nodding in the direction of the middle-aged lady and dog.

"Absolutely."

Then there was Shupe, the Shetland sheepdog mix, surprisingly being walked by thin, senior Kathy; thirty-something Muriel walking Honey, a black Lab mix; and Warren walking Rover, a Scottish terrier mix.

For fun, Nella walked up to each of them and said hello, then bent to pat the pups. "Have a wonderful walk," she said.

"We've been at this for twenty minutes," said Warren, a senior with thin gray hair and a happy smile whom she'd seen before. "My buddy Rover here has accomplished a lot. Good boy!" This was directed to Rover, who had begun sniffing in the grass.

All this made Nella eager to walk a dog, too. She told Scott that, and he accompanied her inside the second building.

There, among several other pups, he introduced her

to Baby, a pug mix, got a couple of leashes that were hanging on the wall, then took Herman, a Chihuahua mix, from the same kennel as Baby.

Once they were back outside, Nella took a deep breath and smiled. "This is fantastic," she said, bending once more, this time to pat Baby and Herman.

"And it can distract us a lot," Scott reminded her—not that she really needed the reminder.

"I understand," she said. "I see Telma and Camp up ahead. Let's go there and take them aside and make sure they know what's going on—and you can be sure I'll be observant of everything and everyone that's at all near me."

"Good girl." Scott nodded toward her with a look that suggested he knew he was addressing her as he would an obedient dog.

Which only made Nella laugh. "Of course," she said. "Now, let's go, Baby." The chubby little pug with the flat nose looked up at her as if understanding at least her name, if not exactly what was going on. "Let's beat Scott and Herman to reach Camp and Telma."

Then, maneuvering carefully around the humans and pups, Nella sped up in the direction of the other managers.

"Good morning," Telma said as Nella caught up with them, then looked down. "So you're a pug fan?"

"Love 'em," Nella said. "Especially Baby." She knelt to hug the little pug, who snorted at her, making her laugh.

"Are you heading to breakfast soon?" asked Camp.

"In a few minutes, after Baby and I finish our walk."

Sweet Baby and Herman both accomplished what was needed fairly quickly. Of course both Nella and

Scott did what cleanup was necessary, then took them back to their enclosures.

Their speed was a good thing, since the others who'd been walking dogs were also settling them back in their habitats, some sweetly promising it was temporary and they'd all find new homes soon.

Nella hoped that was the case—and also hoped there would be more rescue dogs brought in to care for and find new homes for.

Scott and she exited the building together. "Come on," he said. "Breakfast time." He began walking ahead of her to the admin building.

Nella followed closely behind. She realized she was hungry—for the information Scott would impart, even more than food.

Chapter 9

Scott didn't have to unlock the dining area door. Everyone here had access to it and went in and out all the time.

Of course, as part of the orientation to the shelter, Scott always warned incoming residents to be alert everywhere, especially in an unsecured place like this one. And though the indoor eating area's doors remained open, the place had some degree of security since it was behind the fencing surrounding the whole location.

Knowing how he'd wanted this facility to be, Scott had made sure the design of the dining area on the lower floor of the residential building was large and inviting, with a good-sized, brick-walled kitchen off to the side, which contained several refrigerators and freezers, along with a large gas stove, ovens and other major equipment as well as a good supply of cookware, plates, glasses and utensils.

At the moment, he was glad to see breakfast being served as usual at one end of the dining room by a staff member, Sara, who'd most likely cooked it, and Telma, who'd probably supervised her cooking and the area earlier. Sara wasn't as fond of animals as the others were, so she rarely walked dogs, although she did help to feed, and clean the cages of the smaller rescue pets in the last building along the pathway.

So why had Scott accepted her at this shelter? Her parents were friends of Scott's parents and his aunt Pat—his uncle Andy's widow—and though he hadn't completely described what he was up to here, his folks knew he was involved in helping people in need and not only animals. So how could he resist their plea?

Today, Sara wore a yellow Chance Animal Shelter shirt over jeans. Middle-aged and quiet, Sara always appeared sad. That was unsurprising, considering the history that had brought her here. She had been a cook at a well-known gourmet restaurant in San Diego, but her boss, a married and controlling much younger man, had begun sexually harassing her. She'd reported it, as she should have, but the guy had been smart and turned the tables on her, purposely tainting something she'd cooked and serving it, making a few of his customers ill.

He had promised he would kill someone and ensure she got blamed for it if she ever talked about it again.

And when she quit and started to leave, she'd been the one who'd been poisoned, in a way that no one could prove it had been her boss. Nor could she prove he'd threatened to do it again if she ever spoke about it.

Which had boosted Sara to the top of Scott's list of whom he believed the recently received threat involved—except that Sara had been here for more than six months, so why start this now?

In any case, after his investigation of the situation, Scott felt fine having Sara be the shelter's primary cook for the residents. He knew, with her background, she would do all she could to ensure the food was safe to avoid any further suspicions against her. Plus, Telma was frequently around to supervise the kitchen.

Scott knew Nella was eager to obtain background stories of all staff members and figured she would find Sara's particularly interesting when she learned about it from him or from Sara herself.

"Let's wash up and get our breakfasts first," Scott told Nella, who had remained near him as they entered the eating area. "I'll eat fast, then talk to the group."

"Fine." Her head turned back and forth as she surveyed the dining room. "Nice place for a large group of people," she said. "Looks like it can accommodate a lot more than our current staff and managers."

Scott nodded, pleased at her perceptiveness. "That's the whole idea," he said. "We'll make room for as many people as we can, just like we can also add dogs and cats and other pets to our animal areas." They'd reached the end of the extended table covered with long beige tablecloths—washed often, and never coated with dog fur. Food was laid out on it, and Sara and Telma were in the middle helping to scoop portions for the couple of people in line in front of Nella and him. Scott picked up a plate and took some cantaloupe and grapes from a couple of the first bowls they came to.

"I like this place," Nella said, putting the same fruit onto her plate and adding some cherries. She picked one of the cherries and began eating it, soon depositing the pit and stem back onto her plate.

"Glad to hear that," Scott said. And he liked her— that was his next thought, but he kept on going in the line, not looking back at her again, getting some scrambled eggs, a pancake and wheat toast.

He also liked how she greeted Sara by name, even though, as far as he knew, they'd barely seen one another before. But he had introduced them, and Sara, shy as always, nevertheless managed to say, "Hi, Nella. Hope you like our food."

"I'm sure I will."

Scott led Nella to one of the tables that had people sitting along the sides, but spaces at the end. She said in a low voice, "Maybe I should make plans now with Sara to talk to her."

"Why?" Scott asked.

"It's not just Sara I want to talk to, of course, and I'll probably wait till later anyway, till sometime between meals." After putting her plate down, Nella remained standing and approached Scott so the bottom of his right shoulder touched the top of her left one—and they could keep their conversation confidential. "You're aware that I want to get to know each of the staff members and what brought them here. Since I understand that my job is mostly to protect them, knowing their backgrounds can only help…and it might also help to figure out who sent that text. I think, under the circumstances, this is a good time to follow up on it. My being new here will be the excuse, and maybe I'll get a sense of whether any of them feels particularly threatened by anyone from their pasts or otherwise at the moment."

As always, in the short while Scott had known Nella, he liked her attitude. "Good idea," he said. He wouldn't mind hearing how things went and could get an update from her later.

And he still planned to head to the police station to talk to some of his contacts.

When Nella offered to get him some coffee from a separate table at the far end of those holding food, he accepted. "Just black is fine," he said.

Another reason to appreciate her.

He was finding a lot of those. Maybe too many. But he planned to take advantage of her helpfulness in as many ways as possible to help keep this place thriving.

And perhaps to help figure out where that threat came from. But he would be the one to deal with it.

Whatever else happened around here, Scott intended to keep everyone safe.

And now that also included Nella.

Breakfast was good. Nella enjoyed it. Nothing stood out as gourmet, but there was enough food, and enough variety, that everyone should be full and happy.

Scott sat across from her. At the far end of the table, Alice sat near the two men, Warren and Leonard. Other people Nella hadn't yet met were at a nearby table.

The staff member sitting beside Nella, a chair between them, was, coincidentally, her new friend Bibi.

Which was a good thing. Nella turned to her and said, "I loved the dog walking this morning. I'd like to do even more after breakfast. I'm not sure what the protocol is around here, but would you accompany me?"

Bibi seemed to be inserting quite a bit of food into her mouth with each bite. Today, her Chance Animal Shelter T-shirt was gray.

Bibi responded to her question. "Oh, we're pretty much free to go around the whole shelter whenever we want, particularly if we're dog walking. First thing today, though, I'm lined up to visit the cat house and give the kitties a little attention. Would you like to join me there?"

"I'd love to," Nella replied. She wasn't sure whether she'd get much time to speak privately with Bibi, but she'd do her best to work something out. "I know I wasn't near you after we reached the dog shelter area, but I did see you in the distance, walking a little terrier mix, right?"

"Yep, that was Mocha. She's a real sweetheart, and I'm not sure why she hasn't been adopted yet."

"We'll have to work a little harder on that," Nella said, "though I figure most of the pups here are sweet enough that they should get adopted fast."

"It usually takes a while." And for the next few minutes, Bibi informed Nella about the adoption process at this shelter, including how the available animals got publicized on the internet.

Nella figured that had to be the only thing about the shelter to show up on the internet.

Nella noticed some movement out of the corner of her eye and turned to see Scott rising. He nodded at her, then walked toward the food table but stood in front of it rather than getting anything off it and faced the crowd.

"Hey, everyone," he called. "Can I have your attention? Got a couple of things to talk to you about."

There had been an undercurrent of conversation in the air, but that sound lowered, then ended. Nella could see Scott well from where she sat, but the people on the side of the table where he was now standing all moved their chairs around so they could watch him.

Scott soon began talking, projecting his voice. "I've heard from a couple of my sources that there are some new rumors flying around about the nature of our shelter, though I don't know how public they are. I'm going to check into it and use some other resources to try to make it clear that this is an especially wonderful animal shelter that also invites homeless people to volunteer, and that's all—although of course claiming our residents were homeless is just part of the impression we want to convey for your protection. But if you hear anything yourselves, be sure to let me know—whether it's from a friend we allow you to access, or a media source or...well, hopefully we won't feel threatened by any of it, but we need to know and deal with anything, if any of it's true. Okay?"

He began looking around the room, and Nella got the impression he met the eyes of nearly everyone he focused on.

The last ones were Camp, in the middle of the same side where Scott had sat, and Telma, who'd moved from the serving table to Nella's side of her table and now stood watching Scott. Sara had joined her there, too.

Both managers just watched Scott and nodded, saying nothing. But one staff member, Warren, stood and called, "What does this mean? Are we in danger of losing our new identities? Are we in danger, period?"

"Not if we can help it." Nella hadn't meant to interrupt, even in a positive way, but she recognized Warren's fear.

And she also was the one who'd first seen the threat that caused Scott to talk to everyone—the threat he didn't want to pass along to those being protected.

If it had been more specific, she figured things would be different. But no one person had been mentioned.

Just someone who'd been taken in to live here.

Warren was a fairly short, senior man. He had a lot of gray hair, and not a lot of bulk on his body. And of course he wore one of the shelter T-shirts, a brown one.

"But we don't really know you," he called out toward Nella, his hands on his hips.

"She's one of us." Scott, arms crossed, glared at Warren. "Just like you became one of us in the past few weeks."

Then Warren wasn't one of their longest-term staffers, Nella thought. He could be the reason for the threat, too.

"Yes, I am one of you," she said aloud. "But I'm new here, and though I've met most of you, at least to say hi, you don't really know me. I'm a former officer with the Los Angeles Police Department, so I know how to enforce the law." Inside, she cringed, waiting for the questions to come about why she'd left the LAPD.

She had no intention of mentioning the task force and what had gone wrong.

"Well, you're in good company." Warren's tone was a bit gentler. "Our other three managers are with the Chance PD, or at least they used to be. So why did you leave that great, big police force to come here?"

Nella had of course considered how to answer this, and she waved her hand toward Scott when he appeared ready to jump in again and respond. "That was part of the reason," she said. "It was big. I learned a lot there and enjoyed it—as much as anyone can enjoy a job where you can be in danger a lot of the time. But it taught me that I really wanted to help other people in danger even more than telling citizens what to do to obey the law. One of my fellow officers heard me say that, one who knew about the Chance Animal Shelter, and he suggested I look into this. So here I am. And my continuing goal is to do everything I can to help our staff members in all ways they need help."

All of that was true, even if it wasn't complete. Warren was nodding, lower lip out as if he approved what she said. Nella then glanced toward Scott. His brows were raised in what she interpreted as an expression of approval, too.

"All right, then," Warren said. "You seem okay."

"So do you." Nella shot him a smile. "And I hope to get to know you better. Maybe we can grab some coffee here together later today or sometime soon and just talk."

And she hoped then she would learn the reason for Warren being here.

Just like she wanted to know the reasons for all staff members being here.

Plus, while they talked, she would ask some questions that she planned to sound innocent—but might tell her whether Warren was the subject of the menacing text.

After breakfast, though, she'd already made plans to go with Bibi to the cat house, and she would definitely follow through with that.

Breakfast was over. Scott met quickly right outside the door with his managers, including Nella. He stood with his back to that door, watching as some staffers exited. The managers stood in front of him.

Telma's brown hair was longer than usual, and he wondered if she was purposely letting it grow or simply hadn't taken the time to get it cut. Camp's blond beard seemed more trimmed than he usually kept it.

And Nella? She looked damned good to him, with her dark brown hair and attentive, lovely face and brown eyes.

"Now, here's how the rest of the morning will go," Scott said to them. "I'm going to give Nella a more detailed rundown of what her duties here will be, then head to the Chance PD to ask some questions. Telma and Camp, you'll follow your regular routine."

Scott had Nella follow him to his office, where he described that routine to Nella as part of his ongoing description of her job. "First and foremost," he told her as she sat facing him across his desk, "you need to stay aware of who is where, and what's going on—and if anything appears dangerous, especially now, after that text. Otherwise, the managers like Telma and Camp, and now you, mostly walk around the shelter observing staff members as they provide attention to the animal residents, including more dog walking. And talking to them. Getting a sense of their states of mind that day. Before that, though, one of you will go into the reception building and exchange the dogs housed there for others within the shelter, so our canine residents always have new things to see and learn—and so do the staff members. I'll teach you some more as time goes on about how we help to find those pets new homes, or you may just see it in action. Also, please spend at least an hour or so every day in your office at the computer, familiarizing yourself with what's going on in this area and if the cops are involved with anything they've made public."

"Sounds good." Nella asked him a few questions, mostly about how to choose which staff members to work with—which he indicated usually was random— and when they should contact him if they thought they saw a problem.

"Anytime, of course," he told Nella, "and right away. And all I've described to you is flexible. For example, I know you have other plans today—talking individually to some of our staff members." He added that to inform the other managers. He was aware that Nella had made other arrangements since she wanted to spend at least a few minutes with each of those staff members to get to know their backgrounds. He was fine with that. It was a good idea for the residents to get to know the new manager a bit by talking with her. And it didn't hurt for them to retell their stories, not only to inform her of why they were there, but also to talk about it more with someone who would care what they said and knew they were here with new identities.

Most important to him and the shelter, though, Nella might get some idea of whether any staff members were feeling threatened, or had been in touch with people they shouldn't have contact with, or any other bit of knowledge that might help them figure out why that threat had come in, and which resident it referred to.

"In the future, after you've talked with everyone a bit, we'll want you to do as Telma and Camp do—which is more general, and more protective of the whole facility."

"Sounds good to me," Nella said.

"Great. Now, go to it, all of you. I'll see you later."

Chapter 10

Nella watched Scott walk quickly along the pathway, toward the front of the building. She assumed he was going to his office.

Telma and Camp remained facing her as they still stood near the doorway from which staffers exited in groups.

"I'll be interested in joining you to work with the staffers the way you do," Nella told them. Which was true. She'd caught glimpses of what they did before, but wanted to understand it in more depth, including any moves to protect them.

"And I'll be interested in hearing what you get our staff members to tell you—and why you're doing it." Camp's light eyebrows that matched his beard rose over his hazel eyes as if he would be skeptical about whatever she said. The young man had his arms crossed over his thin chest.

"I can tell you why right now." Nella might not like his attitude, but they had to remain friendly coworkers. "That threat. I want to talk to the staff members to try to figure out who it was talking about. Plus, I'm interested. I know people get into terrible situations they have to flee, and I'm here because I really like the idea of a place that can help them regroup, change their lives. Remain safe. But to help them, it's a good idea to know what happened to them before."

"Yeah, but we already know that."

"*You* already know that," Nella contradicted. "And I could dig into the computer files if Scott lets me." Although she hadn't yet even had time to review the file that contained her job description. Even so, she had a good idea of what she was supposed to do, thanks to their discussions so far. "But I think it's a better idea to hear it firsthand—and also to let the people who tell me know that I give a damn and will do all I can to make sure their horrible pasts will no longer affect them."

And to figure out whose horrible past might already be poised to bite them again. But these two knew about the threat now. They must also know the value of figuring out who the threat was aimed at.

"I think it's a good idea," Telma finally chimed in. Her arms were crossed, too, but her posture was more relaxed than Camp's. The expression on her attractive face seemed in sympathy with Nella. "Let's discuss them later, though, to learn if any of them adds something to their story we should know about."

"Exactly," Nella agreed. "That's what I have in mind. We managers are all working together here, right?"

"Of course," Telma said.

Camp nodded. "I just wanted to make sure you understand and agree with that." His gaze appeared to bore into her, as if he wanted to read her mind.

"Well, now you know. And right now, I'm going to the cat house, since I've already asked Bibi if we can get together this morning, and that was where she said she'd be after breakfast."

With a smile and a wave, Nella started walking along the pathway between buildings, hearing some dog barks and again seeing a few staff members out walking dogs.

She liked this place and how the animals were treated. She would like it even if it didn't also exist to help people in need. But this way... Well, she was happy in many ways to be working here.

She would be much happier, though, when she figured out that threatening message and made sure no one was harmed by whoever had sent it.

As she walked toward the end of the path, she saw Bibi ahead of her, talking with Alice. Bibi waved, and Nella joined them.

"How are you doing this morning, Alice?" Nella asked. "Bibi's going to introduce me to some of the cats. Are you joining us?" She hoped not. That would prevent her from asking Bibi the questions she intended.

"No, sorry. I'm going to visit the small animals for a while. They might not need people to be happy, but I want to try to help them anyway."

Alice might have a different identity now from the Ann she used to be, but she didn't look much different—except that now she was smiling, not crying. She still appeared middle-aged, but her light brown eyes looked happy, not bloodshot. She again wore jeans, but this time her shirt, a gray one, featured the shelter logo like everyone else's around here.

"Sounds good," Nella told her. She knew enough

of Alice's background to continue suspecting, thanks to the timing, that the threat was a result of this new staff member's coming here. But she felt certain Scott was checking into that, asking his contacts at the police department. Since no one had zeroed in on Alice or her abusive stepson, it must not be clear that he sent the threat.

So Nella definitely considered a part of her new job to include dredging out information about other staff members whose pasts might be catching up with them.

"We'll talk later, okay?" Alice asked Bibi, who agreed. And Alice walked away, into the cat house, where the small shelter pets were kept in the back room.

Nella would have to make sure the door was closed between the rooms so Alice couldn't hear what they were saying. But that was the protocol anyway, to keep doors shut to make sure different kinds of animals didn't mingle. And that people remained safer, too, in closed quarters.

"Okay, kitties," Bibi said. The smile on her round face suggested her love of cats, maybe as much as her love for the many dogs around here.

Nella followed Bibi inside the cat house and was glad to see that the door at the far end of the rows of cat enclosures was, in fact, closed.

"I've already met a few of them," Nella told Bibi, "but not many."

"Which ones?" Bibi asked. She had passed the rows of benches along the wall and stopped beside the first enclosure, a large fenced-in area with several cats inside. They all appeared to ignore one another, which might be a good thing. Certainly better than if they didn't get along, Nella thought.

"Meower, Kitty and Blackie, I think." Nella peered

into that first enclosure to see if she recognized any of them.

"Some of my favorites." Bibi's grin was as large as a Cheshire cat's. "Here's what we'll do. I'll take one cat out at a time for each of us, and we'll sit over there." She pointed toward the benches. "We'll hug them for a few minutes, then put them back and get others out to hug. Okay?"

"Great idea." Nella hadn't spent a lot of time in her life hugging cats, but she didn't mind starting now, especially if it helped them get used to human contact—which could help them get adopted more easily.

Nella sat down on the bench at her right and waited till Bibi returned with a moderate-sized black cat.

"Is this the Blackie I met before?" Nella asked, accepting the warm, furry kitty into her arms. She held him tightly enough to tell him he wasn't going to get the opportunity to wander around out here—after checking to ensure that he was, in fact, a he.

"Yep. That's the name on his collar."

Nella held him even more closely, enjoying his softness and his purrs, though not particularly liking the way he attempted to squeeze his way out of her arms and get away.

Bibi sat down on the bench near her holding a silver cat around the same size whose black stripes resembled those on a tiger. "This is Nala," she said. "She looks like an American shorthair, though I doubt any of our residents here are purebreds."

"She looks sweet," Nella said. "And her name is similar to mine."

Bibi laughed, as she did a lot—but this time Nella decided to take advantage of their sitting here and Bibi's good mood.

"Just so you know, I realize I'm new here at the shelter but I want to do all I can not only to help the animals, but our staff members, too—like you. I think I can help best if I know your backgrounds, or at least as much as you'll tell me, rather than just looking them up in the computer. Would you mind talking to me?"

Bibi's smile vanished, which didn't seem a good sign. But then she said, "I understand, but I hope you understand it's hard to talk about it—especially since it's all in my past and I hope it stays that way."

"I get it," Nella said. Blackie squirmed in her arms again and she used that as an opportunity to look away momentarily. "You won't need to tell me your prior name or anyone else's." Scott would have that information anyway, if they needed it. "And I recognize that the information I'm asking for might be hard for you to talk about. But please tell me your background."

"Okay." Bibi didn't sound happy, and her round face was all but buried in the fur of the cat she held. Her legs swayed forward and back beneath the bench where she sat. "I just hate to think about it, let alone talk about it. It was…it was my ex-husband."

Bibi's story was interesting, sometimes surprising. She'd come from a wealthy family, and her grandparents had left her a substantial sum of money. She had married her college sweetheart, and he'd assumed all her money was his, too. He'd started attempting to spend it, and when she stopped him he got abusive.

"He beat me," Bibi said, beginning to cry. "I eventually moved out and went to a lawyer and started divorce proceedings, but he came after me and found me and beat me some more, demanding that I give him at least half of my money. I think he wanted to kill me."

Bibi had learned about this place from a cop trying to

help her. She put her sister in charge of her money, with her lawyer's supervision. "Maybe someday I'll be able to get at least enough of my life back that I can retrieve it from her. But for now, I just want to go on living."

"I get it." Nella hoped Bibi was right about her sister. But only time would tell. "And—well, I hate to even suggest this, but is there any possibility your ex knows what you've done, where you are?" At Bibi's shocked expression, Nella continued, "I'm just asking so I can be sure I provide as much protection here as you need."

Bibi shook her head. "If he knew about me and where I was, he'd stomp in here right away and hurt me. He's that kind of horrible person. Act first, take consequences later."

Interesting, Nella thought. That possibly ruled him out as a suspect in the threat, which so far, at least, was only a text, not a barging-in ex-husband.

"I get it," Nella told Bibi. "If there's anything else you think of that you haven't told me or the other managers here, please let us know. For now—I think we have more cats to hug, right?"

"Oh, yes," Bibi said, and she stood up, holding Nala. "Time to take you back to your enclosure," she said to the cat. "And pick up someone else."

Walking into the Chance police station was always enjoyable for Scott, even though he didn't belong here anymore. At least ostensibly he didn't, despite remaining a cop who was undercover in an unusual way.

He had put on a light jacket over his Chance Animal Shelter T-shirt and zipped it up. No need for anyone to associate him with that place while he was here—except for those, of course, who already knew his involvement.

He'd parked on the street outside, in Chance's small

civic center, where the station was located in the middle of town. Now he walked across the entry room to the large reception desk and said hello to Officer Penny Jones, a fairly new recruit, who was on duty. She looked almost too young to be a cop, even with her blond hair pulled up in a bun at the top of her head and her dark, questioning gaze, but Scott knew she had done well in her initial training.

He'd been working here as a cop, too, at the time.

"Hi, Officer," Scott said.

"Hi, Officer," Penny whispered back, then more loudly said, "Hello, Mr. Sherridan. How can we help you today?"

"I've got some questions I'd like to ask Detective Vanderhoff," Scott said. "Could you check to see if he's available?"

Vince was expecting him. Scott had called before. But official police protocol suggested that he request an audience with him here.

"Certainly." Penny picked up the phone receiver, spoke into it in a low voice, then hung up. "He'll be right out."

It only took Vince a couple of minutes to appear in the doorway to the department. As always, the highly regarded detective wore a suit, not a uniform. Scott approached him, his hand out for a shake. Vince's grip was strong, and he peered at Scott through his large glasses and smiled. "Welcome, Mr. Sherridan."

"Thanks, Detective Vanderhoff."

"Let's go upstairs," Vince said. "Assistant Chief Province wants to join us."

That's great, Scott thought. Vince must have told Kara about that threat the shelter had received, and Scott assumed she wanted to participate in their conversation about who might have sent it—and what they could do about it.

"Fine." Scott followed Vince through the door into the area where the offices were located.

They went up to the third floor, where the offices belonged to Police Chief Andrew Shermovski, better known as Sherm, and Assistant Chief Kara Province, as well as others in charge of this police force.

They passed Sherm's office. The next door led to Kara's office and Vince pushed it open. An officer in uniform whom Scott believed was Shelly Dandridge sat there, a middle-aged woman who'd served on the Bakersfield PD previously. "Go on in," Shelly said.

Which they did. Kara's office was spacious. Behind her large, neat desk, his sort-of boss stood at their entrance. Slender and tall, she wore a uniform, although her black jacket hung at the back of her chair. Her hair was black and short and almost feathery, and she was both attractive and professional-looking.

Kara immediately looked at Scott with her dark brown eyes. "Okay, have a seat, both of you. And tell me more of what this is about. I heard some from Vince already."

Scott nodded as both he and Vince obeyed, each choosing a tall black chair facing Kara's desk.

"The gist of it is that, late yesterday, we received a text message on the shelter's office phone that's very troubling." Scott reached into his pocket and pulled out a note card on which he had jotted down exactly what that threatening message contained. "It said, 'You have allowed a person to move into your hell pit of a shelter who is going to be killed. Soon. You should be more careful next time. If there is a next time.'" Scott looked up again at Kara as he put the card back into his pocket.

"I've already had the number checked out," Vince said.

"From a burner phone, I assume," Kara responded.

Both Vince and Scott nodded. "Far as we can tell, it's already out of service," Vince said.

"Despite that, do you have any idea who could have sent it?" Kara's eyes were on Scott again.

"No, although we're more on alert now and checking deeper into the histories of the people we call our staff members—those who we've given new identities and are protecting at the shelter."

Scott would have done something about it anyway but now appreciated Nella's querying of their residents even more.

"Have you done any initial investigation besides checking the phone number?" This time Kara's attention was on Vince.

"Hasn't been a lot of time since we heard about it, and we're not quite sure how to approach it." Vince didn't sound pleased. "But we're on it, and if either of you has any suggestions, let me know. Meanwhile, we've got cars patrolling the area, both marked and unmarked. Nothing seems to be happening, and we hope it stays that way."

"So do I, of course," Scott said, "but I still want to find out who sent that threat. My managers and I will be doing everything to protect the shelter residents—"

"Animals, too, I assume," Kara interrupted wryly.

"Animals, too," Scott agreed.

"Well, we have to find a solution," Kara said—and Scott noticed how she said *we* although he knew that inside she meant *you*. She continued, once more looking at Scott. "You know we like what you're doing there and want to do all we can to keep it going—and more. Increase the capacity and how well it protects people. But we've always realized that the more folks who live there, the more likely it is that what it's all about, besides sheltering animals and taking in supposedly homeless people as volunteers, will get out to the wrong people. And apparently at least someone who shouldn't know about the place now does."

"Unfortunately, that's true," Scott said.

"So if word is out, then we need to do everything we can to protect the real identities of the people there—and again, someone already does know at least one of them."

Scott nodded. "Which makes it even more imperative that we find that person before whoever it is can make an attempt at following through on the threat to kill someone at our shelter."

He'd had an urge to call it his shelter, since it had been his idea. But now a lot of people—and animals—were involved.

"I agree," Kara said. "Vince, I'd like you to work with Scott and look into this more, okay?"

Scott knew it was an order to the detective but nevertheless liked the way the Assistant Chief described it.

"Of course."

"And Scott, you can ask Vince to come talk with the people you call your managers, or have them visit here if you think that would be of help. Your managers are the protectors on-site, right?"

"Right. I think that's a good idea." Although he wished he and his managers were enough to keep the shelter adequately protected, at the moment more help would be great. "As long as that doesn't result in word getting out even more about why and how we exist"

"You know I'll keep it quiet," Vince said, sounding a bit hurt.

"Of course," Scott said. But he was glad he'd given Vince the reminder.

Chapter 11

Nella hadn't realized before how much fun it could be just hugging cats. But she spent the rest of the morning with Bibi doing just that.

Not that her obligations—and concern about the staff members—didn't cross her mind even as she felt warm, soft fur against her face.

So did thoughts of Scott. Was he learning anything helpful at the police station? Would he keep her informed?

It seemed as if lunchtime crept up with no warning. Or at least Bibi soon told her it was time.

"I'll be joining Alice in our dining area," she reminded Nella after they'd returned the latest cats they'd been playing with to their enclosures. "You can eat with us, too, if you'd like."

"Thanks," Nella said. "I'll walk with you to the building but I'm not sure what I'm doing yet."

She was hoping it would involve spending time with a staff member or two other than Bibi, despite the fact she liked this woman. But she wanted to find a way to spend private time with one of the others that afternoon and ask some background questions as she had with Bibi.

Nothing had yet alleviated the fact that Nella felt compelled to check everyone out as quickly as possible in the hopes that the person who was the basis of the threat would somehow stick out so she could do what was necessary to protect him or her—as well as everyone else here.

She exited the cat house with Bibi and Alice, who joined them from the small animal area where she'd apparently spent the entire morning. A couple other staff members—Muriel and Leonard—had eventually come into the cat house and joined Bibi and Nella in kitty hugging, but fortunately that was after Nella had completed quizzing Bibi. Leonard made it clear he preferred independent cats to demanding dogs—although he said he wanted to help them all. Leonard and Muriel had left after about half an hour to go walk some dogs.

Clearly, animal attention was the goal of all staff members, which was great for the shelter pets and the people, too. Dogs and cats required human attention, especially to prepare them for new forever homes.

And spending time with animals who adored them should also help the people's states of mind, and even their physical health, while they were here. Nella had read many articles confirming how relationships with pets could help the mental conditions of people who'd suffered traumas. She assumed the therapist who came here, according to Scott, was aware of that. Nella hoped to meet that person one of these days.

As Nella walked with Bibi and Alice, she didn't say much, but eavesdropped. Neither said anything, though, that sounded particularly stressed or gave Nella new ideas, either.

The outside temperature had warmed since afternoon arrived. But Chance was in the mountains near San Luis Obispo and didn't generally get horribly hot in August, unlike other places in Southern California.

Still, Nella would be glad to eat inside, and air-conditioning could be turned on if the temperature rose too much.

She followed the other women to the handwashing station before they entered the dining area. The long table where breakfast had been served was now laden with lunch foods, cold cuts and salad, where staff members and managers could help themselves.

Nella realized, though, that she needed time to find a grocery store in town to buy supplies for her apartment. It was better for her to eat with the residents to help keep them safe, but she might have some time when it would make sense to eat alone, or at least grab some snacks.

Right now, she needed to determine which staff member would be the focus of her queries that afternoon.

She got into the short line at the table behind Bibi and Alice. Almost immediately, Warren came up behind her. "Great spread, isn't it?" the senior staff member asked.

Nella looked at him, wondering if he was serious. Certainly, sandwich fixings were adequate, but she hardly considered them great.

"Of course," she said nonetheless, and watched the grin on his face grow larger. "I'm sure everyone here at this shelter, animals and people, receive the best meals possible."

"Sure. You've got it. The best possible for here. Me? Once upon a time I was a gourmet, but I'm happy enough with what we're served."

Ah. He'd led into hints of his past, and she hadn't even needed to bring it up.

But lunchtime, with everyone around, wasn't the place to talk about it. "Hey," Nella said, "can I join you for lunch? And I'd also love to walk a dog or two with you this afternoon." She figured, after Scott's discussion with her, that she was appropriately leading into spending time with a resident.

"Sounds good. Which dogs would you like us to walk?"

"Let's talk about the possibilities while we're eating," Nella responded, then put a ham-and-cheese sandwich together with lots of lettuce. She also added some salad to her plate.

When she glanced back at Warren, his plate was similarly filled, although she believed he had sliced turkey instead of ham. He seemed to be mostly using his right hand to put his food together. Was something wrong with his left hand?

Both of them also picked up bottles of water—and Warren tucked his against his body with the same hand that held his plate. They found seats side by side at the far end of the same long table where Bibi and Alice sat.

"So tell me which dogs are your favorite to walk," Nella said, once they were seated across from one another.

"I'm mostly into bigger dogs," he said. With whatever was off about his hand, could he control assertive large dogs well? And if she recalled correctly, Nella had last seen him walking a Scottish terrier mix. "And if you're going to push me about the dog you saw me with yesterday, Rover, well, I like him, too. And others. In fact, I can't tell you any of the dogs here that I wouldn't like to walk."

"Ah, got it," Nella said. "I did recall seeing you with that Scottie, Rover. But who would you like to walk this afternoon? And who would you suggest I get so we can accompany you?"

That was a good topic of conversation. This guy seemed to be fairly senior, but his mind was clearly intact, at least with respect to the dogs here at the shelter.

And he seemed eager to finish eating so they could do as they'd been discussing and walk some dogs.

Nella hurried, too—although she kept watch around the dining area in case Scott showed up. She wanted to find out how his meeting went at the Chance PD as soon as possible.

And hoped he would tell her everything about it.

But he didn't appear before both Warren and she finished their meals—faster than the others at the table, which now also included Doreen and Muriel, both of whom Nella also wanted to talk to about their backgrounds.

But soon Warren and she waved goodbye to their still-eating tablemates and dashed to the kennel area.

There, Nella allowed Warren to make the choices for them. She wound up leashing Honey, the black Lab mix, for a walk, and Warren decided on Bruno, the Doberman mix.

They both grabbed leashes and biodegradable plastic bags and led the dogs from their enclosures to the grassy area around the perimeter of the shelter walkway. Warren appeared to use both hands equally well now.

"Feels good out here," Warren said right away. "Not too hot and not too cold. Are you from around here?"

"I'm from L.A."

"I'm from near there. The weather is similar."

"Right," Nella responded.

She watched as Warren manipulated Bruno's leash and told the dog, "Heel." Bruno immediately obeyed.

"You have him well trained," Nella observed.

"I only know a few commands, but we're all told to work with the dogs and teach them to obey." Warren looked sideways at her with brown eyes surrounded by sagging skin. His thin gray hair lay flat on his head—not that there was any wind that day to move it. "That should make them easier to rehome, you know?"

"Yes, that makes sense," Nella said, recalling that Scott had told her she'd probably learn about how pet adoptions were handled mostly by watching it in action. "When do people come in to check out the animals and see if they want to adopt them?"

"Nothing regular, though I heard a family's coming in late this afternoon."

Nella felt a pang of worry along with her pleasure. Some strangers here after the threat? But surely there was a procedure in place to check them out. "I hope they find their new family member. Do any of us get to watch?"

"Not us staff members. Being seen even here isn't a good idea. Wish I could, though."

"I understand." Nella paused. "You know, Warren, I'm really happy to be a manager at this shelter. I'm a former cop, as you probably know, and I want to do everything I can to keep staff members like you safe." She of course wasn't going to mention her primary concern right now. "One way I hope to be able to help is to understand people's backgrounds better. I don't want to know your real name or anything like that." Because again, if it became imperative to know it, she would ask Scott. "But will you please tell me what the situation was when you decided to seek help here?"

Warren stopped walking, and therefore so did Bruno, which additionally caused Honey to stop. They all stood still on the grass with the front wall of one of the kennel buildings at their side.

Warren stared straight at her then, his expression cold and remote. "I don't like to talk about it."

"I understand," Nella said. "But as I said, I think I can help you better if I know where you're coming from."

"I come from near Los Angeles," he responded, then started walking again, Bruno at his side.

"That's not what I mean," Nella said. "I'd like to know the situation that brought you—"

"It was my damn business partner!" Warren seemed to explode as he again stood still. "I was walking outside our office one day—we were into real estate sales—and all of a sudden a car came tearing around the corner, aiming straight at me. It wasn't his car, but a bigger one, a heavy SUV. And I saw his face grinning as I dove out of the way. Broke my arm." He held out his left arm. This explained why he sometimes seemed to favor it as he did again now, taking most of the force of the dog's leash with his right hand. "Otherwise, I was okay. And after I told the cops and tried to get back to work, things kept going wrong. I couldn't prove anything, damn it—but I figured it was all caused by him, and if I didn't get out of there I'd lose not only my business but my life, too."

He paused then, and Nella, wanting to say something supportive, said, "That had to be really hard."

"I'll say!" He exploded again. "Fortunately, I'd already separated my money out of the business—and that might be why he was after me. I've got it hidden away in secret accounts…but you don't need to know that. I'm just here till I feel I can take my life, and my business, back. Once my health is better, since my arm still hurts. I'll do it, you know. Soon. I've only been here about a month, but I don't want to stay forever and I'm not getting any younger. And I'll do anything to try to make things right again." He again looked directly at her, and she could see the determination on his clearly aging face.

"I understand," she said. "And I'll do all I can to protect you while you're here—and maybe help you get your strength back."

Could Warren be the subject of the threat? If his business partner had found him, that would be logical, since the guy had apparently already tried to kill him.

Now Warren raced to the top of Nella's list of those to protect most.

She would talk to Scott about him as soon as she could.

But as far as she could tell, Scott hadn't yet returned from his outing at the police department. And she was happy when, as Warren and she returned the dogs they'd been walking to their enclosures, Telma hurried over to them.

"We've got two families of potential adopters arriving in about ten minutes." She'd mostly looked serious when Nella had seen her before, her dark brows often set in a frown over her hazel eyes. Not now. In fact, those eyes were sparkling. "That's the way we handle things around here," she said. "We ask interested people to schedule a time by way of our website, and we vet them as well as we can before agreeing to that schedule. More than one group at a time seems fine, as long as there aren't too many."

In other words, the managers would need to keep track of those visitors. Staff members would of course be in protected status. And, as Nella had assumed, the potential adopters had gone through at least some sort of vetting process.

"Sounds great," Nella said. "Just tell me where you want me."

"I will," Telma said. "And let's all keep our fingers crossed that some of our animal residents find their forever homes today."

In unison, it seemed, Warren and Nella raised their hands and crossed their fingers. Nella laughed.

"Lead me to it," she said.

It was almost three o'clock. Scott hadn't intended to stay at the police station as long as he had, and then he'd wound up having lunch with Vince—which got extended because Vince was full of questions that Scott had no intention of answering about the shelter while they were out in public, so he returned to Vince's office at the station to discuss them.

But the conversation ended well—especially since Vince called in K-9 Officer Maisie Murran and her dog Griffin, a golden retriever.

"Hope you don't mind," Vince said, "but I mentioned you might have an issue at the shelter, and Maisie said she'd love to talk to you about bringing Griffin for another visit and to patrol the area."

Maisie, with short blond hair and in her black uniform, nodded toward Scott as she said, "go" to Griffin so the dog approached Scott to sniff him. "Anytime," she said. "You know we enjoyed the last few visits."

She and Griffin had visited three or four times in the months since the shelter had opened, just out of interest.

But having an official K-9 visit the shelter, and also the area, now and then might be really helpful after the threat they'd received. Scott didn't know where the danger might occur and wanted to utilize every asset he could.

"Good idea," he said.

"Oh…and I also know of a retired K-9 whose former master just passed away," Maisie said. "It might be a good fit to let him move into your shelter, too."

Scott liked that idea. "Let's keep in touch and plan for your visit," he said. "And sure, that K-9 sounds like a great idea."

Maisie lifted her hand in a salute, said goodbye and left the office.

"That went well," Vince said.

"Yeah," Scott agreed. "I'll look forward to seeing Maisie and Griffin around. You can tell her the specifics of what our issue is, of course. I trust her to keep it to herself."

"Right," Vince said. "You know I like your shelter and want everything to go well there. And I'm always glad to help you any way I can."

"Thanks," Scott said. He shared a brotherly hug with his helpful coworker and left his office.

Scott stopped for some supplies on his way back to the shelter, particularly because there wasn't much in the apartment he temporarily occupied. Plus, he picked up a few things for Nella since he doubted she'd had time to grab anything so far.

He got some additional items, too, since he had an idea how to spend the evening.

When he finally got back to the shelter, he was delighted to see the managers, including Nella, introducing some potential adopters to a few resident dogs.

The moment Nella saw him, she quickly walked over to him. "This is so wonderful," she said. "These people all seem inclined to adopt, and Telma and Camp told me they'd been scheduled for today and already had background checks so they can even take dogs home with them."

"That's the intention," Scott said. He'd set up a procedure for vetting potential adopters, making sure not only that their backgrounds and homes looked good, but that they were often met face-to-face by managers, too, before visiting the shelter.

And the staff members knew they were to stay in their apartments, or perhaps in the community room upstairs in that building, and not be seen. Not that it was likely any would be recognized, as few had lived near Chance before their arriving.

Introductions all took place in the reception building, and visitors weren't allowed to roam the grounds on their own, though they were most often taken to the shelter areas to see the dogs. There, they selected one or two to meet with in person who seemed appropriate in accordance with the forms the adopters had filled out, describing the size, temperament and more that they were seeking and sometimes mentioning specific dogs shown on the shelter's website. They were then taken inside to the small meeting rooms near the reception area to interact, one at a time, with the dogs they liked, their potential new family members.

Today's two families consisted of both parents plus kids—two in one case, and one child in the other. In the family with two kids, both the mother and father were lawyers, and in the other the mother was a server at a local restaurant and the father worked at a car service station—different backgrounds, but they all seemed to love dogs, especially the ones they chose after getting to meet several possibilities.

When it was over, Scott was glad he'd bought a couple of bottles of wine. Celebration was in order, and he'd invite the staff members to join in later in the dining building.

For now, he and his managers said goodbye to the adopters. "Keep us informed how things go," he said. "Our rescues are always welcome back, but we hope you have a wonderful life with them."

"We will," chimed the little girl who was an only child. Her family had selected Herman, the Chihuahua mix.

"Us, too," said a teenage boy whose family had decided to adopt Shupe, the Shetland sheepdog mix.

As they all started to go, Scott was surprised when Nella said, "Wait a minute, please." He'd been glad, when he'd returned and headed to the reception area to meet the potential adopters, to see she was now wearing a Chance Animal Shelter manager's shirt. The black shirt hugged her curves nicely—but he wasn't supposed to notice that.

And he wasn't surprised when she was the one to step forward and hug both dogs who had just found new homes. "Bye, Herman. Bye, Shupe." After the adopting families said goodbye to the managers and left out the front door that was locked behind them, Nella pivoted toward Scott.

"I don't know how you ever got the idea for this kind of shelter," she said, reminding him a bit of his earlier conversation with Vince. "But it's fantastic in so many ways." Tears filled her brown eyes, and she approached him and grabbed his right hand, which she held tightly, moving it to her mouth so she could briefly kiss it. "Thank you so much for hiring me."

"Thank you so much for working here," was his return, his gaze first meeting Telma's, then Camp's. He'd assumed they would roll their eyes in exasperation, but both looked engaged and Telma was even a little tearful.

Which only made Scott happier he had begun this place and that it had been successful in protecting people.

So far, at least.

But he still had to figure out the meaning of that threat Nella had seen—and soon.

Chapter 12

And if seeing those emotional adoptions wasn't enough, Nella found herself about to have another wonderful experience that evening.

Well, it might not be wonderful. That remained to be seen. But as she headed away from the reception building and into the rest of the shelter with Scott, he told her he had gone on a shopping expedition for himself while he was in town talking to the cops—and also brought some supplies back for her.

"Far as I know, you haven't had an opportunity to stock your new apartment yet, have you?" His blue eyes narrowed as if he could see into her mind for the answer to his query.

"No, I haven't," she said as they stepped onto the concrete path in the middle of the shelter buildings. "Thank you so much. Just let me know how much I owe you." Of course she wondered what he had bought and how useful it would be, but it had to be better than her prior status of having almost no supplies.

"Just consider it part of your salary," he said with a grin that lit up his handsome face. Which made her smile, too.

Telma and Camp walked ahead of them. Some staff members were out there, too, which apparently was fine. They couldn't have been seen by the adopters as long as they remained in their apartments, but they'd been okayed to go out now that the adopters had taken their new family members home.

What time was it? It must be near dinnertime, Nella realized. They all were probably heading toward the shelter's dining area.

"Any idea what's for dinner tonight?" Nella asked Scott.

"I definitely know what we're eating," he replied, "although I don't know what the rest of the crowd is getting."

Nella stopped walking and looked up at his face as he stopped, too. "What do you mean?"

His raised brows and a slight grin suggested he knew exactly what she asked and why she was asking. "Well, I told you I got us some supplies. That included food. Now, I'm not any kind of great cook, but if you're okay with frozen dinners with embellishments, I'll take care of our cooking for tonight."

"But—"

"And I can bring you up-to-date on my conversations with the cops."

What could she do but agree?

And the idea of joining him alone for dinner—truly alone this time, not out in public, and where they could talk about anything—really sounded good.

Still… "That's fine, as long as we check on everyone who's eating in the dining area first, then check on them again later, too."

"You're really getting into this protectiveness stuff, aren't you?" Scott's tone sounded teasing, but the look he leveled on her appeared appreciative.

"Of course," she said. "I'm here, aren't I? And I'm sure you'd say you're even a whole lot more protective than I am."

"Yep, I'd say that," he said. "And it's true." He winked at her, which nearly made her laugh, but instead she kept her face blank.

"Maybe," she said, "and maybe I'm a lot more protective than you."

"We can argue about it over dinner," he said. "Right now, like you said, let's go visit the eating area to make sure all's okay. I was planning to anyway, since I intend to propose a toast. I've already left a few bottles of wine there."

All seemed fine in the dining area, Nella was glad to note. She checked the long tables where people sat, as well as those where others were just getting their food, and counted faces.

The staff members were all there, which was a good thing, as well as Telma and Camp. Telma, who stood near the food table, was helping to serve things, although, since she'd been with them at the adoption, she couldn't have been the one who'd cooked. Nella assumed it was Sara but wasn't going to ask. They'd already settled on some kind of routine long before she arrived here.

Telma's gaze landed on Scott, and she waved a serving fork in his direction. "We've got some good turkey tonight," she called.

"Thanks, but I'll pass." Scott had approached the serving table, with Nella following. He joined Telma behind the table and talked loudly, this time so others could hear. "I want you all to join me in a toast to this shelter and to all of us, and today's great dog adoptions." To Telma, he said, "I'll get the wine from where I left it under the serving table, and I'd appreciate it if you'd bring out some glasses."

Which she did.

Scott popped into the kitchen and returned to where the tables were, holding a corkscrew. A couple bottles of wine—both red—were open in a minute. Scott poured small amounts into the glasses, and Telma, Sara and Bibi took charge of making sure everyone got a glass.

Scott raised a glass after everyone else had been served. "To the Chance Animal Shelter," he said loudly. "And to all our staff members and our managers and of course our animal residents. And this evening, I'm adding a toast to our adopters of the day, and to Shupe and Herman. May they all have wonderful lives together, and may the rest of us also have the best of futures here at the shelter and, possibly, otherwise."

He lifted his glass higher, and everyone else lifted theirs, too. "Hear, hear," resounded through the crowd, then Scott took a sip.

So, then, did Nella. She wasn't a wine connoisseur, but she liked its sweet yet tart berry flavor. She wondered whether Scott had brought a bottle to his apartment for them to taste later. She hoped so—although the last thing she wanted was to start feeling high. She wouldn't want to use that as some kind of excuse to herself to make advances toward Scott, or to react favorably if he began making advances to her.

That just couldn't happen.

She took a few more sips as Scott and the others did, too. Then Scott said, "Hey, everyone. Nella and I are going to leave now. We won't be joining you for dinner. There are still some procedures I need to tell her about—like more about our adoptions. And now that I'm living in an apartment here for a while, I thought we'd go over it there."

"You two, in private." That was Warren. He sat at a nearby table and was clearly quite a character. Nella made herself smile at the implications, ignoring that the thought had crossed her mind, too.

"If you're being suggestive, it's a great idea." Nella's turn to talk to the crowd. "Only, if any of you pop in to watch the fun, you'll be disappointed since we'll just be discussing those procedures Scott mentioned."

"Darn," Warren said.

And in fact, Nella found herself pleased but a little disappointed, too, when their dinner in Scott's apartment was, in fact, totally professional. First, they stopped at his place to pick up the food and other supplies he had obtained for her and brought them to her apartment. Quite a few, including paper products and basic food such as cheese and crackers.

Then they returned to his apartment. Whatever else he had picked up for himself, he had also bought the fixings for chicken Alfredo and a salad, which they ate at the small table in the living room area. They also had wine from a bottle he had kept for himself.

All they did that evening was talk about the shelter and its policies for bringing in new staff members and adopting out pets, and the fact Scott hadn't gotten any more information after his friend the detective investigated the threatening text.

It was enjoyable being in Scott's presence, of course.

And Nella knew and appreciated that it was necessary for them to talk about all the issues and any information and suggestions Scott had for dealing with them.

The most potentially helpful news was that a police K-9 officer would patrol the area and visit soon, and also had a senior K-9 in mind to begin living in the shelter.

Which reminded Nella again about how she had observed some K-9 training while with the LAPD. Maybe she should try it here to improve how the dogs were taught to obey, even before the pretrained K-9 joined them.

The dinner Scott prepared—with her help—might not have been gourmet fare, but it was tasty. And, though Nella tried not to dwell on it, the company certainly made it special.

As the evening drew to a close, they did as they'd discussed before and went downstairs, first to the now-empty dining area, then outside, where none of the staff members were walking around. They were probably all back in their apartments, as they should be.

There was, in fact, one more fun outcome. Scott, gentleman and protector that he was, walked her back to her apartment and waited while she used her keycard to open the door. Then he came inside and walked through the place to make sure all was in order.

As he prepared to leave, he closed that door, took Nella into his arms, and said, "Well, no one took you up on your offer to come and check on us, so—" He pulled her tightly against him. So tightly that she could feel that he was aroused—as was she.

Their kiss was the hottest yet—but went no further. "See you in the morning," Scott said, his voice raspy.

"Yes," she said as her mind churned on the possibility of inviting him to stay—not for the whole night, but a little longer. But her common sense took over, and she pulled away, hoping her reluctance didn't show. "See you in the morning."

Leaving Nella there on her own was right, of course. Scott refused to allow any disappointment into his mind—and ignored how his body had reacted when he'd been with her. Bad move, no matter how enjoyable it was. He was her boss.

He went back to his apartment, finished cleaning up after their meal and turned on the television, where he channel-surfed, mostly looking for news. Not that anything related to the threat would appear. But he hoped for some further ideas to investigate it.

Nothing.

And so he took a walk around the shelter to ensure its security. Alone.

He figured Nella would be doing the same, if she hadn't already.

It wouldn't have hurt for them to do it together—except the together part. Better that they do it separately, as long as all seemed well. Which it did. If he'd seen any indication it wouldn't be safe for her, let alone the others in their apartments or even the animals in their enclosures, he would have acted to stop it.

And soon he went to bed. Also alone. But, despite all his good sense, wishing Nella was there, too.

Bad idea, in some ways, for them to be sleeping so close, yet so far away.

Chapter 13

Nella got up a few times that night, put on some outer clothes and visited the shelter area after strolling the floor where the apartments were, including hers.

Everything had seemed fine. No other people out and about. And even though she felt certain Scott was doing the same thing now and then, she didn't see him, and she didn't call to ask.

In the morning, she woke fairly early, showered and put on her clothes for the day—including a light blue Chance Animal Shelter T-shirt, which she loved.

She figured some people might already be out walking dogs this early. That could be a good thing, particularly if she could latch on to someone she hadn't yet interviewed to learn their story. On the other hand, though she wanted to keep her momentum up, she didn't need to quiz residents each time she got together with one of them.

Though if she did, she'd get the information she needed faster...

In the shelter area, Nella saw a couple of people walking dogs far ahead of her, toward the end of the path, but she went into the second building. There, Muriel was just getting terrier mix Mocha onto a leash.

Seeing pug Baby in the next enclosure, Nella retrieved a leash, too, as well as treats from a container on the wall. "Can we walk with you?" she asked Muriel.

"Sure! Did you have fun with the cats yesterday? I did, for the short time I visited."

Nella was delighted that they had a mutual conversation topic to start with. "Oh, yes. I'm more of a dog person, but seeing the cats up close and personal while I hung out there with Bibi taught me that I can probably fall for any lovable pet."

"Me, too." Muriel also wore one of the shelter's T-shirts, a beige one that seemed to enhance the deep color of her complexion. Nella had the impression Muriel was a happy person despite being at a location where she was in hiding, since she seemed to smile all the time.

Would she keep smiling when Nella asked her questions? The idea wasn't to freak her out, but just learn enough to help determine if she might be the target of the threat.

Outside, Muriel gave Mocha a couple of commands. "Sit," was the first, and the cute little terrier obeyed. "Okay, come." That, too, was clearly an instruction Mocha knew, but Muriel had to repeat it before she obeyed.

"Does Baby know those?" Nella asked Muriel.

"Yes. I've worked with her, too."

Sure enough, when Nella said "Sit" to the pug, Baby

sat, and wriggled a bit as if eager for the next command, which Nella gave quickly. "Come." And Baby stood and dashed off a bit, pulling on her leash, which made Nella laugh. "Well, she's at least partly obedient."

Nella considered again using the skills she'd observed at the LAPD as part of her job at the shelter. She would not be able to turn all these dogs into K-9s, though it should be enjoyable to work with the one Scott had mentioned as a potential new canine resident.

But it certainly wouldn't hurt to try to teach the dogs she worked with here a bit more obedience, as Muriel evidently did.

"Most of our dogs aren't great about following commands," Muriel said as she started walking forward after telling Mocha "Heel," which the terrier did.

And Baby? Nella decided to work with her some more. Those treats she'd picked up should help with that.

Using a tone that was clearly a command, she soon got Baby to sit again, stay, then come and heel. Next came down, stand and follow. Then the same commands again, authoritatively, in a different order, and Baby started to really obey. It didn't hurt that Nella followed each with a treat. Did trained K-9s always get treats? She wasn't sure, but it didn't hurt with the dogs around here.

"Wow, you're good at that," Muriel said. She sounded surprised, and Nella figured it might be because she might have been less than strict before with some of the commands she gave.

She laughed inside at Muriel's surprise, though. "Thanks. It's fun to work with them, as you know."

"Of course."

But that wasn't what Nella really wanted to do here with Muriel. They were walking alone with these dogs, although a couple of other staff members headed out of another building with canines at their sides. Even so, Nella figured this was a good time to talk.

"You may have heard I'm being unbearably nosy with our staff members," she began, "but I've figured that quizzing each of you myself will help me figure out the best way to help protect you. So—"

"So you want to know why I'm here." Muriel stopped walking just long enough to get Mocha to also stop and start pulling at her leash. "Heel, Mocha," Muriel said, and started walking again, as did Nella with Baby— who followed the heel order perfectly this time.

"That's right."

"We've all discussed this with each other, you know," Muriel began. "In most cases it's been ex-spouses, boy-friends or girlfriends, relatives or bosses who drove us into the need for new identities. Me? It was a security guard in the office building where I worked as a para-legal."

Good to know, Nella thought. "Please tell me about it," she said.

"I pointed out a couple of times when some things went wrong, as with people getting into the building when they shouldn't, things getting stolen and all, and believed it was his fault, maybe even his planning, so I told the building manager. I couldn't prove anything, though, and the guy kept his job—but he was furious and wanted revenge."

When she paused, Nella asked, "How did he go about it?"

It turned out that the security guy really knew his stuff and never left any actual evidence that Muriel could have used to get him arrested, or even fired. "I started having incidents first in my office, then at home, where taking the wrong step, eating my food or whatever, could have killed me, and the local cops got frustrated trying to prove who did it. Nothing indicated for certain it was the guy I knew it was. A few cops even seemed to believe at times that I was trying to set him up—although fortunately I had some cops on my side, too, which is why I'm here." She shook her head. "They're still trying, as far as I know, to find out and prove the truth, and I hope not to stay here much longer, but having a new identity, even temporarily, has helped me survive. See, I also have some PTSD from when I served in the military before becoming a paralegal."

"Got it," Nella said, reminded of her own wonderment about whether she, too, had PTSD from what had happened in her life before she'd come here. She then had to ask, "And have you had any indication that your security guy knows what you've been up to, or that you're here?"

Muriel was another one whose background could have led to that threat. Of course, that was possible for all this shelter's residents.

"No." Muriel came to a stop, though, and therefore so did Nella and the dogs. "Do you have any reason to suspect he does?"

Nella wondered if Muriel's PTSD was kicking in, so for now, at least, she decided to attempt to calm her. "Not at all," she said. "But again, I want to know the worst to try to provide the best help."

"Got it." Muriel started walking again. "But—well, if you ever think otherwise, please let me know. I do have my outside resources who'll at least try to help again. I want to leave here as soon as I can, so in some ways maybe it would be good if my personal menace came after me in a way he could finally be stopped."

"Maybe." Nella realized her tone was dubious. To ease Muriel's state of mind, and to help both of them and the dogs enjoy their walk, she asked her human companion about her favorite pets and how being with animals helped calm her life.

A short while later, they both took their pet companions back to their enclosures. "Ready for breakfast?" Muriel asked. "I am."

"Sounds good to me, too," Nella said. "And—well, if there's anything else you think I should know, or any way I can help—"

"I'll definitely let you know," Muriel said. "You're a really good manager, Nella."

That made Nella smile. "And you're a really good staff member," she responded.

She started to walk with Muriel toward where breakfast would be served. On the way to the eating area Nella's phone rang. She pulled it out of her pocket and saw the caller was Dan Poreski. "I'd better take this," she told Muriel. "I'll catch up with you in the dining room."

Muriel walked ahead as Nella moved to the side of the path, watching as others appeared, heading toward breakfast.

"Hi, Dan," Nella said, glad to hear from her former boss. "How are you doing?"

"The more important question is how are you doing?"

"Fine," Nella responded. Well, she might be worried about all those under her protection, but she really wasn't doing too badly, all things considered.

"Great," Dan said. "I've really been thinking about the idea of starting a similar shelter to that one here in L.A., like I mentioned before. I want to come and see your place soon, possibly tomorrow, Saturday. Would that be okay?"

"I'll have to check with the director." Scott already knew Dan, so he'd probably be fine with the idea. Even so, Nella would ask. "I'll let you know as soon as I can."

"Very good. Oh, and I'll be bringing Jon along. He's also interested in opening that kind of shelter, and I want him to see what it's about so he can help if I decide to follow up on it."

Great. Well, Nella wasn't surprised. And if Jon could help Dan move forward—if he decided to—it certainly wouldn't hurt to see him again.

"Fine," Nella said. "I'll get back to you soon." She hesitated, then asked, "Oh—and anything new to report on the escaped gang members?"

A slight pause, then Dan said, "No, but we're still working on it, of course."

Nella felt sure they were. And for the moment, she wished she was there to get revenge, as she'd wanted before. But that moment passed quickly.

"I hope things work out and that I get to see you soon," she told Dan. And she meant it.

Scott had seen Nella in the shelter area walking Baby alongside Muriel with Mocha. He'd stayed away, standing in the cool air outside the building where breakfast would be served, since their body language as they talked in what appeared to be a serious conversation suggested to him that Nella was quizzing Muriel about her background while apparently working with the dogs on their obedience.

Though he said good morning to some staff members as they walked past him into the building, he wasn't ready to go in yet, so he checked his phone for anything new from the Chance PD, although nothing of any note appeared to be going on. Nothing likely to affect the shelter anyway.

He remained there when Nella and Muriel took the dogs into their building and emerged quickly on their own.

He saw when Nella got on her phone, and Muriel headed his direction, toward the eating area, without her. He remained there anyway, waiting for Nella.

Which was silly, he knew. But he wanted to talk with her. Eat breakfast alongside her.

Find out who she was talking to—and if she had learned anything more to help determine who'd issued that damned threat.

That was his excuse anyway.

He also figured she'd inform him if she found anything useful he should know.

Enough, damn it. She was his employee. He didn't need to hang out with her any more than he did with any of his other managers.

Their dinner last night, talking over pertinent matters about the shelter, didn't change that.

Nor did their brief and inappropriate good-night kiss.

He started to enter the building—then saw Nella end her call and walk in his direction.

Well, it wouldn't hurt now if he remained here and asked for any updates she might have.

She reached him quickly. "Everything okay?" he said.

"If what you're asking is whether I got Muriel to talk to me, I did. She probably didn't say anything you don't already know, but we should discuss it. And something else, as well. But after breakfast, since we ought to go inside and join the group, and they don't need to hear any of the stuff I want to talk over with you."

Which pushed Scott's curiosity up a notch. But Nella didn't sound as if anything was urgent, so it could wait.

Besides, whatever it was gave him a reason to spend some time with her alone, after breakfast, and—

Enough already, he ordered himself again.

Soon, they were in the line to pick up food. Sara helped Telma and Bibi dish out eggs and more, so he figured she was done cooking for that morning. Cooking remained Sara's primary function since she still hadn't cozied up to any dogs or most other animals.

Scott got two fried eggs, over medium, plus some toast. He noticed that Nella stuck with scrambled eggs and toast.

They soon sat beside each other at one of the tables farthest back from the one containing food—after they both also got coffee. Scott made certain to sit where he faced most of the others so he could watch them and their surroundings. All seemed fine.

Until Muriel stood and approached them.

"I've been telling people about how you did such a great job training Baby this morning," she said to Nella. "We all try with whatever dogs we're walking, of course, but not as many commands as you gave her, and not always with such good results. Maybe we could all work together later this morning, and you could give us a lesson. I think we have another potential adopter coming in this afternoon, right?" She looked toward Scott.

"Probably not today, although we'll have some soon," he said. He didn't mention it, but Dr. Moran, the therapist who came weekly to talk to some of the residents, would be there that afternoon. Some were already scheduled to meet with her, including their new-comer, Alice.

"Well, if you can show off a dog who knows some commands, that adoption is more likely, right?" she asked Scott.

He nodded.

"I'd be glad to show you all what I know, but I'm hardly a skilled dog trainer." Nella was looking at Muriel now.

"That's not what I saw," Muriel responded, her hands on her hips.

"The more we all do to help each other, the better," Scott said. "And I'd love to see what you can do." He smiled at Nella, who nodded.

"Okay," she said, "but only for half an hour or so this time, if that's okay. After that, I'd like to talk to you." Since he'd met up with her here this morning, he'd had a sense she had something besides Muriel on her mind and now he felt certain of it.

"Fine," Scott said. "For now, let's bring on the dogs."

Chapter 14

"Hey, where are you two going?" asked Warren as Nella and Scott stood and started walking away from the still-filled table. Warren had sat across from them beyond Kathy and Leonard and now he stood to face them.

"In a bit, we'll work with a few of you to see who can train dogs the best," Nella replied. "Why don't you finish here and go grab a dog? Rover or Bruno? You like them best, right?"

"That's right," Warren replied. "Sounds good. Let me finish my breakfast and go get a dog, then I'll find both of you and whatever dogs you're training. We'll have fun. You can teach me, and maybe I can teach you, even though you're both in charge together, of course. Right? Yeah. Anyone else interested?"

A few other staff members volunteered to join them.

"Good. See you later." Warren plunked himself back down and grabbed a piece of toast from his plate.

Scott led Nella to the table where the coffee sat. He filled a paper cup and put a sleeve on it. "One to go," he said. "How about you? I gather you want to talk a little before we get any dogs out."

"I'd love some." Nella was perfectly happy also grabbing a cup of coffee before getting together with Scott to describe her earlier conversation with Muriel. Plus, she wanted to ask if it was okay for Dan to come here tomorrow to research this place with the idea of possibly setting up something similar in L.A., as she'd mentioned to Scott before.

That, of course, reminded her that Jon would also be coming. She would have to talk to them about the missing gang members, of course, and might show her appreciation again for the way Jon helped her on the task force. And in case he appeared to have anything else on his mind about her, she knew she could be cordial without giving him any ideas about following up with her, even on a friendly basis. She didn't need to feel guilty that she wasn't as interested in him as he was in her.

"Let's take a quick peek into the cat house," Scott said. He clearly wanted to spend a little time on this conversation since that building was at the other end of the path, but that was fine with Nella. They would still have time to work with the dogs and staff members soon. It was fairly early in the morning.

As they started down the path, cups of coffee in their hands, Nella said, "I assume you want to know how things went this morning in my conversation with Muriel."

"That's right," Scott responded, and so Nella told him what Muriel and she had spoken about.

"I feel sorry for her—as I do with so many other staff members," Nella finished. "She shouldn't have had to deal with a malicious security guy that way. I'm glad she remained friendly with some cops, but I wish I could tell from what she said whether her security nemesis has found her here. He might have the resources to locate her."

"You're right." Scott stopped on the pathway near the building that included the cat house. "But that might be too obvious. Plus, since her circumstances were special, and her original tormenter had potential resources to find her, I'm still in touch with the police who sent her here in the first place. I gave them a call after the threat, and they're still keeping an eye on the guard. Best they can tell, he's just doing his normal thing of ostensibly protecting people and property in whatever building he's supposed to be monitoring—and he seems to be going after another woman employee there, so they've made themselves a bit obvious, plus I gather the company's PR department has told him to back down."

"So our threatened staff member probably isn't Muriel." Nella looked at Scott, who nodded. As their eyes met, she felt her usual unwanted interest in the guy and remembered Warren's teasing.

She had to be more careful. Her feelings might be showing.

"That's what I think," Scott said. "Even so, the therapist I mentioned to you before will be here later today, and Muriel is one of those scheduled to see her, as is Alice and a couple more. Now, should we go say meow to some cats?"

Nella smiled. "One thing first, though."

She felt glad that some of those in need got an opportunity to talk to a therapist and eventually to get beyond the heartache they must still feel from their pasts. She'd even talked to a therapist once after losing Lou on the gang task force and thought she'd felt a little better—although remembering what happened still hurt.

She took a sip of coffee as they stood there and she explained to Scott how Dan now wanted to do something about his own interest in opening a shelter similar to this one. "He wants to come check out the Chance Animal Shelter tomorrow," she said. "And he wants to bring along Sergeant Jon Frost, who also worked with me, including on the gang task force." She tried not to allow her tone to give away her opinion of Jon joining Dan, but she apparently wasn't totally successful.

"Is there anything the matter with both of them coming?" Scott's face had taken on a concerned frown. "If you're okay with it, I am, but if not—"

"Then I'll let Dan know it's fine. Jon can be a bit over-the-top at times, but he's basically a dedicated cop and a good guy—especially if he wants to help Dan open a people and animal shelter in their jurisdiction."

"Okay. Just keep me informed. I had no problem with Dan knowing about this shelter and even sending me a wonderful new manager—"

He winked at Nella, which got her pulse pounding, and then he took a sip of coffee. So did she, wishing this time that it was something a bit stronger, like that good wine Scott had shared. But not in the morning.

"I'm not so sure about the *wonderful* part," she said, "but this new manager is certainly glad to be here. For a lot of reasons. Including getting away from that ugly gang stuff. Dan admitted that a few members still haven't been rounded up."

"Really?" Scott looked her square in the face. "Is Dan working on it?"

"I'm sure he's trying to." Nella didn't want to talk about it anymore. She'd at least mentioned it to Scott, who should be aware of it. But now she said, "Are you ready to get some dogs out and work with them along with some staff members? I'd like to—and when I was with Muriel this morning I pulled out some memories of K-9 training that I've observed that encourages immediate obedience, and tried using it with Baby."

"Our Baby? Pug Baby? Wish I'd seen that."

"I can show you as part of our demo. And when I was strict with her—and gave her treats when she obeyed—she really did a pretty fair job."

"Great. Well, you can train Baby and some of our staff members—including Warren—and maybe me, too," Scott said. "Oh, and by the way, you should know there's a facility called Chance K-9 Ranch nearby, where people are taught how to train their dogs as pets, service dogs and K-9s."

"Interesting. Maybe I'll try to visit someday."

With that, they turned and strode through the cat house, then the small animal part of the structure at the far end. Nella enjoyed seeing all of them but didn't take the time to remove any from their enclosures, or even reach inside to stroke them. This time. She'd come back when she had a chance.

Soon, they returned to the outer area where some staff members had begun to congregate. Telma and Camp were there, too.

And Nella felt good that she and the others were going to work with some dogs and get them even more prepared to find their forever homes, while also giving the human residents here at the shelter something worthwhile to perk up their spirits.

* * *

Scott watched with both pleasure and amusement as a few staff members ducked inside a couple of buildings and came out a short while later with leashed dogs.

Nella, Telma and Camp joined them. Scott felt tempted as well, but for now he would just watch.

This was, after all, the secondary but still important reason for this shelter to exist. Finding new homes for needy pets was what they were ostensibly all about, the face they put on for the rest of the world. It was true, though it wasn't everything.

And having dogs trained certainly made them potentially more adoptable to people seeking new pets to bring home.

"Okay, now, everyone watch Nella," Muriel called to the others. She had the little terrier mix, Mocha, with her, and the dog appeared better behaved than Scott remembered, sitting on the paving beside Muriel and staring up at her as if awaiting a treat.

Warren was there, too, of course, since he'd committed to join this class while they were in the dining area. He had brought out Bruno, the Doberman.

The dogs with most other staff members besides Nella, including Bruno, didn't seem as obedient as Baby, and maybe Mocha. Some sat beside their current handlers, and others pulled at the ends of their leashes, sometimes sniffing one another. Fun to watch, but that wasn't what they were all there for.

Scott focused his attention on Nella, who similarly had Baby on a leash beside her. He was too far away to hear the commands she gave, but he could see some of her hand signals. They included sit, come, stay, heel, the standard ones, as Baby appeared ecstatic to obey them right away. It didn't hurt that Nella gave her a treat with each successful obeyed command.

Then she did a couple more things that appeared possibly a result of watching police K-9s being trained. One was retrieve, and she threw what appeared to be a sock she'd pulled from her pocket. At first, Baby appeared confused, but Nella gave the command again and walked the dog at heel to go get the sock. The next time, apparently, Baby knew enough to retrieve it herself.

Interesting that Nella, though clearly not an expert, knew a lot about dog training. All the more reason for this shelter being perfect for her—and for the animals she worked with, as well as the staff members she could teach these skills to.

"Okay," Nella finally said, "I'm done. I don't know many other commands, but why don't you all work with your dogs now and see how many you can get them to obey? Do you all have treats with you?"

They apparently did, and Scott figured they'd been forewarned.

They spent another twenty minutes going over commands in the warming sun of Chance's midday. As far as Scott could tell, most dogs appeared at least somewhat obedient—a good omen for their eventual adoption. The experience also introduced some helpful skills to the staff members who stayed at the shelter—even if they eventually left and had dogs in their lives.

"Okay, everyone," Nella finally called. "You're all on your own. You can continue working with the dogs you have with you now, or take them back to their enclosures. But I hope I've been at least some help."

Apparently they all thought so, since suddenly the mostly silent enclosed shelter area was filled with sounds of humans clapping and cheering and calling out thank-yous.

Scott cringed a bit. He didn't like the idea of the shelter being obvious for any reason. But late in the morning like this it was unlikely there were many people nearby, and even if there were, people inside animal shelters could certainly cheer the resident pets for some reason or another.

He nevertheless decided this would be a good time to go into the office and check the security camera monitors to be certain no one lurked outside wanting to find out what all the noise was about.

As he turned to head that way, Nella joined him, Baby still leashed at her side.

He stopped. "Good show," he said. "I'll cheer you on like the others, if you wish."

"What I wish is to bring my friend Baby back to her enclosure and take a breather. It's fun giving training demonstrations, even short ones, especially since I didn't know I had the skills to do it particularly well." Her face was flushed a bit, which didn't detract from how lovely it was. And she appeared a bit flustered, as if she was embarrassed.

"You clearly do." Nodding, Scott turned and said, "I'll go with you to return Baby inside, then why don't you come with me? I'll be doing some administrative stuff for the shelter—heading up to the office, checking some security cameras, that kind of thing. As a manager, you need to learn more of that, too, and not only work with animals and residents. And I may have another potential new staff member coming in a few days whom I'll want you to interview."

"Sounds perfect." Her smile lit up her face, and he had a sudden, unbidden urge to give her a kiss. A brief, nonsuggestive one, certainly—but definitely not a good idea here, where some staff members including Warren, as well as Camp and Telma, had formed their own circle and were each working with a dog.

Nella and he quickly returned Baby to behind her indoor fence, and Scott felt a little sorry for the dog, since at the moment there weren't any other pups in this part of the building.

"I hope she doesn't get too lonesome right now," Nella said, echoing Scott's thoughts.

"I'm sure it won't be for long," Scott responded.

He watched Nella hang the leash Baby had been wearing on a hook along the wall where most of the other hooks were currently empty. He noticed she didn't return any treats to the jar hanging on the wall and figured she must have been generous to the obedient pup in her charge.

Soon, they were outside again, walking with their backs toward where all the training was going on, but their goal was the offices near the entry to the shelter.

In a couple of minutes, they entered one of the front buildings and walked upstairs to the offices. "Want to look at the security cameras with me?" Scott asked.

"Do you think there's a problem?" she countered, looking ill at ease.

"Not really, but I want to be sure the street looks normal, not much traffic or many pedestrians outside, after all that noise in here."

"Good idea." And so, Nella accompanied him into his office, where they'd be able to look at the screens showing what was picked up on the security cameras.

Scott had them set up so there were multiple camera recordings in rows on the same screen to start with, although he could always zero in on one or another if anything looked interesting. He could also access them on his phone.

At the moment, all appeared normal. Cars drove by on the street, and no pedestrians were visible in the area, not even walking dogs across the street in the park. He also glanced at the pictures within the shelter, but the only thing interesting there was also where the training was going on.

"When and where does the therapist arrive?" Nella asked Scott.

"Not till this afternoon, and she'll see people in rooms off the hallway in the entrance building. No reason for her to come inside. She has been well vetted, of course, but this is easiest."

"Sounds good," Nella said. "I'm going into my office for a few minutes now. Mostly because I've been eager to study that file you talked about that describes all the duties of a manager here. I've glanced at it now and then when I've had a brief chance to stop in my office and like what I've read so far, but I'd like to spend more time with it."

"Fine. I'll spend a little more time in here, although I'm not so concerned about our outside environment now."

He watched Nella's back as she walked out of his office. He liked the way she walked—as if determined to reach wherever she was heading, and yet she had a feminine sway to her body.

He needed to cut that out. She was doing well as a shelter manager. Very well. She got along with those they were protecting—staff members and animals. She got along well with the other managers.

And she got along well with him.

But that was because, despite their shared kisses, she was very professional.

Well, so was he, most of the time. He got down to business, which for the moment involved checking his email.

But a muted scream suddenly startled him. Nella?

He leaped up and exited his office quickly. "Nella?" he called as he headed a few doors away toward the office he had designated as hers.

"I'm out here!" Her shaky voice sounded as if it came from the reception area, and Scott pivoted to head that way.

In moments, he saw her. She stood behind the reception desk, the shelter cell phone receiver in her hand. She was staring at it. She looked terrified—no surprise after that scream.

But what did she see?

He took the phone from her and nearly hurled the receiver against the wall.

Last time the message had been ambiguous about who was being threatened.

Not this time.

The message today said:

You were warned. You should have gotten rid of the latest person to move into your hell pit of a shelter so she could be killed elsewhere. But you didn't. And we know where you are. That bitch Nella Bresdall will be killed there. Soon.

Chapter 15

Nella stared at the message, wanting to delete it.

Better yet, wishing it wasn't there.

"Damn!" Scott exclaimed, reaching for the receiver. "Same phone number as last time?"

"I—I don't know," Nella responded, hating how halting and raspy and—well, not at all like a professional officer of the law—her voice sounded.

But then, most professional cops weren't confronted with threats like this, with no clear source. No one to go after and bring in for questioning—and for whatever punishment was available for an attempt at intimidation, a death threat, a verbal assault like this, or whatever a prosecutor would choose as the official charge against the perpetrator.

Whoever that might be. And assuming he—or she—could be found and taken into custody.

"Any idea who might have done this?" Scott still held

the phone, pushing buttons and staring at it, moving the screen view around as if it would reveal who sent it.

She hoped Scott didn't do anything to accidentally erase that horrible message or otherwise cause it to disappear in a way that it couldn't be investigated adequately—never mind that she'd had an initial urge to get rid of it. She knew that, as a law enforcement professional, Scott definitely wouldn't do anything to intentionally delete it.

Who was she trying to kid? They hadn't figured out who was behind the last, less distinct threat. They probably wouldn't be able to determine who had sent this one, either.

But they had to try. *She* had to try. And succeed.

And protect herself.

She sat down on the chair, hunching her shoulders. Damn. She straightened them. Made them solid and tight.

And cop-like.

"I don't know who sent it." Nella liked how her voice now sounded at least a little more professional. "One of those gang members still on the run would be my guess, though. I'm glad, at least, that the threat's not against one of our staff members—although we can't completely discount that possibility even though I'm specifically mentioned this time."

"Of course. But we need to make sure everyone here is adequately protected."

"Including you." She turned to look at Scott. He stared back at her.

"Yeah, you're right. I'm not being threatened, but I'm here, and whoever wants you or anyone else at this shelter is going to have to go through me. Which means I'd better be adequately protected, too."

Nella smiled grimly. "You got it. And..." She couldn't help hesitating, but she knew what she had to say.

"And what?" Scott prompted.

She didn't look at him as she said, "I'm leaving. Whoever it is said they're after me. By hanging around, I'm endangering all our staff members who need protection. At least I can protect them a bit by getting away from them."

Scott grabbed her arms and pulled her back to her feet. He glared into her face. "You're not going anywhere. I don't intend to make you a staff member and alarm the others, but we'll protect you, too. Got it?"

"But—"

"You are staying here." He spat each word out without looking away from her. "Got it?" he said again.

"Got it." She wished she didn't sound so meek, and she looked away from him, but only for a few seconds. She refused to even consider the fact that this could trigger her possible PTSD symptoms, too. She squared her shoulders, stared more fiercely back at Scott and forced herself to act the way she wanted to. "Okay, then—what are we going to do to find this creep? As I said, my first reaction is to assume it's one of the gang members my task force failed to bring in. They knew I was designated in charge of that raid. And like I told you, Dan said a few are still out there, so that's a logical guess."

"Could be." He smiled a bit, as if happy with her new attitude. "Okay, here's what we'll do."

Nella wanted to continue watching Scott's face as he spoke—but as she did she noticed the window on the side of the room beyond him. Could someone be out there with a weapon, ready to shoot inside?

Or somewhere outside the fence, hiding behind a car parked along the nearby street?

Or—

She realized Scott had kept talking. She'd let him know her additional concerns in a minute—but remained determined not to sound too scared and wimpy. She needed to plan how to better protect the facility. And not just herself.

"I'll call one of my Chance PD contacts now, then Telma and Camp and have them come in here so we can tell them what's going on," Scott was saying. His eyes appeared glued to hers, as if he wanted to see what was happening inside her head.

Nella didn't particularly like that, but the only way she moved was to plant herself between the window and Scott.

"What are you doing?" he asked—then looked past Nella. And shook his head as he grimaced. "If you're trying to protect me, don't bother. First of all, when I redid this place I made sure all the glass was bulletproof, even assuming someone could see inside a room this high with no other buildings around for them to look in through windows or off roofs or whatever." He drew closer and grabbed her shoulders with his strong hands—and moved her so he was between the window and her. "But here we go. I'm protecting you, not vice versa."

Nella gave a short bark of a laugh. "Got it," she said, not that she would let that be the end of it.

"So anyway, after I—we—inform the other managers what's going on and make sure they're on highest alert, you and I are going to the Chance PD station no matter what my contact says." He paused and looked over Nella's head as if pondering something, then back at her. "I could just leave you here behind the protective walls and fences, but I not only want to talk more to people there but also get you away from here, temporarily, at least."

"Okay," Nella said, "but—"

"I know," Scott continued. "That might not be the best idea if we're being watched, since whoever made the threat could consider it an indication we, or you, don't believe him, and that could cause him to act. But I'd rather he know where we're going, see us at the police station, recognize that we have resources there. And in case you're wondering, even though I don't have an armored car, mine does have some safety features that'll help if we're attacked. Which I don't think we will be, at least not today."

She thought about asking him why not, but didn't. Scott seemed to be thinking aloud, weighing possibilities, going with the ones he considered most applicable.

Not that he could really know. But she recognized that he would do anything to protect her, as he would anyone here.

She didn't want to die, of course. But she also wanted to protect the shelter and its residents.

And she trusted Scott.

Before she could respond, though, her phone rang. She checked it. It was Dan. Oh, yeah. He and Jon wanted to come by tomorrow. Bad idea now? Or a good one?

She answered quickly, but before he could talk she told Dan she'd call him right back. Then she reminded Scott of the request.

"I'd like to say yes," she told him. "Not give the threatening creep any control over me. And besides, it won't hurt to have more cops around."

Scott seemed to ponder it, but only for a few seconds. "Yeah. Sure. Go ahead."

Nella called Dan. That had, in fact, been the reason for his call.

"See you tomorrow," Nella told him. "Be sure to let me know what time." Then she hung up again and turned to Scott. "All right," she said. "When do we head to the Chance PD?"

After speaking with Vince at the Chance PD, Scott called Telma and told her to come to his office—and bring Camp with her.

Both seemed outraged when they saw the threatening text. "We'll take care of you," Camp said immediately. He had taken a seat in the boss's office, but now he stood, folded his arms, and walked to Nella's chair. His expression was grim.

Telma didn't stand, but she seconded Camp's statement. "You're one of us now," she said, also crossing her arms. Her dark brows were often set in a frown over her hazel eyes, but her expression now was more of a furious glower, as if she were glaring directly at the person who'd threatened Nella.

"Thanks, both of you," Scott said. "But at the moment the primary duty for both of you is to make sure no one here at the shelter is endangered. In case you didn't know, Dr. Moran is coming this afternoon to do therapy work with some of our residents, so you'll have to ensure the comings and goings work safely, too. At least she only sees them in one of the rooms in our secure entry building. I'm taking Nella with me to the PD."

Now, Telma stood as Camp had. "But—"

"Until we know more about who it is, where they are, whatever else we can find out, we need to rely on our fellow officers as well as being cautious around here. Maybe it'll seem as if we're ignoring the threat, taunting the menace or whatever, but we need to show we're not intimidated. That Nella isn't intimidated. Although we will be careful…"

"I agree with Scott," Nella told the others. "I'm… well, a bit intimidated, of course. But I don't want it to show. And the more information we can get about whoever it is, the less likely that person is to harm anyone at the shelter."

"Except you," Camp said.

"Not on my watch," Scott shot back. "Now we're going to get ready to go. You two are in charge here. Okay?"

"Yeah," Camp said resignedly.

"Okay," agreed Telma.

"Now, don't tell our staff members anything specific, but remind them to be careful, even around here. Got it?"

Camp and Telma agreed with that, too.

"Oh, one more thing." Scott explained the pending visit tomorrow from Nella's previous cop cohorts. "It won't hurt to have more authorities present, even for a short while," he finished. Scott rose then, and so did Nella. "You okay with visiting the Chance PD with me?" he asked her in front of the others. If she said no, he might just listen to them and leave her here.

"I'm ready to go. Doesn't matter if I'm a bit scared. We need to nail this down. Let's go." And she strode toward the office door, which he hadn't locked.

This was one of the times he wished he had built some kind of protective garage at the shelter, but he hadn't. Now he led Nella down the steps and around toward the rear of the entry building, then out the back door—which he did have to unlock. He went first, leading her to the parking lot behind the shelter, where his special SUV was parked. Before Nella came through the door, he walked around, observing the area—potentially making himself a target if anyone was there stalking her. But he stared at the open parklike area directly across the street and saw no activity, and little activity at the few commercial buildings beyond it—a hardware store and a sports gear store.

Most important, he didn't see people at all, let alone anyone looking in this direction, so he returned to the door and got Nella out, immediately ensconcing her in the passenger seat of his car.

He had bought a very special vehicle when he got involved in creating this shelter—in case he had to transport some of the residents in protective custody someplace else, when they were in danger.

Soon, Nella and he were both locked inside, and he drove them quickly to the Chance PD's headquarters. Instead of parking on the street as he usually did these days, since he was no longer an obvious member of the department, he parked in the back lot among the vehicles owned by police officers and the brass in charge. There was a space not far from the door, and he took that—once more preceding Nella outside the car, though he saw several cops milling around in the lot and no civilians around to worry him.

While driving, he'd used his car's phone system to notify Vince Vanderhoff they were on their way—and why. He gave Vince the phone number used to send this threat so he could get a department techie working on attempting to learn the source, but doubted anything more useful than the search the last time would come of it.

His phone rang as he reached for the handle of the driver's door, and he answered it with the car's system.

"You here yet?" That was Vince.

"Just arrived. Parked in back. We're about to come in."

"Fine. Look at the door." Which Scott did. The back door to the station opened and four officers emerged, each striding out as if on duty—which they clearly were. Each had a hand on the butt of his or her holstered service weapons.

"I think Vince is ready for us," Scott told Nella, and, with the cops hanging around them, they got out of the car.

Soon, Scott and Nella sat in Vince's office. The visit was helpful, Scott believed, although so far there was no indication of who'd sent the threat. It had come from a burner phone, surprise, surprise.

Vince, wearing a suit as usual, was cordial to Nella and, in his raspy voice, asked about her time on the LAPD, including the gang task force. Scott hadn't told him much about Nella's background despite Vince's involvement in checking out potential new staff members before they were accepted at the shelter, so Vince had clearly done his homework. Scott did mention that Nella was anticipating a visit from a couple of her previous coworkers but gave no particulars.

While they were there, Vince had K-9 Officer Maisie Murran join them with her dog, Griffin. She hadn't yet started patrolling the shelter area with Griffin but promised to do so tomorrow to potentially notify whoever was issuing the threats that the place was under police protection. She and her brother Doug, with his dog, Hooper, would go around the entire neighborhood during the next few days so it didn't seem that the shelter was their reason for being there—to better preserve its covert purpose.

Plus, she said she looked forward to stopping by more often to talk to some of the staff members and also see the shelter pets. And also have Griffin sniff things out as an extra precaution.

"Oh, and yes," she told them, "that retired K-9 I told you about hasn't found the perfect forever home yet, so I think I'll be able to get him to become one of your shelter animals soon—but you'll have to promise to treat him like family."

"I'd love to," Nella said immediately, and Scott agreed.

Maisie and Griffin left then, but not before Nella had given Griffin a hug.

After Maisie and Griffin left the office, Vince took Nella and Scott on a walk around the station, though not in the reception area, where strangers could walk in off the street. But he did introduce Nella to several of the top brass there, including Chief Andrew "Sherm" Shermovski and Assistant Chief Kara Province. Vince must have told them in advance what was going on, since both appeared concerned and told Scott to keep them informed about anything they should know about.

Then, Vince walked them to Scott's car—along with a couple of armed officers who didn't appear to be there to protect them, but Scott was certain they were.

As the brass had done, Vince told Scott to stay in touch—and let them know if any further protection was needed.

"It is," Scott said, "but other than nasty texts we don't really know where the danger is coming from, so we'll just have to stay alert."

"Absolutely," Vince said. "And those patrols we

started around your neighborhood after the last threat? I'm going to get them increased a lot—though still by mostly unmarked cars."

"Thanks, bro," Scott said to his detective buddy, and gave him a guy-hug before getting into his car and starting the drive back to the shelter.

Nella still refused to panic about herself and would do everything she could to ensure the safety of others. Or so she told herself as they returned to the shelter and headed inside via the reception area. Of course Scott didn't let her get out of his car till he'd looked around, and then he walked very close to her, as if attempting to shield her in all directions with his body.

Very sweet, she thought—but the last thing she wanted would be for him to get killed instead of her.

Not that she wanted to get killed, either. Especially by one of those horrible gang members who had eluded her task force. Could it be that the one who had killed her partner, Lou Praffin, had located her and wanted to bring her down, too?

That wasn't going to happen. She wouldn't let it.

She hoped.

Well, she'd at least let Dan know tomorrow what was going on now. She hoped nothing like this would happen if he started a similar shelter.

Scott and she were now outside but behind the shelter's tall, protective fences. They had walked through the reception building and around the ones behind it, including the dining area. Scott had pointed out the closed door behind which Dr. Moran was undoubtedly now talking with one of the staff members. "Probably Alice," he told her.

Camp, who evidently was guarding this end of the

long walkway, immediately joined them. Nella assumed he had been watching a significant bunch of staff members walk dogs along that pathway, and she saw Telma at the far end, apparently also observing more protected residents walking dogs.

"Everything okay?" Camp asked.

"No news, but the shelter's under added observation now," Scott said.

"Good." Camp paused. "Nothing new here, either. Everything appears normal, although Telma and I have switched places often and also each walked upstairs in the entry buildings now and then and looked out windows to check for anything unusual. Didn't see anything, though. And I accompanied Dr. Moran inside and told her we've got some current security concerns, and I've also kept an eye on who she's seeing when."

"Good. We'll all stay alert. And I'll check in often with Vince."

Nella had noticed Telma heading in their direction. "So I assume you checked with our buddies in the local PD," Telma said when she reached them, "and they've already taken whoever sent that message into custody."

Nella knew she was kidding, but the frown she had last seen on Telma's face when Camp and she had been shown the threat was now replaced with a falsely angelic look of peace. Nella wished she could throw that sarcasm right back at her, but she just said, "What? Do you mean you want them to have all the fun? No, we're going to be the ones to solve this."

Telma just laughed. "Okay, tell me what you want me to do now." She looked at Scott.

"Just act normal. In fact, let's all observe and work with our staff members who're dog walking right now.

Okay?" He looked first at Telma, then Camp, but Nella figured he was really wanting her opinion.

The others agreed, of course. So did she.

And as Camp and Telma both walked away toward some staff personnel, Scott said, "Of course we're all on alert. I'm going to pop into the offices to check for any other messages, and, as I said, I'll keep in touch with Vince."

"Why am I not surprised?" Nella asked, trying to sound droll but relaxed.

She actually felt pretty good, fairly safe, for the rest of the afternoon. She wound up walking Baby again and giving her commands while staff members watched and imitated her once more. A couple were residents she hadn't yet interviewed—Kathy and Leonard—but now it seemed pointless to try to get more background information about those under protection here. They weren't the ones the threats had been directed at, after all. Or it certainly seemed that way.

But still, Nella would keep her concerns for everyone else in mind.

And do all she could to protect them.

Without, she hoped, losing her own life.

Chapter 16

Nella was glad the staff members remained unaware of the threats, including today's against her—even though they had most likely been reminded by the other managers to stay alert and careful. That assumed, of course, that Telma and Camp did as they'd promised before Scott and she headed to the police station.

No matter what those under official protection were thinking now, the rest of Nella's afternoon was enjoyable, working with them and Baby and other dogs. Of course some staff members visited the therapist for their individual appointments. And at one point Nella went into the entry building and got a glimpse of Dr. Moran as she said goodbye to one and greeted another. No time to introduce herself.

She had only been at the shelter for a few days, but in some ways it already felt like forever. Working with the canines had seemed to be a sort of panacea for the staff members under protection, since taking dogs for walks apparently helped them keep their minds off everything else.

Now Nella was pleased to continue to help train them all—the people to work with the dogs, and the dogs to obey their handlers. That helped her keep her mind off her own problems—somewhat, at least.

Later, she was glad Scott was willing for both of them to join the other people at the shelter for dinner in the dining area. She didn't look for safety in numbers, for she would do anything to protect everyone here, even run away, if it came to that. But it helped her feel at least a little better to have others around.

She sat beside Scott, as seemed her norm these days—but this time it wasn't just because she wanted to learn more about the shelter from him.

She wanted to protect him, as absurd as that was, even more than everyone else around here. And as a former cop, she would know the best way to deal with anyone who burst in here to attack her, or would figure it out fast. She didn't carry a weapon despite having one in her room, as Scott had instructed the managers, including her, to avoid carrying because of the potential additional stress it would levy on the staff members to see weapons around—although she was aware of some places guns were hidden. She knew a full range of self-defense techniques, of course, but how useful they were would depend on the situation.

Now, as usual when they ate in this facility, Scott and she sat at one of the long tables, and other residents surrounded them. Bibi and Warren sat across from them, and Alice sat at Nella's other side, while Muriel sat beside Scott.

It was fun to see how they all matched in their Chance Animal Shelter T-shirts, although of course the colors varied and only a few said Manager. Nella still wore her light blue one, so she matched Bibi, Alice and Muriel. Warren's was black, and Scott's was gray.

Tonight's meal was beef stew, cooked by Sara, as usual—in another gray T-shirt—who also helped to dish it out at the main buffet table. It was delicious—although Nella didn't have much of an appetite.

Still, the company helped to calm her, especially Scott's. Without specifically mentioning what they'd been up to that afternoon, or that Dr. Moran had been around, he managed to praise those around them for their excellent work with the dogs. He also reminded them dog socialization and training was a great function for this shelter, and that dogs and people all had similar reasons for being here—and all humans, at least, had to remain alert and careful.

Nella thought about adding something but figured it might only scare some of their residents without giving them a way to add to their protection, so she stayed quiet while smiling wholeheartedly at Scott.

After dinner, they joined a few residents visiting dogs in the kennel area inside the reception building and other dogs deeper within the shelter, ending up at the cat house and also visiting the small pets in the back.

Along the way, Nella got to pet Baby again—her favorite dog here. But Nella was in no position to adopt the sweet pug and hoped that one of these days someone wanting a new forever family member would come to fall in love with Baby.

Eventually, the other residents began disappearing into the apartment building, but Nella insisted on remaining outside as long as Scott did. They both said goodbye for the night to Camp and Telma, who both offered to stay in one of the empty apartments in case their protective services were needed, but Scott promised to call them if he sensed any trouble. They soon left for their own nearby apartments.

"I'm going into my office for a few minutes to check some things on the computer before I go to bed," Scott told Nella when they were alone in the main shelter area. "Will you go with me?"

"Why, so you can protect me?" Nella didn't mean to sound irritated—but the alternative would be for her to beg to remain in his presence for her own safety and comfort, and she wasn't about to do that.

"If necessary." Scott aimed a half grin down at her as he took her hand and started walking.

She had little choice but to join him. At least no one was outside to see them holding hands.

It didn't take long for them to reach the nearby building, and they walked up the steps to the offices. While Scott headed for his own director's office, Nella forced herself to head to the reception area and look at the phone there.

Would there be another threat?

But no, there were no messages at all, which made Nella take a deep, calming breath.

"Everything okay?" Scott had joined her pretty quickly.

"Yes," she said. "How about with you?"

"Just give me five more minutes to check emails—but I thought I'd just drop in on you here in case…there was a good reason."

"Thanks," she said. "I'll read any general shelter emails while you check your own." Plus, if she had time, she'd use the opportunity to read another small portion of her instructions as manager.

Scott left the reception office but returned a few minutes later—five, in fact, as he'd said.

"Any exciting emails?" Nella asked.

"Not on my computer. The general shelter ones?"

"Nothing there, either," Nella told him. She'd even had a couple of minutes to start the next instructions section. "Unless you're excited about some dog food ads."

"We've got our sources already," he said. "But thanks. Are you ready to call it a day?"

"Only if I can call it one really difficult day."

"Absolutely."

He didn't take her hand this time when he led her down the stairs and into the building next door, nor up the stairway to the floor containing all the occupied apartments.

But as far as she could tell, he was fully alert, looking all around them inside and outside the buildings, listening for anything unusual—as was she.

Nothing struck her as requiring any attention. And soon, they were outside her apartment.

She pulled her keycard from her pocket and unlocked the door. She had an urge to invite Scott in—to look around and ensure everything was in order there. But she could do that herself.

After all, she was a cop. A cop on alert.

Still, when he insisted on preceding her inside, she felt a lot better. He locked the door behind them, then walked around, examining each room, even each closet and under the bed.

"Looks okay," he finally told her in the apartment's living room, near the door. Though she'd been checking, too, she let out a sigh of relief. "I'll head to my place now, but call me when you wake up in the morning."

So he could protect her again tomorrow, she figured.

She appreciated it.

She appreciated him.

After assuring him she'd call, she walked up to him and put her arms around him, planning to give him a brief good-night kiss.

Only it didn't turn out so brief. The feel of his hard body against her. The relief that she remained safe and alive, at least for now.

His arms around her, pulling her close..

She reveled in the feeling. But she wanted more. Much more. And she had the sense he did, too.

Bad idea. He was her boss, and they were together because they were caring for people in protective custody—and animals, too. But that was all.

Yet she didn't let go of him. He didn't let go of her. She felt his hand go down her back—stopping at her buttocks, which he caressed lightly, then moved his hands away.

Well, she did the same with him—and liked his butt. A lot. Did she have to make that clear? Seduce him? Let him know she was ready for him to seduce her?

A continuation of this was a bad idea. Wasn't it?

Well, hell. Her life had been threatened. Shouldn't she take advantage now, while she could, of something she'd been craving—if she were honest with herself— but had sloughed off as forbidden and inappropriate?

"Care to visit my bedroom again before you leave?" she said against his mouth as it continued to search hers, tasting her tongue as she tasted his. Beef stew? Maybe. But it tasted a whole lot better than that.

"That sounds like an invitation," he whispered.

"Well, RSVP, then."

Which he did, by keeping his arm around her while leading her through the door into her room.

But they stopped at the doorway. "Much as I'd like for this to continue," Scott said, looking down at her, "it's really not a good idea, since—"

"Since it's not politically correct. You're my boss, not just my coworker, which could be bad enough. But know what? Whatever we do here will be entirely consensual on my part, and I'd be willing to tell the world—although I don't especially want the world to find out."

"You're really something, you know?" he said, smiling sexily at her. "Well, in case anyone asks, it's entirely consensual on my part, too."

In moments, they were on the bed together. First thing, they each removed the other's Chance Shelter T-shirt, which made Nella laugh—but only briefly.

His hands caressed her upper body, first her back, then around to her front, where he gently took first one breast, then the other, into his hand.

"Here, let me," she whispered, and she reached around to remove her bra. Next, she reached for his belt.

They both stood and removed their own jeans. Nella stared for a moment at the planes and angles of Scott's carved, muscular chest, then down toward where his shorts bulged.

She drew closer to pull off those shorts, and he used the opportunity to also pull off her underwear.

They were both naked, standing there, staring—but only for a few seconds. Scott again took Nella's arm and this time drew her down to the bed, where he stroked her breasts again, then moved downward to caress her most sensitive, most needy area—while she took the opportunity to clasp his erection in her hand and pump it gently.

Nella's breathing was uneven and fast. So was Scott's.

"Are you sure?" he began, as if she might back away now. As if she could resist what was right in front of her.

"Are you?" she countered breathlessly.

"Oh, yeah." No doubt sounded in his response, although he did exit the bed for a moment, which made her wonder if he'd lied...but he hadn't. He just bent to grab his jeans, get his wallet out of the pocket and extract a condom.

He quickly pulled it onto himself, while Nella watched and yearned to be touching him again herself.

Only... He was the one to touch her again first, to direct his fingers down to that very sensitive area of hers.

Then, kneeling over her, he bent forward and guided his erection so it entered her slowly at first—and then more decisively.

In moments, he was pumping as she responded from below him, moving upward, holding his butt as he moved...

Nella wanted it to last forever, but in very little time she found herself coming, even as he, too, arched in climax.

"Oh, Nella," he groaned, as she let out a low, brief sound of final pleasure.

Wow. He hadn't intended for that to happen when he followed Nella into her apartment. He had just wanted to verify that it remained safe, then leave. Or, at worst, sleep on her sofa for the night so he could continue to ensure she wasn't under any immediate threat.

But now he lay on her bed. He had wanted her from nearly the moment he met her, but he'd also immediately recognized how inappropriate that was, since she was his employee.

A very versatile and skilled employee, caring about the people he had hired her to help protect as well as the animals. And even the other managers—and, apparently, him.

She was a professional. A cop.

And now he realized she was a whole lot more—not only a woman who had appealed to him for her professionalism and beauty, but that beauty was more than just her appearance.

What they had just done had been probably the sexiest brief encounter in his life. He smiled in recollection of their conversation before, that it had been consensual on both their parts. He definitely appreciated her statement.

And, inhaling deeply as he worked to get his breathing under control, he realized he wanted more.

But not tonight. He had to be sensible again.

Right?

For a moment, he listened to her breathing settle down a bit, too. He was partly on his stomach, with his left side on her as she lay on her back. His left arm was over her body, which was bare beneath it. He considered moving it so his hand could caress her. Again.

But he continued to simply lie there. Any movement he made could spoil this moment if she reacted by pulling away.

"I didn't expect that." Her voice broke into his reverie, and her breathing once more became a bit irregular. "Did you?"

"No," he said. "But did I want it? Hell, yes!" He might as well be honest. It had been mutual, consensual, after all.

And damned wonderful.

"I… Would you like to stay here tonight?" Now Nella was pulling out from under him. She rolled to face him where he still lay, on his stomach now.

If she didn't remain there, neither would he. But the answer to her question was a definite yes.

Still, they had more to consider than what they'd done—and whether they could continue with any more physical enjoyment.

"Yes, I'd like to stay." He rolled over. "I *will* stay, after that threat. But our staff members aren't aware there was a threat against you. We could announce my staying here as part of my job, to protect you as well as them, which would be true. This way, if any of them see us, they could think the shelter isn't as safe for them now because we won't seem to be on duty."

She sat up and folded her arms across her breasts. Because she was seated, he couldn't see her other vulnerable, wonderful, sexy body parts at the moment.

"Well, since Telma and Camp reminded them today to be careful, we can always hint tomorrow at the reason why."

"Yes, we can," he said. "And that would make it more logical for me to move in here with you for a longer time, too."

Nella laughed. "Yes, logic is important—though I suspect that at least some others around here won't believe you're just sleeping in my apartment to protect me and might even wind up teasing us about it."

"Logically, as it turns out." Scott moved around some more so he could sit beside Nella on the bed. Put his arm around her. Pull her close again.

"Yes, logically." And Scott felt himself grin broadly as they kissed once more, their bare bodies tight against each other—and his most excited body part growing much more.

"So shall we?" she whispered against his mouth.

He let his hands answer the question.

Chapter 17

Nella appreciated how Scott rose first the next morning, very early. He kissed her awake, touched her hair, looked her in the eyes and said, "Good morning."

Then he showered, dressed—and peered out her apartment door while she stood behind him, wearing a robe and nothing else. But nothing that morning was suggestive, either.

They had work to do.

Plus, they would have visitors, although Nella wasn't sure about Dan and Jon's timing.

"No one there," Scott whispered. "But be careful anyway. Stay alert. I definitely will. And I'll see you in a little while." He edged his way into the hall and left.

For a moment, she felt bereft. Last night had been amazing. Making love with Scott, and not just once, had even taken her mind off the threat against her life—at least some of the time.

In any event she felt that, even if she lost her life after this, at least she had experienced the most fantastic sex she could ever imagine. She had enjoyed the first time, and each one after that somehow got better, and better...

Sure, she'd had boyfriends now and then. The ones who were cops liked to assume they were in charge, so she had just enjoyed the moments as best she could, then stepped away from each of them.

Those who hadn't been cops didn't seem to know quite how to be in a relationship with a law enforcement officer, so those hadn't lasted long, either.

She forced herself to shake off any feeling of loneliness. She would see Scott that day—and they would both be who they were supposed to be. Last night was wonderful, but it was most likely one unique, unrepeatable experience.

Now it was her turn to get ready for the day, which she did. In about half an hour, she left her apartment—and locked it after herself. No one was in the hall then, either.

Next thing was for her to fulfill her duties of getting into the company of some of the people in protective custody and walk dogs with them. Make sure they were okay.

And shove to the back of her mind, as much as possible, the threat against her life. She would remain alert, though. And not just because Scott had told her to.

A short while later, she had Baby on a leash and they joined staff members already walking dogs—the early morning crew, as she had begun to think of them: middle-aged Darleen with Pebbles; thin Kathy with Rover, the Scottish terrier mix, since Shupe, the dog she'd walked before had been adopted; Muriel walking Mocha; and Warren walking Bruno.

Warren. Had he spotted Scott anywhere near Nella's apartment? Was he going to say anything?

Fortunately, he didn't. The guy was his lighthearted self that morning, but apparently had no particular teasing goal in mind. He most likely had slept through the night, seen nothing. A good thing.

"How you doing?" Warren asked after settling in to walk beside Nella and Baby with Bruno.

"Just fine." Nella wasn't about to tell him otherwise. And, in fact, she was doing a whole lot better than fine, despite the threat.

Thanks to last night with Scott.

"That's good. Looks like Baby and you are bonded, right?"

"I do like the pup," Nella said, and stopped walking along the grassy area long enough to bend down and give Baby a pat on the head. The dog turned and looked up at her with a sweet look on her pug face, making Nella smile. "And how are you doing?" she asked Warren when she stood up again.

"Well enough."

They quickly caught up with the other walkers next to the tall wooden fencing that surrounded this area.

Nella wished she could look outside it to make sure all was well. Perhaps see one of the K-9 officers patrolling the area with their dog.

And maybe spot some of the police cars Detective Vince Vanderhoff had assured Scott would also be patrolling—although he'd said they would mostly be unmarked, so she probably wouldn't recognize them.

And she didn't know exactly when Dan and Jon would arrive this afternoon, but she'd check with them in a bit to schedule the time.

Warren and she finished walking in about half an

hour and returned their dogs to the appropriate enclosures. No extra time at this hour for any training. That could come later. Right now, it was time for breakfast.

Nella and her companions washed their hands, then started collecting their food and drinks. She didn't see Scott.

Was he okay?

And why was she worrying about him? He wasn't the one who was threatened.

But he had vowed to take care of her, and after last night she recognized, despite all reasons against it, she had really begun to care for him.

She soon sat down at a table with the people she'd been walking dogs with earlier. A short while later, Scott strode in. She'd saved a place beside her in case he wanted to join her—which he soon did, after getting his own food and coffee.

"So guess what, everyone," Scott said before he sat down. "We're going to get a few more rescue dogs this afternoon. It's always a good thing to increase our doggy population, and it's all the better since we had a couple of adoptions the other day. Telma and Camp are going to head to a San Luis Obispo shelter that I've been in touch with and choose them for us."

Nella couldn't help wondering if those rescues would include the former K-9 Scott had discussed with Officer Maisie Murran at the police station. It might be a bit early for that to happen, but knowing Scott, he was probably pressing to have it occur as soon as possible.

Even so—Nella leaned toward Scott and said softly, "Do all managers get the opportunity sometimes to help pick out our canine residents to help rehome them here?"

He put down the slice of toast he'd been raising to his

mouth and said, "Yes, and one of these days you'll get the opportunity, too. I'd love to see who you pick out, and I'm sure you'd do a great job selecting dogs likely to find forever homes quickly. But not until…" He let his voice trail off, then took a bite of his toast without looking away from Nella.

"I get it." She knew her tone sounded grumpy. "That's just another reason we should find—you know."

Scott tilted his head and clearly attempted to glare, but instead he laughed a little. "Yeah, that's a really good reason."

Nella finished her breakfast before Scott finished his. She stood and walked to the side of the room, where she called Dan.

"Yeah, we're coming," he said. "Unfortunately, we had some things come up at the station so we'll get there around two and only be there for an hour or so this afternoon."

"Okay," Nella said. "See you then." Good. She could now schedule the approximate time of their arrival.

She returned to her seat beside Scott, then started conversations with Darleen and Muriel—about dogs, of course. Both wanted her to work with them more on training, not just walking, and they discussed the kinds of commands Nella used most frequently. She confirmed that she, as a cop, had learned quite a bit just by watching trainings of official K-9s now and then.

Before they finished, Camp, at the next table with Telma, rose and called, "Hey, everyone. Like Scott said, we're heading out to bring in a few more rescues. We won't know who until we meet them, but I thought I heard a few of you over there—" he pointed toward Nella and those she'd been speaking with "—will be ready to help train whoever we find to help make them more adoptable. Right?"

"You got it," yelled Warren, who hadn't participated in the conversation but he'd been close enough that Nella figured he'd been eavesdropping.

"Great," called Telma, who had also risen. "That means we need to find only almost-perfect dogs, and you'll all help to make them perfect, right?"

Nella couldn't help feeling proud of the whole group as the response was both laughter and clapping.

She liked these people. A lot. She wanted them all to be okay.

Herself, too.

Damn those threats. And damn whoever was making them. She didn't want to be nervous about her own life, like she was now. She wanted to do her job. Help staff members. Train dogs.

She glanced toward Scott, who was looking at her in a way suggesting he knew what she was thinking. He appeared both concerned and caring—and not just because she was one of his managers.

A shiver went through her as she recalled their night together. Not that she'd forgotten it, or ever would.

"I can't wait to work with our newcomers, whoever they are," she said softly to him. "And continue working with them and others." She knew he would interpret that to mean she wasn't stopping her life or her dreams because of the threat.

And she wasn't surprised when he surreptitiously moved his hand from his lap toward hers and squeezed her hand under the table.

Scott understood Nella's frustration. He understood she'd want the opportunity to help choose additional shelter animals. But that was just one more thing to add to the list of matters beyond her control until they found the source of the threats and got whoever it was into custody.

He was frustrated, too. He wanted this over with in a completely positive way for Nella, and for the shelter. He wanted control over the same things that must be frustrating her.

He wanted her safe. And here. As a manager for a good long time.

And after last night? Well, he wasn't sure where that might lead, but he wanted to find out in a positive way, under his and Nella's control.

But for now, he had to act in a professional manner to try to clean up this mess as quickly and safely as possible.

And so, in addition to his prebreakfast contact with the shelter in San Luis Obispo from which the latest canine residents would be chosen, he had spoken with Maisie to learn when she and her brother would patrol this area with their K-9s. She hadn't arrived yet, but would definitely come this morning, with Doug planning to come soon, as well. Stopping in for a visit would be fine, too.

Scott intended to make a grocery run around then, as long as things seemed in order here, and also depending on when Nella's friends arrived. That way, he, too, could conduct a bit of an investigation of the area, and maybe see Maisie and Griffin, too. Dr. Moran wouldn't be coming today, so he wouldn't have to worry about who the therapist would be seeing, and when.

Camp and Telma wouldn't leave on their outing till this afternoon, so they could remain in charge of security while he briefly left the shelter. Which he did, around eleven o'clock. At that time, he ensured Nella was safely in her office going through emails—and that no further threats had been texted or otherwise received.

"So you're okay if I leave for a little while?" He studied her lovely face as he asked. She'd been concentrating on the computer when he had walked in and still appeared reluctant to look away.

Or was that a delayed reaction to their night together...?

"I'm fine with it, as long as you stay safe." She'd already mentioned that her friends wouldn't arrive until the afternoon. "And let me know what you find out—about the patrols and all around here, helping to protect the shelter, right?"

And you, he wanted to say, but she knew that. He didn't need to remind her. And so he just glanced around. The office door was ajar, but no one was outside. He bent and gave her a brief kiss. "Right," he said, then left.

He didn't bother calling Vince, since the detective might not know exactly where Maisie and Griffin were patrolling. And he didn't want it to seem too obvious that he was searching for them, in case the shelter was being observed.

But it wouldn't hurt to be utterly obvious that he was driving around searching for anything, anyone, that could be dangerous—and was ready to act should he find something. He would keep his weapon hidden, of course. And joining whatever unmarked Chance PD cars were canvassing the neighborhood, but not trying to hide his presence, could be of some advantage.

As long as he remained careful and didn't put himself in unnecessary jeopardy.

Once he got inside his car and locked it, he drove slowly around the shelter. There weren't many other vehicles, so if the place was being watched he would be fairly obvious.

But there were a few, and a couple appeared to also be cruising slowly, as if the drivers were observing the area and the shelter, perhaps looking for other people—pedestrians or drivers.

A few blocks away, Scott located Maisie and Griffin, along with another couple of cops in uniform as Maisie was. They were far enough away that a stranger unaware of the shelter's background might assume they were merely police on patrol with no specific goal in mind.

But Scott knew better, and if the shelter was under a suspect's scrutiny, that suspect would know exactly why the K-9 cop, dog and others were there.

As Scott passed, he wasn't surprised that they peered into his car. Maisie waved, then turned to the other cops she was with, and Scott assumed she was telling them who he was and why he was there.

He continued circling the area for a while, watching for anyone who looked out of place. Of course he couldn't be certain that all the cars he saw were unmarked police cars—and there were some regular cop cars, as well. But he didn't see anything or anyone that appeared out of place or dangerous.

Nor did he see anything out of the ordinary when he headed to town and quickly bought a few supplies.

He decided finally that it was time for him to return to the shelter and take over his protective obligations there, so Camp and Telma could go on their outing to pick up dogs.

When he parked in his regular spot, he was surprised

and pleased when Maisie joined him there with Griffin. "Mind if we come in and visit?" she asked.

"That would be great," he said, meaning it. Having a uniformed cop strolling the premises, particularly a K-9 cop, would make the staff members feel good. Him, too.

He quickly unlocked the door to the parking area and led them inside, leaving his shopping bags in his car for now.

"Anything in particular you'd like us to check out?" Maisie's expression was both quizzical and determined as they stood inside the fence, and as usual Scott got the impression that the pretty blond officer liked for her golden retriever and herself to do their job well.

"If you don't mind just patrolling and making sure nothing strikes Griffin as a problem, that would be great."

From what Scott gathered over the next half hour, Griffin enjoyed being greeted by the staff members and trading sniffs with the dogs they were walking. He wasn't surprised when Nella joined them too, and grinned a lot as she talked with Maisie and petted Griffin.

And, fortunately, during the long walk outside and short ventures into shelter buildings, nothing appeared to strike Griffin as an inappropriate sound or scent.

Soon, Scott accompanied them both through the reception building as they prepared to leave. "Let's do this again soon," he said. "Everyone seemed really glad to see you—and so did I. And I'm glad Griffin seemed relaxed."

"Me, too." Maisie smiled at Scott. "We'll be glad to come back. And you know, I assume, that I'm having that retired K-9 turned over to your shelter this afternoon, right?"

"Right," Scott said. "And thanks for that, too."

He walked out with them then to pick up his purchases from his car.

Chapter 18

At a little before two that afternoon, Nella received a call from Dan. "We're here. Just parked in the lot behind your shelter. Do we come in the back door?"

"No, please come around to the front. I'll meet you in the reception area."

Under other circumstances, Nella would have gone outside to meet them. And it might have been safe even now, thanks to the police patrols in the area—including Officer Maisie and her wonderful K-9, Griffin, who had visited the shelter that morning.

But instead, after hanging up, she walked from her office, where she'd been hanging out, into Scott's. "My friends are here. I told them to come into the reception area."

"Good. Let's go welcome them."

She figured his protectiveness about the shelter—and about her—was the reason he was joining her, and she appreciated it. She appreciated him, as usual. "Great," she said.

He preceded her down the steps and along the hallway, then waited for her to catch up before unlocking the door into the reception room. He entered there first, too. Which made her smile and shake her head—and silently thank him.

Both Dan and Jon were standing, watching as the two of them came in. "Hi, guys," Nella said, and introduced Scott to them. Of course, he had already met Dan by phone calls and emails, so they greeted each other enthusiastically.

Dan, off duty, wore a button-down shirt and dark trousers, but no suit jacket. Jon was dressed more casually, most likely changing out of his uniform before they left L.A.

"How are you?" Jon approached Nella with arms out as if he intended to hug her. She slipped sideways and smiled at him, drawing closer to the other two men. She thought she saw dismay cross his face but ignored it.

Jon was a guy of moderate height, with thick, short blond hair and pale blue eyes. Nella considered him reasonably good-looking, but she had no interest in him other than as a cop who'd been her superior officer, since he was a sergeant.

And she'd had even less interest in him when he'd started flirting with her—and became somewhat pushy, as if, because of his higher rank, she should do what he wanted. He hadn't been abusive, but he had been annoying.

She had been appreciative, though, when he had acted somewhat as her backup on the task force. But she'd figured if she emphasized that now, he might take it as an expression of her interest.

"I'm doing well," she responded. "I hope you are, too. And it's so great that you're both interested in starting a similar shelter in L.A. This place is amazing."

"Tell us about it," Dan said. "And show us around." He looked from Scott to Nella. Dan hadn't changed from the last time Nella saw him. He appeared interested and relaxed, with a bald head and good build for any cop, including a detective like him.

"So tell me what you want to see, and what you want to know," Nella said. "Scott will be most able to help with both, but I'll do my best."

For a few minutes, they sat on the chairs in the reception room, and Nella was the one to respond to most questions about how they protected both people and animals here. "I love it," she finished. "It's fun taking care of all of them."

"So you intend to stay here, at least for now," Dan said. "But if we do open something similar in L.A., could you come help?"

Nella aimed a glance at Scott. "Depends," she says. "Maybe, but I doubt it would be permanent."

"Then you really like it here." Jon didn't exactly sound thrilled.

"And everything's going well for you here?" That was Dan. Should she be honest with him?

To some extent, at least. "More or less—although there've been some texts that seem to indicate at least someone knows what this covert facility is about and isn't happy." She didn't say that the last one had mentioned her. "I can't help wondering if maybe some of those gang members could be involved."

Okay. That had to tell them she was concerned about her own safety.

"We're still trying to find them, like I said," Dan

told her, his brow furrowed. Okay, nothing new there. They'd been trying before. And she didn't really know the source of those messages anyway. "Did those texts—"

She interrupted before he could finish. "Know what? It's time to take you on a tour of this wonderful place." That was okay, since they were cops, and Nella had already gotten Scott's approval. "Just Scott and I are in charge at the moment since the other managers are out collecting some new rescue animals for us to take care of. You'll probably meet a few of the staff members who are under protective custody inside. Most visitors aren't permitted to come inside and meet our residents, but your situation is different from most."

Once again, Nella allowed Scott to precede her, with the others following as they went through the door, through the entry facility and past the first dog kennels, then outside to the main shelter area. Nella happily explained all they saw. And sure enough, some staff members were walking dogs as they got into the center area.

"Nice place," Jon said, not sounding particularly happy. But Nella and Scott introduced both visitors to some of those staff members, explaining that they were police who happened to be visiting but not much else.

A short while later, Scott got a call—and Nella was excited. Camp and Telma were on their way back to the shelter with three dogs they had chosen to add to the group of current canines needing new homes.

Nella didn't ask any questions about those new dogs, though she wondered if one of the three was the retired K-9 that Scott had been told about by Officer Maisie. She hadn't had the chance to ask Maisie about it before. Even if the K-9 did move in here, though, Nella knew she couldn't rely on the dog to protect her from any threats. Of course, she didn't want to rely on Scott, either.

She wanted to take care of herself.

But under these circumstances, she needed to be flexible and smart, and accept all the help she could get.

And help those new canine residents as much as she could.

While they waited, she decided to give her visitors a brief demonstration of more of what she and the staff members did. She saw Warren walking Bruno, and Muriel walking Mocha. "Come with me and watch this," she told Dan and Jon. With Scott beside her and the others following, Nella went into one of the buildings and got Baby out of her enclosure.

"Do you want to work with anyone now?" she asked Scott.

"I'll just watch you," he said.

"Okay." Taking the lead, she got the others to practice fairly simple commands like sit and stay, down and come with their dogs, and even try paw—which Baby seemed to get fairly quickly.

"See?" she said to Dan—and to Jon, who remained beside him. "This is what we do."

After about ten minutes of intense doggy training, Nella decided it was time for them all to take a walk in the shelter area—again demonstrating to Dan and Jon what they did here.

"What do you think?" she asked Dan quietly as Baby continued walking beside her, and Scott moved away to talk to a couple of residents who weren't working with dogs just then. "These folks all have hard pasts, but their presents, and hopefully futures, are enjoyable and productive. They all get vetted before they are accepted here as residents, and they all appear appreciative and helpful and even happy."

"Got it," he said. "And I like it. I'd like to learn even more. But we need to leave in a little while. This was, unfortunately, a quick visit we managed to fit in, despite how busy we are at the station. We'll want to come back soon, though."

"I understand," Nella said.

"But what about you?" he asked. "What you said before. Are you sure you're okay here?"

"Of course," she responded. It was true. She would make certain of it.

As they headed toward the entry buildings, Nella stopped as she saw Telma and Camp exit a door and walk toward them. Telma held the leash of a golden poodle mix, and Camp held two leashes, one with a pit bull mix and the other a German shepherd.

"Hi," Nella called out excitedly. Knowing how good at their jobs the two managers were, she assumed all three dogs got along well with others, although Nella would be careful since she still had Baby under her control. She allowed Baby to lead her in the other dogs' direction.

They each traded nose sniffs with Baby, and none appeared vicious or territorial in the least.

"This is Cheesecake." Telma waved at the golden poodle mix whose leash she held.

"And these are Samson and Spike." Spike was the shepherd, and he immediately sat and looked at his current handler, Camp.

Well-behaved? It certainly appeared so. Could he be the retired K-9? If so, Nella felt hopeful that Spike would be a great asset to the shelter.

Scott, who had been watching from near the dining facility door, caught up with them now. He immediately joined Nella and whispered in her ear, "Spike's the former K-9. Maisie got him released to us today."

Nella couldn't help grinning.

The staff members, though they appeared curious about the new arrivals, did their jobs well and all continued to walk the dogs under their control.

Dan and Jon stayed back, but they clearly were watching.

"Looks like some good choices," Scott said to his managers.

"Yeah, we kept in mind what we thought you'd say about each possibility at the SLO shelter," Camp said drolly. "I wasn't certain about this pit bull, Samson, till I got down on my knees in his enclosure and he came over and began licking my beard."

Nella found that amusing, if a bit distasteful—literally. "And Cheesecake?" she asked Telma. "I assume she didn't lick your beard."

"Not hardly. But she met my eyes and sat down the moment I entered her enclosure. It was like she was telling me she knew who I was and what I was looking for, and that she wanted to come with me."

"Delightful!" Nella couldn't help exclaiming.

"What about that—who is it? Spike?" Warren had joined them with Bruno as they stood at the edge of the walkway. "Why did you choose him?"

"I'd imagine the answer is in that guy's ancestry," Scott replied, looking from Camp's face to Telma's and back again. "A German shepherd? Why not bring a smart and lovable dog here to help him find a good home?"

"He looks a bit old," Warren countered. And he did. Spike's black-and-tan coloration had some gray in it, including on his muzzle. But he was alert, and clearly very friendly. He even pulled on his leash till Camp allowed him to get close to Warren, as if he recognized this man was talking about him.

Maybe he did.

"So, Nella, do you want to test these three to see how well they know commands?" Scott asked her, which also suggested that Spike was the K-9.

"Absolutely. Here. I'll give you a command first." She held out the end of the leash she held. "Take Baby back to her enclosure." She paused before adding, "Please."

"Will do." Scott accepted the leash. His gaze back at her seemed more amused than offended, fortunately.

She liked the idea that he remained standing there for a few minutes after telling an obedient Baby to sit. He watched as Nella ran Spike through a group of dog commands she had heard given to K-9s, some of which she had tried here before—a lot of the normal ones for dogs plus fetch, follow, stand, and more. And dear, well-trained and clearly excited Spike obeyed them all.

Would he protect her or anyone else from threats? She had no doubt that he would, if they occurred in a manner that was clear to him, like a person jumping on her and starting to beat her.

But there were so many other ways that the threat could come true—such as her getting shot. Or the menace doing something even worse, like attempting to burn the whole facility down to get to her.

Well, Spike might not be able to prevent those kinds of things, but Nella figured that, with his background, he would alert her and the others if there was a person nearby causing a dangerous situation.

Nella recognized she might have to count on that,

just as she had come to rely on Scott to do anything he could to find the source of those threats.

Even though she still wanted to take care of herself in all ways. And to bring down those final gang members at last, assuming they were the source of the threats.

Better yet, Dan and his group should do it. But she didn't say anything about it to the two men standing behind her.

For now, Nella handed Spike's leash back to Camp while she worked briefly with Cheesecake and Samson. She was delighted that both appeared willing to work with her, even though neither seemed to know many basic commands—yet.

"Cheesecake, heel," she said to the poodle as she attempted to take her for a walk. Cheesecake sat and looked at her, as if she was curious but not knowledge-able about what Nella wanted.

Nella remained patient as she got the poodle to stand and walk with her, and it only took a few minutes before she appeared to get it, that she was supposed to walk beside Nella, at her heel. And obey even more com-mands. Then, when the training session was over, she snuggled up to Nella, acting utterly sweet and adorable. Was she a potential therapy dog?

And Samson? His initial expression as he regarded Nella when she gave him orders appeared bored. He didn't obey her, either, at first. Then, almost as if he was shaking his head in exasperation, he started to obey each of Nella's commands as soon as she demonstrated to him what she wanted.

Hooray! Success. Nella felt proud of herself, and prouder of the dogs.

And, most importantly, she had begun the process to help Samson and Cheesecake find perfect new homes fast—especially one for Cheesecake, where her wonderful personality could be utilized to help people.

Spike, she hoped, would remain her companion for at least a while.

Till there were no more threats or reason for her to worry about her safety.

Scott hurried as he finally returned Baby to her building, fastening the latch on her enclosure's gate so she was secure and safe. Then he returned to the area near the offices where Nella was saying goodbye to her LAPD colleagues.

"Sorry we couldn't stay longer, especially after the long drive here," Dan was saying. "But I saw, and learned, a lot. What you've got here is wonderful—especially considering the source of the people who work with the shelter animals." He had bent closer to Nella as he spoke, clearly not wanting to upset any of those people, though none was nearby at that moment.

"I liked it, too," said Jon. "And the way those residents act with the dogs, and are treated themselves—it looks really great."

Scott liked that his idea for this shelter might expand, thanks to Dan. And he'd noticed that Nella seemed a lot closer to Dan than to Jon. But right now Jon continued praising all he had seen here, so Scott had nothing against him.

In a few minutes, they finished their goodbyes. "We'll be in touch, of course," Dan said. "And maybe visit again soon." He looked at Nella. "And—well, I'm not exactly sure what's going on, but you know you're always welcome to return to work with us if things aren't going well here."

Yes, Nella had mentioned to them what was happening, even if she hadn't been specific about what those text messages contained. And she had told Scott she was willing to leave if the shelter was being threatened.

But he thought that was the worst thing she could do just then.

He wasn't surprised, though, when Jon reiterated Dan's invitation. "That's right," he said. "Come back to L.A. anytime. That could really help us dig in to start a shelter like this, you know. And—well, we've always got your back."

Maybe so, Scott thought. Well, so did he.

He was glad when both men finally gave Nella a parting hug—brief ones, not particularly emotional, fortunately. They waited for Nella to unlock the door into the reception room. Scott followed the three of them and watched Dan and Jon leave—and felt relieved, even though he loved the idea of their opening a similar shelter.

But he didn't like the idea of Nella going back to L.A. for any reason. Especially now.

"Are you okay?" he asked her once the others were gone and Nella and he stepped into the hallway beyond the reception room. He watched her lock the door. No reminders needed, of course.

"Sure," she said. "And I do hope they work on developing a shelter like this. It's such a great idea."

He couldn't really read her emotions as she looked into his eyes. Sorrow that her friends were gone? Pleasure that they had enjoyed what they'd seen here?

Something else?

"You know what?" she said as she started walking down the hall toward the first kennel area.

"What?" Scott asked.

"I want to spend a little more time with our new canine shelter residents."

"Then let's go," he said.

In a few minutes, they had rejoined the staff members who were still working on some of the commands Nella had been teaching them. Nella took over with Cheesecake, Spike and Samson, one at a time.

Scott was delighted to see that the staff members seemed almost spellbound as they watched her, then determined as they tried the commands again themselves.

Nella was certainly one major asset to this shelter.

He wouldn't let anything happen to her despite the threats. Period.

And he hoped she stayed there, despite the open invitation to return to L.A.

Eventually, the afternoon faded into evening. Nella clearly recognized it. "Let's all take one more long walk around the shelter," she said, "then think about our dinner."

Which was a cue for Sara, who had also been watching the dogs and their handlers that afternoon, to dash off and start cooking.

Scott watched as Nella appeared to take on Spike as her primary dog companion. He had hoped that would happen. But would Spike be able to guard Nella adequately?

He'd talked with Maisie again earlier, after she had handed Spike to Telma and Camp to bring here for security. No, Maisie and Griffin hadn't detected any sign of gang members hiding in the area, waiting to take their revenge on Nella. Neither, apparently, had any of the cops who'd been with Maisie or in the patrol cars.

Which didn't mean that wasn't the source of the threat.

"Hey, where are you?" Nella had stopped walking

the dog. "You look as if you're planning something pretty worrisome for this shelter." Her words and tone were teasing, but he could see the questions in her eyes.

"Worrisome? Nope. But I'm getting hungry and I'm eager for dinner."

"Me, too." Warren had apparently been eavesdropping, which, considering what had been said, was fine.

So for now, Scott put all his musings aside and helped the staff members, who had all now completed their final walk around the shelter, return the dogs in their charge to their enclosures.

He showed Nella the large enclosure in the reception building's kennel that he had decided to designate as Spike's when the K-9 wasn't with her. If anyone came inside the shelter who shouldn't, that was a likely area for it to happen, so they could listen for Spike's bark—at least for tonight.

Once they had enclosed Spike, Scott said to Nella, "Are you ready for dinner?"

"Sure, but I'd like to check the offices..."

He'd been planning to do that, too, but only once he had ensured himself that Nella was surrounded by other people, at dinner. But they were close to the office building, so he agreed. "As long as we do it quickly."

And Spike didn't bark.

Fortunately, there was nothing unusual in the texts and emails either of them, or the shelter, received. And so he accompanied Nella back down the stairs to dinner.

Nella enjoyed her dinner well enough, though she didn't eat much. But the company was good. As had become a habit since her arrival, she sat with Scott.

A lot of the discussion as they all ate the excellent burgers Sara had prepared was centered around the new dogs. Several residents commented about how well they'd done, and how the managers would find them new homes as they did with other canine residents.

Nella didn't object to talking about finding Spike a new home, and neither did Scott, but she knew the plan was to keep the K-9 here for a while. Considering the protective nature of the shelter, they might not even try to find him another home.

Which was fine with Nella. She liked that dog a lot.

When dinner was over, the usual routine was followed, with some staff members helping to clean the dining area while others were free to go watch television or play cards or whatever for the evening.

Nella just decided to retire to her room. At least there had been no more threats.

Spike was here and on duty.

Same thing applied to Scott, and to a lesser extent Camp and Telma—and Nella too, of course.

So why didn't she feel more relaxed?

She turned on the television in her room and found an old movie on a local channel—a romance.

Which caused her to think about last night, here, in this apartment. With Scott.

As if it had ever totally left her mind.

But she'd be okay here tonight on her own. No threats or other indications of current problems like sinister people sneaking around this area.

Okay. She needed to go to bed. It was getting late, and—

She heard a light knock on the door and immediately hurried to unlock it after asking who was there.

Scott.

Of course she let him in, but why was he here? She glanced around him and saw no one in the hall—fortunately. Everyone had probably gone to bed, or at least to their apartments.

"Is everything okay?" she asked.

"As far as I know." He shut the door and locked it, then towered over her as he looked down with those incredibly blue eyes. "And I want to make sure it stays that way."

"That's great," Nella managed to whisper, even as her body suddenly yearned for the gap of maybe a foot between them to disappear.

It did. In moments she was in his arms, and his mouth was on hers.

He pulled back, though, after an incredibly hot kiss. "Is it okay if I stay for the night?" he asked. "To help ensure all is well."

"Oh, yes, please," she said, and found herself once more tightly ensconced in his arms—even as she felt his hardness pressing against her. "And yes, this is completely my decision, whether or not you're my boss."

All would definitely be well that night.

Chapter 19

The next morning, Scott left Nella's apartment early again, after peering carefully into the hallway to make sure no one was there to see him.

Oh, yes. It had been another amazing night. Sure, he had stayed there because one of his most critical functions right now was not only to ensure the safety of the shelter and all its residents, but also to protect Nella from whoever had issued those threats.

Since the shelter had been mentioned in those threatening texts, he had to assume that the person not only knew it existed and that Nella now lived here, but also where it was.

So where was he—or she? Here? Or someplace far away, attempting to cause a lot of worry—before doing whatever that person was planning?

Which now, apparently, focused on Nella. But why? How? And when?

Well, despite there being no indication of anyone sneaking around there that night any more than the previous day, Scott had wanted to stick around, as he'd told Nella. To keep her safe, he'd assured himself.

But also, if he was honest, as a possible follow-up to their wonderful activities the night before.

Which it had been. Each time they made love, it was more exciting. More intense. More addictive, since when it was over, it wasn't over for long. Each time started with a look or the lightest of touches.

Yet despite being so physically involved, he had managed to maintain a reasonable degree of vigilance—listening for any unusual sounds other than residents sometimes strolling the hallway outside, even checking the shelter's security camera footage on his phone now and then when he wasn't in bed with Nella.

Scott knew he would be tired all day, but so what? And, as unprofessional as it was, would there be more that night?

It would be better if they caught the suspect first, and then their lovemaking could also be a celebration.

Not that they were developing a relationship. She was his employee, and now also one of those he needed to protect. No emotion could get in the way.

So this would be just another day at work. Special work, of course, at this shelter that had been his idea, his creation, a place that protected not only people with changed identities but also animals needing safety.

And, most important, for the moment, it also contained Nella.

They had agreed to meet in the dining area for breakfast in an hour, after Nella showered, dressed and joined staff members in walking dogs again around the outdoor shelter area.

She'd made it clear that, as much as she liked Baby, the dog she would mostly walk now, and for the foreseeable future, would be Spike.

To start the day off right, Scott headed into the office building and upstairs. He checked the main shelter phone first, holding his breath while he looked for any more threatening texts, but there were none.

Next, he scanned the footage once more from the security cameras both outside and inside the shelter. He had only glanced at it occasionally during the night, on his phone, so he could have missed something. But there weren't any people showing, and the few cars outside just rolled by. So, nothing there to worry about.

Then he checked the shelter email. Nothing particularly exciting in it, or his own that he accessed with the desk computer—and just to be careful he also looked at Nella's, since he'd told her not to change her password and he was still able to get into it. She wasn't likely to receive anything personal here on the shelter system anyway.

Nothing. Good. And he was getting a little hungry—for food, and for Nella's company again. Time to head to breakfast.

Nella had a difficult yet fun time early that morning as she joined the staff and headed to breakfast—after she had walked Spike, accompanying a few other residents walking dogs. But now, where was Scott?

She tried to focus the conversation on the three new dogs at the shelter. Everyone was happy to talk about them, including those who hadn't yet walked Cheesecake, Samson or Spike but were begging for the opportunity.

All three dogs were involved in that day's early morning walk.

"I'll let some of you take a few turns working with Spike sometime," Nella said more than once to staff members who asked, although she wanted to keep Spike mostly to herself. It wouldn't hurt, though, to allow others to work with this special dog sometimes. "But he seems pretty smart and fairly well trained already."

Fairly well trained? Heck, he was about the best dog Nella had ever observed or worked with—though there weren't many of the latter.

And she believed that the smart, alert K-9 would let her know if anything seemed amiss.

She felt uncomfortable being the only manager around that morning. Telma and Camp hadn't arrived from their homes yet, and she still didn't know where Scott was.

She didn't feel as if she was in danger, though—did she? Well, she remained alert while walking Spike, so she wouldn't allow herself, or anyone else around here, to get hurt.

But staying alert was a challenge, since her mind kept returning to her night with Scott, and how wonderful it had been. How inappropriate it had been.

And how she wanted it to happen again. Tonight, if possible. And additional nights...

Forget that. For the moment, she was the only one in line at the buffet table and she prepared to grab a plate.

Her cell phone chirped in her pocket, indicating she'd received a text message. Odd. She wasn't expecting to hear from anyone despite keeping her phone turned on. She pivoted without picking up a plate, maneuvered around the chatting people in the area and walked back to the dining room's entrance.

She looked at the number from which the text had originated. It wasn't familiar. Probably just a robocall. Even so, she pressed the button to read it.

And froze.

It must be from the same person who had left threats on the shelter's phone. Last time, it had warned the shelter that she would soon be killed there.

This one said,

You are still there, bitch, even after what I said before. Your coworkers haven't gotten rid of you. If you want that shelter and the people who live there to survive, leave. Go home. I have decided not to kill you—yet— if you return to L.A.

She gasped and nearly dropped the phone.

She needed to get out of there. Any appetite had fled. So had her nerves. But where would she go now? Back to her apartment to pack up and—

"Good morning." Scott was now beside her, obviously pretending they hadn't seen each other earlier. Then he asked, "What's wrong?"

She couldn't speak, couldn't tell him, but her expression must have been so panicked that he reacted by scanning her with highly concerned eyes. The phone remained in her shaking hand.

He gently removed it from her grip and looked at it.

"Damn." His tone was hard yet muted. "Enough of this crap." He looked her straight in the face. "And don't even consider paying attention to what it says. Your leaving here, even to return to L A. as it says, will only put you in further danger."

"But the threat against this shelter. Again. I just can't take the chance—"

"We're all taking the chance. After all, this is Chance, California." His attempt at a joke failed to make her smile, but she appreciated the effort. "Look," he continued, "we're already investigating the source of those outrageous threats, and this one only makes it worse. It's even more personal against you. Apparently, whoever it was expected we'd throw you out after the first two, and since you're still here—which that person clearly knows—they're just trying a different approach. Well, none of them will work, and I'll do what I can to step up the effort to find that person."

Nella looked him straight in the eye. "I appreciate it, but—"

"But I'm getting hungry, and I bet you are, too. Let's go grab our breakfast." He handed her back her phone after looking at it once more. "I'll get in touch with Vince soon and let him know about this latest threat."

Nella stuck her phone back into her pocket but felt as if it was setting her on fire.

Rationally, she recognized Scott was right. Giving in, doing what that person demanded, wouldn't solve anything.

She actually managed to get some food down, although she mostly sipped coffee. And discussed more about dog training with the nearest staff members, Alice and Warren—and with Telma and Camp after they joined the group.

Scott remained quiet, but she felt certain about what was on his mind.

It was on hers, too.

"So you going to let me walk Spike today?" Warren asked loudly from where he sat a few people down, facing her, interrupting her thoughts and waving a piece of toast.

She had to act normal, despite what was happening in her mind. "Nope," she told him. "Your training skills are getting too good to work with a dog who already knows it all. I want you to take Cheesecake out and teach her something."

"That's what I want to do," Alice said. "But I'll take Samson. He's pretty smart."

Several other residents who planned to walk dogs when they were done eating entered the discussion that began to focus on the various skills of the canine residents, as they often did. But this time Cheesecake, Spike and Samson were the main subjects, being compared in skills and friendliness with those who already lived at the shelter.

Nella loved listening, although she didn't contribute any further to the conversation. Instead, despite Scott being right beside her, also apparently listening, her mind started heading in a different direction.

Who was threatening the shelter—and narrowing in on her? And why?

The only possibility that made sense was what she had considered before—some of the gang members who'd escaped from her task force wanted some kind of revenge against her, since she'd been in charge.

What—their killing her partner, Lou Praffin, hadn't been enough?

And—well, was this logical?

She might be able to find out if she actually returned to L.A., not to obey the threats but to look for those gang members and capture them at last.

Maybe. If she survived.

There was one possible way of finding out more, which she planned to do after breakfast.

Scott, perceptive guy that he was, apparently noticed that she must be thinking something different. He leaned toward her. "You okay?" he asked softly.

"Sure." She made the word sound decisive, though the opposite was true—and perceptive Scott probably knew it.

Even so, that was the position she would take.

"When you're done eating, we can leave," Scott said. "I'm finished."

"Great. Let me just get some more coffee." Nella immediately rose, tossing smiles at the people around her, who continued talking about the dogs she was so fond of.

And yes, she was fond of these people, too. If her presence was putting them in danger… Well, she would at least follow up on the thought she'd just had and try to decide what to do next.

Even as the phone in her pocket caught her attention again, despite no sound or motion erupting from it.

Only the memory of that most recent, horrendous text. And her wonderment why there was apparently no security on her phone number.

Scott and she both refilled their coffee cups after bussing their dirty dishes into the kitchen area. "What do you want to do this morning?" he asked.

"Walking dogs with staff members is always a good idea," she said, although her mind also suggested that she begin packing. But she would wait for the phone conversation she intended to have before deciding for sure.

"Okay," Scott said. "I'll do some walking with you."

"Really?" He was often there, but nearly always just watched everyone else walk dogs.

"Sure. Let's go up to the offices for fifteen minutes

or so, and I'll make my call. By then, everyone else should be done with breakfast and ready to get to work."

"Sounds good," Nella said. That would give her time to make her call, too.

"And in case you're wondering, I'm also following up on a couple of possible adopters who are interested in visiting, maybe even later today."

She couldn't help smiling at that—both at what he said, and the fact that Scott was adeptly changing the subject. "Great! I'd love to get involved with that, help introduce them to whichever of our pets they're interested in."

As long as she was still here.

And she probably would be, at least later today. If she made a decision to leave, it most likely wouldn't be immediate.

Unless she learned that the threat to the shelter was imminent, of course.

Which of course it could be…

She didn't want to focus on that. Not now. "You ready?" she asked Scott, nearly prancing beside him to get going.

He gave her a questioning look. "Yeah, I am. But why—"

She took a sip from her coffee cup, poured just a tiny amount back in from the urn to replace it, and said, "I'm not letting any concerns ruin my day."

He could interpret that any way he wanted, but she felt certain he'd recognize it was a result of that latest threat.

And would assume from what she said that she was listening to him and staying here, notwithstanding the attempt at intimidation.

Which was true… At least for now.

"Okay, let's go," he said. Nella turned to look at the people still sitting around the tables. Most seemed involved in conversations—about dog walking and training, she figured.

Well, under other circumstances she'd have been delighted to stay there and join them.

But right now, she had that phone call of her own to make.

In a few minutes she was in the room designated as her office. Both Scott and she had entered the general office area first, and he checked the shelter phone for any more nasty texts.

None, fortunately. And Nella hadn't received any more on her personal phone, either.

Now, with Scott in his own office with the door closed, she settled more comfortably into her desk chair and stared at the wall across from her, where there were a few pictures of rescued dogs. Then she pressed the button to reach the person she figured she needed most to talk to right now—her former boss, Deputy Chief Dan Poreski.

Dan answered immediately. "Nella. How are you?" His voice sounded a bit raspy, but definitely friendly.

"Fine, Dan, and you?" Okay, the niceties were necessary, she supposed.

"Just fine. Are you calling to see if plans are in the works yet for us to start a shelter like yours here in L.A.? If so—well, we're talking about it, but nothing's happened yet." He paused for a second, then continued, "We're waiting for you."

Nella laughed. "Well, that's one of the reasons I called, but you'd better not wait for me. The other reason is…well, is there any way I can convince you to ramp up the search for the remaining gang members?"

A hesitation. Then—"Why do you ask? We didn't talk about it much when I was there, but… Did you get another text message about the shelter? I assume you think those guys are the source. And that…well, you didn't tell me what the text said, but it's threatening somehow, right?"

Nella drummed her fingers on the desk. His response clearly meant he hadn't attempted to increase the search yet. Might never. But he'd guessed at least part of the reason for her concern.

"Well, yes," she answered, hearing the coolness in her voice. "And I'm tired of it."

"Me, too." Dan's tone sounded gloomy, but a bit more energetic when he continued. "Look, I'll try to ramp it up a bit more than we already have. And Jon and I could schedule another time to come up there to see you again, talk more about the shelter—and this. Soon, okay?"

"Right, soon," she said, not believing it.

"Better yet, you could come here both to advise us about the shelter and to discuss your situation more."

Sure she could. Scott would be furious.

And so would she—since she might be putting herself in even more danger and still not get the menace to back off.

"I'll think about it," she said.

"Whatever you do, please be careful," Dan said.

"Of course," she responded, and felt even more depressed and worried as they hung up.

With clearly nothing accomplished.

Sure, Dan seemed to give a damn about her, but was what he was doing enough? She doubted it.

Nella had an urge to throw something and looked at the computer and tissue box and other items on the desk.

But that wouldn't make her feel any better.
Only resolving the situation would.
She needed to figure out a way.

Chapter 20

It was midafternoon. Scott and Nella were just driving back in his SUV from the Chance Police Department. After the most recent text, he had wanted to have Nella's phone checked by the tech staff there, and one of the best, Officer Gil Jonas, a part-time technology officer, had been the one to help out. They had also spoken with Vince again and Assistant Chief Kara Province, as well as K-9 cops Maisie and Doug Murran, letting them know about the latest threat sent directly to Nella's phone.

But the fact they'd gone to talk to the authorities didn't give away what the shelter was, even if someone happened to notice who they were or where they came from—only that there was some kind of issue they were looking into. He'd made sure that Nella understood that. She wasn't putting the shelter into any further danger by disclosing this latest incident to the local police and getting their additional help in trying to solve it.

"You doing okay?" he asked her now. She certainly looked okay. She sat straight in the passenger's seat, staring out the windshield as if assessing every business in town that they passed, every person on the sidewalks, every car they saw going the other direction, to determine which contained her enemy. The shelter's enemy.

And therefore Scott's enemy.

"Yeah," was her curt reply. She looked over at him. "I just wish there'd been something to lead your coworkers to the source of that text, even though it was sent from yet another burner phone—of course."

"Of course. And I just hope your buddy Dan finally gets his people to locate the remaining gang members so we can determine at last whether you're right and they're the ones making these threats."

Which was the logical assumption, but if it wasn't them, Scott and the Chance PD needed to know that, too, and figure out who it really was.

And stop them.

For now, he was doing what he could to help Nella get through this.

"So, are you ready to be the primary interviewer of our visitors this afternoon?"

"Absolutely," Nella responded. He was delighted to see her smile at him. This was a wonderful distraction, he figured. The shelter had been contacted by several potential adoption families, and one was coming to visit this Sunday afternoon—after some really deep vetting by Telma, Camp and Scott. The last thing they needed was to allow someone inside who could be the person menacing the shelter—and Nella.

They soon reached the parking area behind the shelter. Scott parked the car and reached into his pocket for the keycard for the door through the back fence.

He got out of his car and started walking over to help Nella get out—and protect her when she did.

Only—he was immediately shocked and furious when she not only got out on her own but began running across the street. As soon as he looked where she was headed, he understood. A dog ran loose in the park area. No people were around at all, let alone any chasing him. And he appeared ready to run into the street.

"Nella, go inside," he yelled at her. "I'll come back out and get him."

Which was when a car started barreling down the street toward the dog—an old brown sedan, with darkened windows so Scott couldn't see the driver.

"No!" Nella cried, and continued running.

But the car didn't seem to be after the dog. Instead, it veered toward Nella.

"No!" Scott echoed, knowing there was no time. He'd already clicked open the rear door to his vehicle and now dug down into the back padding—where he had stashed a weapon.

He aimed it toward that driver he couldn't see.

But the driver must have seen him, since he started zigzagging, then gunned the engine and zoomed forward—without hitting Nella or the dog.

"I— I— Thanks," Nella called to Scott, sounding almost hysterical. But did she change what she had been up to?

No. She dived forward into the park and soon, somehow, caught up with the loose dog—a Jack Russell terrier mix. Sweeping it into her arms, she hurried back across the street to where Scott still stood near his SUV after putting the safety back on and thrusting his gun into his pocket and out of sight.

Some people near the businesses at the sides of the park area—the hardware store and sports gear store—had apparently seen some of what happened, and a couple headed in their direction. Scott immediately herded Nella toward the shelter door, which he finally unlocked, then locked again behind her.

He had used his phone to take pictures of the rear of the fleeing car so the make could be identified, and he believed he'd also gotten the license plate number.

Was that the same person who'd been threatening Nella?

Damn! If he'd only had a way to stop that car. Take the driver into custody, then check into background information.

But now… He held his hands up toward the approaching, concerned people. "Everything's okay now, folks. But did any of you recognize the car? The driver? The dog?"

No one appeared to, but Scott nevertheless called Camp and told him to come out here right away, briefly explaining what happened and telling Camp to interview the people who'd drawn closer because of the car.

But Scott figured they wouldn't be able to supply much, if any, useful information. One of the guys, a youngish Asian man, said, "That looked like my neighbor Bill's old car, but I thought he traded it in for something else."

So it could have been stolen from a used car lot, if

that was the case. Well, it wouldn't hurt to get whatever information this guy could supply.

And right now, Scott hid his fury. With Nella, for going after that dog. He could understand why, but she also knew she was under threat. And the person who had threatened her might have let that dog loose to bait her—and been driving that car.

But he was also furious with himself for not being in a position to stop it.

Camp arrived, and Scott took him aside, then sent him over to conduct the interviews.

And Scott headed inside the shelter.

"What a cute little guy," Bibi said when Nella approached, holding the dog she had just rescued. Bibi was in a group of staff members clustered near the food building, working on training dogs with the commands Nella had been teaching them. Bibi was working with Honey, the highly intelligent black Lab mix who seemed to get the hang of the commands easily.

"Yeah, he is, isn't he? But don't let us interrupt you." Still, Nella allowed the staff members present to make a fuss over her new charge, including Muriel, Kathy and Leonard.

"What's his name?" Bibi asked.

"I don't know." Nella hadn't had time to check for a collar with an ID tag, but she did now, and there wasn't one. "Why don't we just call him Jack for now?"

"That's appropriate," Bibi said, and the others agreed.

"Right now, I'm going to take him in there." Nella gestured toward the nearest kennel building. "Since he was a stray, I have to assume he's hungry, so I'll give him a little afternoon snack." Nella would ensure that

Jack got onto the same schedule as the other dogs as long as he was here, with two meals a day plus treats for obeying commands and otherwise.

First, though, she intended to ask Scott to take her to a nearby veterinarian so she could get Jack scanned for a microchip. Too bad Scott hadn't yet found a vet to hire here, as he was attempting to do. That would save time and be easier. But for now they would rely on the one they'd been using. It would be a whole lot better if they could find Jack's owner right away.

Where was Scott now? She found out after taking Jack inside the nearest kennel building since he joined them immediately. All the other dogs were outside with staff members, so the fenced enclosures at the perimeter of the large room were all empty.

No sense putting Jack behind a fence just yet, but Nella got some kibble and wet food from the usual cupboard and put it in a bowl for the white-and-brown dog, then placed the bowl onto the floor nearby. The poor little guy leaped right at it, scarfing down the food as if he hadn't eaten in days.

Maybe that was the way he always ate, but people here at the shelter would learn that if he wound up staying for a while.

And as Nella watched him, grinning and pleased that she'd done something else to help the stray, she saw Scott come in through the main door.

"Looks starved," he commented, also looking down at where Jack inhaled his food.

"Yes, poor thing. I'm glad I saw him when I did and was able to grab him." She knew her look and tone were defiant. She recognized she had put herself in danger and had known better. But she had possibly saved this cute little life, and she had no regrets, since neither of them, nor Scott, was hurt.

"I'm glad you're both okay," Scott said. He drew closer to Nella, as if he intended to put his arm around her, but instead just stood there, still looking down at the pup, who was now licking the empty bowl. "And in case you're interested, the car that nearly hit you is probably one reported stolen from a used car lot yesterday. It reappeared just down the street from there a few minutes ago. The theft was reported to the police, and so was the apparent recovery."

"That sounds too much like someone stole it with that specific use in mind." Nella didn't like how her tone quavered, and she crossed her hands over her chest. "I assume it'll be checked for fingerprints under the circumstances, right?"

"Yeah, I've talked to Vince and he promised to let me know the outcome. But you know what I think."

He didn't make it a question. "Whoever it was probably wore gloves and did everything else to ensure nothing was left that could identify him—or her."

"Most likely." This time, Scott moved to plant his tall, muscular body right in front of her with his own hands crossed over his chest. "And if you ever do anything like that again—"

"What? You'll kill me?" Nella attempted to sound joking, and she figured Scott would do all he could to ensure no one hurt or killed, her. But she still felt her eyes tear up, and this time she knelt on the concrete floor and scooped Jack into her arms before rising again. "Hey, little fellow," she said to the dog. "You and I will be just fine now, won't we?" She hugged Jack so their faces met and he licked her, then looked back at Scott. "So, didn't you say I'm to interview some potential adopters this afternoon? When are they supposed to arrive?"

Scott looked at his watch. "In about half an hour."

"Excellent. I'll look forward to it. Any idea which dogs they might be interested in—or at least what size?"

Scott just looked at her, in a way that made her realize he was scared she could have gotten hurt—or worse.

But she was who she was. She might be here to help take care of people under protective custody, but part of the job was also talking care of the animal residents. Which made her feel even more like trying to ensure that other animals, too, remained okay. Like poor little Jack.

Carefully setting the dog down on the floor, she approached Scott, who just stood watching her. "Look, Scott," Nella said quietly, fists now clenched at her sides as she looked up at him while trying to figure out what to say. "Thank you. And I'm sorry if I'm not living up to your expectations as a manager here. But—"

"That's not—" He paused before continuing. "I certainly didn't expect to take on someone else needing protective custody when I hired you, but I can't control that. What I can control is what I do about it. And that's to do my damnedest to make sure you're not hurt, either." He kissed her then, and little Jack immediately started barking near their feet.

Nella shared in that kiss, but both broke away quickly at the cute, shrill noise. "Looks like Jack wants all the attention." She grinned down at the little dog, then back up at Scott.

"I'd say so." Scott was smiling, too, and Nella felt so much better then that the distance that had suddenly, reasonably, begun growing between them had now evaporated, at least somewhat. "Now, let's go wait for those potential adopters."

Scott realized that, no matter how much he wanted to back away from Nella if she insisted on ignoring the realities of the danger around her, he simply wouldn't do that.

And so, he was the one to lead little Jack outside on a leash and turn him over to Bibi to take him on a walk around the shelter path. Then Nella and he went to the reception building to await the potential adopters.

Who became more than potential.

Following the process posted on the shelter website, the Clavers had contacted him before they came and let the managers research their backgrounds and ability to take on a dog and treat it well. Scott had talked to each of the adults on the phone, as well as friends, neighbors and coworkers, as he always did.

It was a family in which both parents were teachers, the father at a local elementary school and the mother at a high school. Their kids were school-age, and they also brought along a grandma who lived with them—and would mostly hang out at home with whatever dog they adopted.

Which happened to be Pebbles, the Maltipoo. Pebbles seemed happy to be hugged and talked to and immediately included in this family that seemed so perfect to take on a new pet.

Nella appeared thrilled. Scott was, too. And even staff member Darleen was okay with it. Though she loved Pebbles in particular, she had already expressed the hope that the Maltipoo would find the right forever home as soon as possible.

At least for this moment, all seemed wonderful here

at the shelter, and for both Nella and him—and for Pebbles.

Scott just hoped it would stay that way—and intended to do everything he could to ensure it did.

Chapter 21

Over the next couple of days, Nella remained alert. On edge. Concerned.

And found herself surprised.

No additional threats, for one thing. No cars coming after her, though of course she remained inside.

Nothing new to worry about—although she continued to worry. After the car incident, which ramped up her fear, she expected something even worse as a follow-up.

But all seemed well. No threats, by text or in reality.

Not that she dared to feel safe. All she could do was wait. And allow herself to worry just a little less. Maybe.

She wasn't the only one. She discussed the lull, if that's what it was, with Scott. He, too, remained alert. He didn't consider the short time much of a lull—but he also seemed to let himself relax, at least a bit. He even visited his own home more.

But he still stayed in his apartment at the shelter at night. And he checked on Nella often and stayed with her, at least for a while, each night.

He also talked more with his contacts at the Chance PD and let Nella know about those conversations. Still no further word on who'd stolen the car—or driven it at her. Whoever it was had apparently been as careful as they'd suspected not to leave prints or other identification in the car, which remained under police control for now.

Nella was delighted when Maisie visited now and then with her K-9 Griffin, and told the managers that she and her brother Doug, with his K-9 Hooper, patrolled the area often.

Meanwhile, Nella's routine at the shelter working with animals, mostly dogs, was highly enjoyable, maybe even more than before. She walked along with staff members as much as possible, accompanying Baby a little less but having Spike at her side most of the time. Fortunately, she didn't necessarily need to have a K-9 nearby besides the visits from Griffin.

Strange, after all that had happened before and the immediacy of the threats? Yes. But she certainly wasn't complaining.

And she did remain wary, for her own sake and for the staff members.

Meanwhile, she had lots of fun with those staff members who took turns working with Jack. Telma was the one to take him to the local vet to check for a microchip, but there wasn't one. If Jack had had a family before, there was no way to identify them.

Of course it was a policy, at this particular shelter, not to send out social media notices about found animals, because the entire point of this place was to remain as private as possible.

They would respond to any inquiries, though, which Scott had shown Nella came in frequently, since the fact that this was an animal shelter wasn't hidden, just not publicized much. And the few other animal shelters in the area let people know to check for lost pets at the Chance Animal Shelter, just as this shelter also told inquiring people about the others.

But no one, no shelter or owner, appeared to be searching for Jack.

Now it was Wednesday morning. "You're our manager in charge for the day," Scott told Nella quietly as they sat at breakfast, after she had taken Spike for a walk alongside Bibi with Jack and Warren with Cheesecake. "We have a potential new staff member arriving around eleven, and I'd like you to conduct the initial interview. I'll be with you, of course."

Nella knew the other managers conducted that kind of interview on their own, so she recognized Scott wanted to make sure her first interview went well. But she figured this could also be another protective effort on his part, a good thing. He had undoubtedly vetted whoever it was, since the person was coming at a scheduled time, as was the general practice.

But with all that had been going on lately, she appreciated that Scott wasn't just assuming what he'd found was the person's whole story. What if it was a gang member, or someone else who'd issued threats—or driven that car—who'd lied and worked out some kind of proof because they wanted access to the shelter… And, possibly, her?

"Sounds good," she told him. "Can we meet first to go over what you know so far?"

"Of course."

They got back to eating, sitting at one of the regular tables with others. Nella talked to some of those staff members and made plans to conduct another brief training session after she watched them feed cats and the smaller animals. As was standard now, she'd already observed some feeding dogs that day, ones they'd walked as well as others, after their earlier outings but before breakfast.

Yes, today all seemed normal around here.

If she kept her mind off those latest threats…

Once more, when she was done eating, she retrieved Spike from his enclosure in the reception building and brought him outside. Most staff members joined her, bringing leashed dogs to work with, including their most recent new residents—Bibi still with Jack, Warren with Cheesecake and Muriel with Samson. The other staffers brought some longer-term canine residents, including Kathy with Baby, Nella was glad to see. As a result, the sort-of class Nella taught just outside the main office building was busy.

With Spike as her companion and example, as usual now, Nella had no problem working on basic canine commands—and she'd been doing it here long enough that she didn't see any staff members having problems with their dogs. Jack, though, did require a little more effort to get him to obey, but he remained a newcomer, after all—and he was an energetic Jack Russell terrier.

She allowed her training session to go on a little longer than usual, which didn't seem to make any dogs, except maybe Jack, obey less. Scott had gone inside the office building when her class started, which was fine.

But she watched for him. When he reappeared, she

figured it was time to go prepare for the interview she'd be conducting in a little while.

"Okay, gang," she called to her crowd. "Class over. Go walk your dogs some more, or play with them, or both."

"Thanks, teacher," called Warren, followed by Bibi's echoing "Thanks" that was then repeated by pretty much everyone.

Which made Nella feel good, especially when she didn't see a single dog balk at heeling beside its trainer as the group disbanded—not even Jack beside Bibi.

She thought about taking Spike right back to his enclosure in the reception building but figured she could do that later, when she went to greet the person she'd be interviewing, who would enter the shelter via the reception room.

For now, she and Spike headed toward where Scott still stood near the office building.

"How'd it go?" he asked as they reached him.

"Really well." Apparently he hadn't watched much, which was fine—though Nella did feel a small pang of disappointment. But he couldn't—shouldn't—be with her all the time, especially when nothing major was going on. And she had seen Camp and Telma observing from this area on and off, so there had nearly always been another manager nearby.

But she had been the manager in charge, which she liked.

Especially when she didn't have to worry about immediate threats against her—or worse, the shelter and any of its occupants.

Was this just temporary? She certainly hoped not. But there'd been no conclusion...

"So what should I do now to prepare?" she asked Scott.

"Let's go to my office. I'll show you the results of my initial research on this woman—who showed me by phone and secure email that she was a viable protective custody candidate, and why it appeared what I learned was potentially correct. Then we'll talk about what you should ask, not too different, though, from the way you treated Alice when she—and you—first got here."

"Great."

That research discussion went well, and Nella felt comfortable waiting with Scott, and Spike, until the shelter phone rang and the interviewee let them know she was in the reception area—which they already knew, thanks to the security cameras. They told the woman someone would be right with her and headed back downstairs—where they first dropped Spike off in his enclosure, and a couple of the other dogs greeted him.

Then they headed to the reception area. Its occupant was a woman who matched the description and photograph Scott had received, midtwenties, moderately deep-toned skin, long black hair pulled back in a clip—very attractive, Nella thought. Except for her haunted, frightened expression as she looked from Nella to Scott and back again.

"Is this—is this the shelter that's looking for people to join the…staff?" she asked quietly. Apparently she'd been given at least some information by whoever suggested she come here or during her initial vetting process.

"That's right," Nella said. Scott remained behind her, holding the door into the shelter open. "Please, follow me," she told the woman.

In a minute, they were inside one of the last interview rooms along the hallway just before the dog enclosures nearby, including the one holding Spike. Nella told their guest to sit down. Then, referring to some information she'd entered into a file on her phone, she began quizzing the woman.

Her name was Angie Black. In her midtwenties, she came from San Francisco. She had recently ended an engagement to the son of a tech magnate who was CEO of a major computer company.

That hadn't gone well. Her fiancé, from a family with such power, had exerted some of it over her, threatened her, abused her horribly and promised more revenge. Soon.

So here she was.

And after a short while and a few phone calls to contacts Scott had at the San Francisco PD, plus a visit to see how she got along with the dogs in the enclosures in this building at the moment—Spike and others of various sizes and temperaments—and a visit from Telma and Camp for their okay, their new staff member, now called Denise, was hired. She'd been told to bring clothes and other supplies as if she'd been heading out on a trip, in case anyone saw her, though she'd been warned to stay silent about where she was going and why.

When asked, she seemed to feel fairly confident she'd not been seen by her ex-fiancé or anyone else, since she'd left in the middle of the night and took her time driving here—but hadn't stopped for anything. She'd loaded up on gasoline and snacks stealthily before getting on her way.

And now she appeared a little more relaxed than when Nella first met her.

Nella, carrying some of the supplies Denise had brought to the reception area, showed the newcomer upstairs to yet another apartment on the floor where hers and Scott's temporary one were located.

Nella still hoped things would change so she could have a choice whether to move someday. But not now. She certainly couldn't count on just a couple days' worth of peace to mean all the threats were over. Especially after the last one.

But, oh, how she wanted to…

Enough. She was a manager, and she had to reassure the new staff member she'd just hired.

"Make yourself at home," she told Denise. "I'll come back in half an hour and take you back downstairs. I'll show you around, introduce you to some of our shelter pets and to some of our other staff members, too, who have different, yet similar, stories to yours."

Of course she didn't mention the recent threats to the shelter, or to her—or the car incident. Scott and the other managers and she would now take care of Denise, so she wouldn't have to worry about those threats or any from her former life.

Not anymore.

Scott had thought Nella was a wonderful person from the moment he had met her. That opinion kept growing.

She had done a great job interviewing Denise that morning. At lunchtime, she'd introduced their new staff member to her new comrades. The others knew not to quiz her on what had brought her to the shelter—at least not here, in the group. If she wanted to talk about it with any of them, she could do so later. And Nella, in introducing her, had made it clear, with no detail, that

Denise unsurprisingly shared a similar background to the others.

After lunch, it was dog-walking time again. Once more, Nella took charge of introducing Denise to the routine, though she did let the young woman know that if she didn't want to walk dogs, at least not now, she could keep cats or the smaller animals company. Before getting a response, Nella showed Denise around the entire shelter complex, including the cat house and the other small animal enclosures inside it.

Scott didn't watch them. He knew he didn't need to. But he did go upstairs to the offices during the introduction to check on a few things—including making sure no threatening messages appeared on either the shelter's email or phone.

Of course the most recent one had come on Nella's private phone, but he felt sure she'd let him know if anything like that happened again.

Or anything else.

Although, thanks to the way he had this place rigged, nothing as scary as that car chasing Nella was likely to happen inside the shelter, against her or anyone else.

He would continue to make certain of that. And never forget, despite the lull of a day or two without threats, that those prior ones still hung over Nella.

When he returned to the central walking area after his visit upstairs, he saw Nella with Denise, who had Honey, the black Lab, leashed beside her—and Nella, unsurprisingly, had Spike.

He approached them. "Everything okay?" He bent to give Spike and Honey a pat, then straightened to aim a smile at Denise.

She still appeared nervous, dark eyes uneasy, but she said, "Yes. Thank you. Thank both of you. I'm so glad

I'm here." Still holding Honey's leash, she reached out and hugged first Nella, then Scott.

Since he'd conducted quite a bit of vetting before he permitted his contacts at the San Francisco PD to send her, Scott felt comfortable with her being here. "You're welcome," he said, and was amused when Nella made a gesture that caused Spike to bark his okay, too.

Chapter 22

Late that afternoon a family and a solitary man came in at separate times to look at pets available for adoption, so the staff members were sent upstairs to their apartments, or to meet in the community room on the floor above.

That was a good thing in multiple ways, Nella figured, because she was able to discuss with Denise on her first day here how the adoptions worked—and also make it clear that no staff members could be seen. The place needed to appear like a regular shelter to visitors, and staffers needed to stay away for their protection. Only managers brought visitors around to see potential pets.

The results that day were uneven. Despite visiting all areas containing dogs, the family didn't find one they wanted to adopt. However, the man chose Rover, the Scottish terrier mix. As usual, the potential adopters had sent information before coming, and Scott had checked them out. Since they'd been approved, the man already had an okay to bring a dog home—which he did.

Nella wanted to cheer. And maybe cry a bit. She would miss Rover, as she missed the others adopted since she started working here. But they all should have much happier lives with their new families, despite the love and attention they received from staff members and managers.

Scott was with Nella as she went inside to let the residents know the results—and to get someone to clean the enclosure where Rover had been living, even though a couple of other pups also stayed there. But it seemed more final to do a last cleanup. More closure for all the people here.

When Scott and she went to the meeting room above the apartments, where most residents were hanging out, including Denise, they were immediately asked whether any adoptions had occurred. Nella let them know about Rover, and everyone seemed excited. She told them then that it was okay for them to come downstairs when they were ready and got assurances from Bibi and a couple of others that they'd clean the enclosure where Rover had been.

On her way back downstairs, following Scott, her phone rang. She didn't get many calls these days, but that worried her less than if she'd heard the sound of a text coming in.

She pulled her phone from her pocket and looked at the ID. Dan.

"Hi, Nella. I'm calling because I've been thinking even more about the idea of starting a shelter here. I've been looking around, conducting research and talking to appropriate people—making sure they understand the need to keep it quiet—and really think I'm making progress."

Nella had stopped at the base of the stairs in the building housing the apartments, meeting room and dining area. Scott, who'd been in front of her, was already outside. "That's great." She leaned against the wall, smiling toward the door where she'd last seen Scott. "I'll be so excited to hear when you've actually got something going. And I'm really glad you're keeping me informed."

"Well, that's the thing," he said. "As we told you, we'd really like for you to be part of the process. And though I know you haven't been at the Chance shelter long, you've already seen a lot more about how it works than we really know. It would be fantastic if you'd return and take charge of getting this off the ground. You could always stay in touch with your contacts there in case you have any questions. Also—well, you've indicated you received some bad messages there. You'd be away from that here."

"Unless they came from those gang members still at large," she reminded him, hearing how chilly her voice had suddenly gotten. "And this shelter isn't secret, just who the staff members are and why they're really here. I assume it would be the same there, so those gang members, if they're the perpetrators, would probably cheer if I get closer to them again."

A silence—and Nella noted Scott back in the doorway, arms crossed. His good-looking face was marred by a curious scowl. Well, she'd tell him later about this call. Or maybe he'd figured it out if he'd been eavesdropping.

"Okay," Dan finally said. He didn't sound particularly happy as he continued, "Look. I'll bring Jon and come back up there this weekend, maybe stay longer this time so you and the other managers can give more insight into what we'll need to do, okay?"

"I think so. Just a sec." Holding her phone off to the side, she approached Scott and quickly, in a low voice, conveyed that part of the call.

Scott nodded. "Okay with me if it's okay with you."

Nella's turn to nod, and she got back on the phone. "Yes, it's fine. But when you know when you'll actually arrive, let me know and we'll schedule the time, since we always schedule appointments with visitors— and that's something you should know in case you do open a similar shelter. While you're here, maybe we can figure out more things to demonstrate for you, okay?"

"Sure." And Dan ended the call.

"Why are they coming?" Scott asked as they started walking outside along the usual dog pathway.

"Because they want to learn more about how to start a shelter like this," Nella told him, "but I'm not intending to go to L.A. to show them what I know."

"Good," Scott said. "It's easier to protect you here."

"Like I'm one of the staff members," Nella grumbled. "But you're right. And I appreciate it. I'm hoping it's all over after that nasty car attack, but—"

"But we can't count on it," Scott finished.

Still, the rest of that Thursday went just fine, with staff members doing their usual thing of caring for the animals. That now included Denise, who'd jumped right in and joined the others. She appeared a lot more relaxed than when Nella had first met her. Of course, she was under the shelter's protection now.

Then there was a visit from a couple of managers of a pet shelter in a town twenty miles away. Coming straight into the reception room, where Nella joined Scott and Telma to meet them, they brought two dogs and a cat that they hoped Chance Animal Shelter would take in and find new homes for. They'd already been in touch with Scott, who'd scheduled their arrival, then took a quick look at the pets—and accepted them: Fräulein, a dachshund mix; Sheba, an Old English Sheepdog; and Silver, a small, gray feline.

Things seemed quite normal for the rest of that day—and night, considering what had started to become normal for Nella and Scott. He stayed at the shelter in his apartment there, despite nothing going on at that moment, at least nothing that obviously required extra surveillance or protection. Although they had to remain constantly alert, of course. And Nella was happy to have him around. It wouldn't last forever, but she would enjoy their spending time in her apartment as long as she could.

She realized she was developing deep feelings for Scott—a bad idea. Did he feel the same? Who knew? They of course didn't talk about such things. They were boss and employee and had already discussed that whatever they did was consensual—but it was all physical. Still, she would enjoy what she could while it lasted.

Friday started out well, too. In fact, very well. After Scott and she met for breakfast—he had gone back to his home very early in the morning—he came outside while she walked Spike with some staffers, two of whom had newbies Sheba and Fräulein with them, and another had Jack. She then did a brief training class.

When she was done, he came up to her and said, "I think it's time for you to learn more about another aspect of being a manager—doing the official vetting process, both for potential staff members and for potential adopters."

"Yes!" Nella was delighted with the idea. It would give her even more insight into what they wanted in both kinds of situations.

Telma and Camp rounded up some staff members to visit cats and other pets after they returned the dogs to their enclosures. As Nella followed Scott to the offices, the thought crossed her mind that what she was about to learn would be essential if she ever wanted to help start and run a place like this, like in L.A. to help Dan.

She immediately erased the idea from her mind. That wasn't on her agenda, and although she didn't mind helping with advice, she had no intention of working directly with Dan to start his shelter. Or his buddy Jon, either. She had no idea how the two of them intended to share duties.

Scott showed her the blank file format she would need to complete for each potential staff member, then the one for potential adopters. They discussed how to fill in the initial blanks, including, with staffers, their names, addresses, who had suggested the Chance Shelter to them, and what was the torment in their life that made such protective custody necessary.

He went over with her some online sites they subscribed to for learning as much as possible about those people. Next was the list of questions to ask the authorities who had referred them here.

After that was the beginning of vetting one of those people who had just recently gotten in touch. Scott told Nella to begin handling it herself. She was delighted. She found it fascinating.

They soon broke for lunch, but though Nella, as always, enjoyed the group meal—including with Scott—

she couldn't wait to get back to the analysis she had just started.

By midafternoon, she believed she had enough information to show Scott, who had gone back into his office, that the person they were analyzing did appear to fit their guidelines.

She stood from behind her desk and started walking toward her office door—when her phone made its noise indicating a text message. She froze. Surely—well, it had been a great couple of days, but her first thought was that she had received yet another threat.

She was right. This one said:

Enough. I left you alone for a while—after I chose not to hit you with the car—but you're still there. It's nearly time. You're nearly dead. Get out now, and I'll back off. But if not, not only will you die, but I'll first tell the world what that damned shelter is all about and make sure the people your residents are hiding from know where they are. And then? Who knows? An explosion?

Nella gasped. Another threat against her—and worse. A threat against all the people being protected here, and even the animals.

But she'd hoped that whoever had it in for her wouldn't harm anyone else.

Now she had to assume the increased threat was true.

It was time for her to leave—unless she could determine a way to truly protect Chance Animal Shelter.

But this was something she absolutely had to show Scott, maybe go with him to the police station again. In any event, the local cops needed to see it. The entire shelter could be horribly affected. She ran into his office.

On the phone, he looked up at her quizzically. He immediately said goodbye to whoever he'd been talking with and hung up. Obviously her panic was showing.

"What's wrong?" he asked. Nella handed him her phone, and he scowled as he read it. "Damn, I was waiting for the next shoe to drop, and here it is. Sit down." He waved at the chairs on the other side of his desk. "I was just talking to Vince anyway, and now I'll call him back. We were discussing the situation, questioning the few days of nothing after those nasty threats and what might happen next. Now we know."

"But— Okay, Scott." Nella stood in front of a chair but didn't sit down. "I really think it's time for me to—"

"Move back to L.A.? Where we can't protect you?"

"Where I can, in a backward way, protect you and the shelter. If that person will let the world know what this shelter is all about, and even possibly blow this place up, I can't stay."

Scott stood and walked around the desk. He handed Nella her phone back, and she noted his other fist was clenched. "Can you be absolutely sure leaving will help? We don't know who it is, or what the actual agenda is, or why. And even if you leave, who knows whether it'll end the threat to your life?" He stepped even closer and put his arms around her. "It's time for us to concentrate even more on figuring this out—with you here, helping. And staying safe."

"But—"

He pulled her closer. "No buts. Got it?" He bent and gave her a short but sensual kiss. "We're together on this and the shelter."

Nella wasn't about to cave—but she also knew she'd better not tell Scott that at the moment. "Okay," she said. "But—"

"I said no buts." Scott kissed her again.

And of course Nella participated gladly despite continuing to shiver. But she also figured she would be able to exit the shelter with support and even protection if she left with Dan and Jon when they visited that weekend.

Scott called Vince immediately. Fortunately, Nella sat down and watched him. If she'd left, he would have had to go with her. He wasn't about to let her out of his sight, not even this late in the day on a Friday.

Would she really attempt to move back to L.A., and on her own? That was exactly what the monster apparently wanted—where he could control or kill her.

She needed to stay here. Period.

And in case she didn't get it, that was part of what he said in his conversation with Vince.

"Hey," he said when Vince answered the phone. Scott continued to stare at Nella as he told Vince about this latest threat. "Whoever it is said they'd not only tell the world about all our residents in protective custody but this entire shelter, too, and its purpose. And maybe even blow it up."

"You're kidding." Scott had put Vince's call on Speaker so Nella could hear, too, and he watched her wince at Vince's yelled response. "Okay, I've pulled back the patrols around there slightly but I'll increase them again, including unmarked cars. I'll also get our K-9 team and others to patrol the entire area on foot even more. But that's not going to prevent whoever it is from blaring out the covert stuff on social media and otherwise. What do you think we should do?"

Before he could answer, Nella said, "Hi, Vince. I'm here, too. I—I think I ought to just leave town. Maybe not go to L.A., though. Just…well, figure out a way to disappear, kind of like our staff members do when they come here."

Scott wanted to jump across the desk and grab her. Shake her. Somehow instill some sense into her.

But Vince responded first. "No way," he said, his voice even louder. "You'd still be giving the suspect just what he—or she—wants. Or close to it. With no assurance of silence or your safety. No, you stay there. You got it? The Chance PD will do all we can to help you and your shelter—without you losing your life."

Yay, Vince, Scott thought. He reacted just the way Scott hoped he would.

"And I'm sure you and the rest of your detective team will beef up your research and resources so we can find this suspect immediately, right?" Scott asked.

"Right."

"I appreciate that," Nella said. "And maybe you can aim more resources toward your efforts, but you've already been trying to find whoever it is."

Scott had been watching her face, and at the moment she seemed expressionless. Her tone was calm and cool.

And she didn't look into his eyes.

"We'll just try harder," Vince said.

"Well, thank you." But Nella didn't sound convinced.

Scott couldn't blame her.

Vince and he finished the conversation after a quick rundown of what the Chance PD would start doing the next day, besides keeping an eye on the shelter that night. Plus, they would have their tech staff start searching all social media sources to see if the Chance Animal Shelter was mentioned—and outed.

If he was consistent, the jerk who'd put them into

this mess would again give Nella a day or so to comply before continuing his battle against her.

Not that Scott would allow her to leave, of course.

For now, Nella stood and left Scott's office, heading downstairs. So did he.

During what was left of the afternoon, he watched as she interacted with staff members as usual, along with dogs they worked with. She kept Spike by her side.

But would that skilled, senior K-9 be able to help her if, in fact, the intimidator did show up and try to kill Nella? Maybe, but it would depend on how the act was attempted.

Of course Scott encouraged Nella to keep the dog with them at dinner, and, later, when Nella retreated to her apartment.

Scott joined her there later, as usual, to be with her during the night. But he felt not only hurt, but damned angry, when Nella wouldn't let him stay.

"I need to be by myself," she told him. "And—well, you need to understand that I will make my decisions by myself, too. I want to protect the shelter and its residents—and managers—the best way I can. Tonight, I'll consider what to do next, whether I stay here as you want, or leave. Thanks for trying to protect me your way. But I need to think this through on my own."

And with that, she gently closed the door in his face.

Chapter 23

Nella missed Scott that night. Terribly.

And not just the sex.

She loved having him around to talk to. To discuss the shelter and where it was going, the new arrivals—both human and pets—the adoptions, the existing staff members and managers, and... Well, she missed talking to him about everything.

And, darn it all, she missed his protective spirit. She couldn't help feeling extremely concerned—for herself, and for the shelter and its residents. Scott always paid attention. He also somehow helped to calm her and make her believe, at least on some level, that things would be okay. That *she* would be okay.

When she got up in the morning even earlier than usual, showered and prepared to go downstairs to walk dogs and work on more training lessons, she missed him even more. She felt as if the perpetrator was hanging around outside, ready to hurt her.

And had maybe already endangered the residents by making their location and backgrounds public.

Could that person find the secret information about the individual staff members? If so, how?

He or she knew about the shelter and its purpose, so maybe they had unlimited resources.

"What am I going to do, Spike?" Nella asked as she prepared to leave the apartment. The wonderful K-9 had been with her all night, sleeping on a blanket on the floor. Now the shepherd looked up at her and gave a little whine, as if trying to respond to her question.

Before she unlocked the apartment door, her phone made its text noise. She froze. Another threat? Had the person already started telling the world about this shelter and its people?

Was Nella about to get shot as she opened the door?

The last was the least likely, considering the shelter's security and the police patrols. But even so…

Nella swallowed as she pulled her phone out and looked at the text. And relaxed a little. The message was from Dan. He and Jon were running late and would be at the shelter that afternoon. They would be at the shelter around two o'clock and had booked a hotel room for that night. Two in the afternoon seemed to be a good time for them.

A silly thought crossed Nella's mind. Could they be the ones issuing the threats? Did they want her to return to L.A. that much, to help them open their new shelter?

Ridiculous. For one thing, they wanted to open a similar shelter, which wouldn't work if they publicized this one's purpose to the world. For another, she was their friend and former coworker. Threaten her life? Why?

Still, she would find a way to question them without seeming to on their arrival. And she recognized that, though she doubted it was the case with them, she considered everyone a potential suspect.

As usual when Nella reached the center of the shelter, she saw several residents out on their morning dog walk. She joined them with Spike, greeted them all warmly and gave the dogs quick pats. Then, they all walked until it was time for breakfast.

Nella saw Scott outside during the walking time, but he didn't greet her, just watched—as if surveilling the place for any obvious danger. Which he probably was.

His ignoring her hurt, but it wasn't unexpected after her attitude last night.

At breakfast, he sat down with Telma and Camp, who were already at the shelter and had begun to eat. Scott didn't invite Nella to join them, but there were several free seats near them, and she was, after all, a manager, too.

She took a chair beside Telma, not Scott, and Spike settled down at her feet. She'd already fed him the regular dog food breakfast that the other dogs got—but she'd picked up some extra toast from the buffet table that she could break into little pieces and feed a small amount to him.

Scott did say good morning as she sat down, as did the others, and he continued to stare as if to see if she had cracked yet.

Well, she hadn't. Not exactly. But she did ask, glancing toward Camp and Telma, "Do they know?"

Both nodded before Scott could say anything.

"Nothing's going to happen," Camp said between gritted teeth.

"Not on our watch," Telma agreed.

But how could they be so sure—especially about whether the shelter and its purpose would remain secret?

Well, Nella told herself, she couldn't be positive, either, even if she left. But...whoever it was appeared to be focused on getting her out of there, which made her continue to believe it was a loose gang member seeking revenge.

On her, though. Not on everyone else.

Which meant she had to leave, at least for a while, to attempt to save this place and everyone here.

It might be serendipitous that Dan and Jon were coming that day, since she could use her desire to help them as her excuse to leave the shelter—although Scott, of course, would know better.

Nothing particularly exciting happened at breakfast, and when they were done, Nella managed to take Scott aside and ask if he'd be contacting Vince again to ask whether the Chance PD's techies had found anything online that was worrisome about the shelter.

"That's my plan," he said.

"Good. I'll come with you." Before he could agree—or not—she called out to the staff members that her training class would be held in an hour or so rather than now.

She and Spike accompanied Scott to his office. And she was relieved when Scott put Vince on speakerphone and heard that so far it didn't appear that word had gotten out about the shelter.

Nella nevertheless adjourned to her office and also did some online research. Not that she was a tech expert, but at least she felt a little more relaxed when she couldn't find anything about the Chance Animal Shelter except the aspects of it that they did want the world to know.

She spent an hour on the computer researching, then studying her instructions again, before heading back downstairs to work with staff members and dogs, then going for lunch.

Around two o'clock, Nella received the call she had been expecting. Dan and Jon were in the reception area. Scott had been observing the lessons, and she let him know where she was heading, and why.

He insisted on going with her. Which felt good. The reception area was more open than the rest of the shelter, although she figured Dan would have told her if anyone besides Jon and he were in there waiting.

Nella, hanging back a bit with Spike on his leash, let Scott unlock the door into the reception area and enter first. Sure enough, the only people present were Dan and Jon. Both wore T-shirts and jeans, clearly not on duty now. Dan had a frizz of hair around the back of his head, as if he was letting what was left of his hair grow a bit. He stepped forward and gave Nella a hug.

Jon also came close to her when Dan and she had released one another but just smiled, his light blue eyes gleaming. Then he petted Spike, who sat down and looked up at him in pleasure. "So, you ready to teach us everything else we need to know to create a place like this in L.A.?" Jon directed his remark to Nella, even though Scott would have been the better recipient.

"Whatever I can." Nella refrained from mentioning that she might have changed her mind again and might return to L.A. with them. "And Scott will help even more." She looked at him with a gaze she hoped was beseeching enough. His outfit was similar to the others', although he wore a Chance Animal Shelter T-shirt.

Just looking at Scott hurt Nella. She didn't know if she was staying or not, and if she left whether she would wind up having to sever all ties with this wonderful, caring man—to help protect not only all the others around here, but him, too.

Fortunately, Scott nodded and agreed. After he unlocked the door, they all exited the reception room down the hall, and into the rest of the shelter.

"As I told you before, this area is off-limits except for invited visitors," she told Dan as they walked together into the central area, which now, as it often did, contained most of the residents walking or working with dogs. "You'll need to ask questions or tell me what else I can help with."

As Nella came toward them with Spike, most stopped, got their dogs to sit at their sides, and looked at her.

It was time for her to provide a class.

She explained that to their visitors. "It's now a fun part of the program for those under protection," she said. "They're here to help with the animals, and taking the time to work with them and teach them helps the people, too."

"Got it," Jon said. "I like dogs, in case you couldn't tell." Which Nella figured after he'd petted Spike. "This will be enjoyable. In fact, if you have a dog available that I can try handling, I'd like to do that."

Nella was happy with that idea. It would be excellent for one of the people founding the new shelter to have firsthand experience like that.

After a little bit of maneuvering about who was walking who, she made Sheba, the Old English Sheepdog who was a newcomer to the shelter, available for Jon to handle.

Nella was happy to see Sheba and Jon do well in the training session, as did the staff members with other dogs. She noted Scott and Dan standing near each other off to the side, watching and talking. Was Scott filling Dan in on what was going on here? She hoped so, especially if there was anything new in the LAPD hunt for the missing gang members.

Or was Scott using the opportunity to tell Dan why she couldn't return to L.A. now for any reason, no matter what her own opinion was?

She worried about that, even as she kept up an excited and pleased front while demonstrating dog commands and helping her students work with the canines at their sides to make sure they all performed correctly.

She had a feeling she needed to talk to Dan about training. Maybe Jon, too. Fortunately, she was impressed with how he worked with Sheba. He would surely be able, without her presence, to handle dog training at the shelter Dan and he would build. But... Well, she was leaning toward helping them in person for several reasons.

When the session was over, while Scott excused himself to go talk to the other managers, Nella and Spike walked with both visitors through other areas of the shelter, including the cat and small animal enclosures—although Nella left Spike leashed outside while they did that. Then they went upstairs to look at the apartment building and Nella's unit, so they could see what one was like. She also took them to the next level to see the small community room there.

After that, she took Spike back to his enclosure, then led the men to the dining room building and invited them for dinner later. "One of our staff members is our primary cook, since she's not as fond of animals as everyone else."

"Got it," Dan said. "But we've got other dinner plans unfortunately."

"And I don't understand it," Jon said, scowling at Nella till his expression changed into a teasing smile. "Why would anyone not be fond of animals?"

She was surprised at how Jon was acting. He wasn't coming on to her at all anymore, which was a good thing. Instead, he really seemed to like animals and to want to get that new, special shelter going and be part of it.

"But how do you feel about people?" Nella said, half-teasingly. She had seen in person that Jon was a good cop, so protecting people in need was probably part of who he was. He'd done a good job on the antigang task force, at least, as her best backup.

The three of them stood in a tiled corner of the empty kitchen near the large oven. "I like them," Jon responded, smiling broadly. "You know that. And I can't begin to tell you how much I appreciate what's being done at this shelter for people as well as animals. The form of protective custody here seems amazing—particularly giving them new identities. I can't wait to be part of something like this," he finished. "And—well, I'd like to know more about why you're not willing to come and help us get it started."

Nella looked from Jon's face to Dan's, then down at the floor. "At the moment, I'm seriously considering coming back to L.A. with you tomorrow."

"Really?" Dan was the first to react, folding his arms over his thick chest, his brown eyes focused on hers. "Why?"

Nella sighed. They should know about the latest threat. They'd heard at least generally about the earlier ones. And this one was the worst—especially if they were going to attempt to start a similar shelter that could come under threats like this, too.

And so she showed them the text message. "I'm torn about whether to stay here while the perpetrator is sought and stopped. I really want to be around to help." She didn't mention that Scott was so insistent about her staying and remaining under his, and this shelter's, protection.

"But it sounds like not only are you in danger here, but so is everyone else if you stay." That was Jon, and he looked down to peer sharply into her eyes with his blue ones. "You've got to come with us, even if you don't want to stay forever. But it'll buy some more time for the authorities to find the perp and save this place— not to mention you."

"I… I'm wondering about that," Nella said. "And whether that perp could be one of those escaped gang members. And—well, can I let you know tomorrow if you'll have another passenger in your car?"

She looked at Dan, assuming he was the main driver. She would want to ride with them for security now, then find a way eventually to get her car back to L.A. if she didn't return.

"Well, one of us will. We drove separately, though we're staying at the same hotel. I wanted to make a stop on my way back to L.A. tomorrow and didn't want to hold Jon to it."

Which probably meant Nella would ride with Jon if she left. Well, okay. He was, at last, behaving like a gentleman.

"Do it," Jon said now. "It sounds like there's every reason for you to come with us—helping to start our shelter, and…well, potentially saving a lot of lives. Including yours."

"You may be right," Nella said with a sigh. "And right now, my inclination is to come with you."

* * *

"That's what she said!" Bibi was nearly crying. Warren and Sara didn't look much better.

It was late afternoon. They had joined Scott in his office. Apparently Bibi and Warren had come into the kitchen a short while ago to get a cooking demonstration from Sara—and had overheard Nella, Dan and Jon, who'd been standing in a far corner, talking. They had remained quiet and just listened.

The three staff members had therefore heard about the latest threat, which was bad enough. But they had also come to count on Nella and her soothing, teaching presence.

They understood why she'd said she would leave— possibly to save all of them. But under the circumstances, they assumed the worst. Nella would get murdered anyway. And the shelter, too, might be doomed.

"Can you at least get Nella to stay?" Bibi finished. Scott was used to seeing her smiling, revealing the gap between her front teeth.

She was definitely not smiling now.

"And save all of us," added Warren. The thin senior looked frazzled. Could his hair have become even grayer because of the stress? "Or let her go, if that will make sure we're all okay. It sounded like she'd be okay that way, too, and so would the rest of us. I like this place. I want to stay here—safely—and even do more to help."

Damn. Scott wasn't surprised that Nella had told her former coworkers about the threat, including that she was ordered to go back to L.A. or face death—and other horrible consequences for the others.

But he'd thought he had convinced her to stay here

under his protection, and that of the Chance PD, which would continue to search for the source of those threatening texts—and also search for anything online or otherwise that indicated the threat of making the shelter's underlying purpose public.

"I—I don't know what to say." That was Sara, who just sat there. She always appeared sad—but not as sad as now. And frightened.

"You don't need to say anything," Scott reassured her. "I'll talk to Nella and see what we can do." He didn't tell them he knew of the threat. He didn't need to. They all assumed he'd have heard, he figured, via Nella or otherwise.

The staffers left his office, and Scott called Vince again. Still no news, but the patrols around the area continued. And nothing had been found on social media or otherwise about the shelter.

So now what? Sara had gone downstairs to plan dinner. The others indicated they would work with some of the animals again.

And most likely inform the other staff members what was going on, if they hadn't already.

Things only got worse, since Nella and he didn't speak much as they ate as usual at the same table at dinner, although she did mention her friends had other plans for that night. Otherwise, she appeared to be attempting to ignore him, although their eyes caught frequently, and she just looked away.

As the meal ended, Nella stood and told the crowd she would be leaving the next day to go help the cop friends who'd been visiting that day start a similar shelter in L.A. She didn't mention the threat—or that she believed she would be saving all of them if she left. In any case, she apparently hadn't bought into his assumption that her leaving would only make things worse.

Most people there were clearly upset by the idea of her leaving, even if only for a while, as she implied.

Then Bibi stood, crossed her arms as if in defiance, and said, "We know the real reason."

Nella blinked. "How?"

"We heard you talking to your friends. And we still don't want you to go."

And all the other staff members nodded in apparent agreement.

"Thank you so much," Nella said, her eyes glistening with tears. "I wish things were different. I'll miss you all."

The rest of their time in that room was filled with hugs and tears from others, as well.

Scott realized he should at least be glad the woman he had most recently hired as a manager had done so well, gotten so many of their residents to care about her.

She left the dining area before anyone else, though. Without saying goodbye to him. Well, that wasn't the end of it. When the other managers had left the shelter and the staff members had gone to bed, Scott went to Nella's door and knocked gently. He saw her peer out the peephole, then unlock the door. She moved away and let him come in, which he did despite the wary expression on her face.

Once she'd locked the door behind him, she asked, "What are you doing here, Scott? If you think you can convince me—"

"I'm just here for one final night with you, Nella," he said, then took her into his arms.

Chapter 24

Nella woke early the next morning, in Scott's arms. He was awake, too, and they kissed.

The night had been wonderful. The end of a delightful affair.

Something Nella would really miss. But would feel better about if her leaving resulted in no one getting hurt, preferably not her, either—but definitely no one else.

"So you are staying here, right." It was as if Scott was trying to read her mind—which wasn't surprising.

"So you seduced me to get me to change my mind." She pulled away from him. But he was possibly right. Her mind had been reeling all night. Changed?

Maybe.

How could she leave this place?

How could she leave him?

Scott drew her closer again. "Not really. You're going to make up your own mind. I recognize that. But—I want you to stay with me, where I hopefully can protect you…and everyone else here. I've got backup here. And from what I gather Vince's tech people are ready to put out some social media posts that could negate any attempts to claim this shelter is anything but a nice animal shelter—by making it seem that other organizations are jealous and throwing stuff out there to harm us. That way, it's less likely that anyone will buy into the possibility this is a people shelter, too, except as a place where apparently some homeless folks can stay if they help the animals, but hey, they won't be in protective custody. Ridiculous. Or at least that's what will be out in public."

"I just wish there were some kind of guarantee that my staying here, with all that help, is the best course of action. I'd love to stay." Partly, she realized, because she loved Scott. She was admitting that to herself now, though not saying anything to him.

And when she left later that day, she would probably never see him again.

If she stayed, she would be terrified that whoever was making the threats would carry through with them. If she left, she would be the only one still in danger.

Yet could she be certain that he—or she—would back off simply because she obeyed and headed to L.A.?

Obeyed. She was good at obeying orders from her superior officers at the police department, of course. But orders from strangers? People whose identities she had no idea of?

"I'd love for you to stay, too." Scott had been hugging her close, and now he whispered into her ear. "There are no guarantees either way, but if you leave, I can't help you. And…we won't be together."

Had he in fact, as she'd thought before, come to bed

with her to get her to change her mind and stay? No, she had the sense that he was saying farewell, too. But even if that had been his reason…

"If I do stay," she said, her mind whirling, "I'll be afraid for everyone." What was the right thing to do?

"But if you go——" Scott began, his lips still near her ear.

"I'll still be afraid for everyone. And so——" Her mind stopped. At the right place? "Well, if you're sure, I won't just give in and obey faceless commands, at least not yet. Nothing happened after the first threats, and we can't be sure he'll follow through now."

"Then you're staying?" Scott backed off and looked her in the eyes. His smile was wide and appeared hopeful.

"For now, at least," Nella said. "But you understand, I assume, that I could change my mind at any moment."

"Yes, I do understand that. I'm already prepared to protect you and the rest as much as I can. And now, I'll do even more, if that's possible, to get this all worked out."

"I know you will," Nella said, and kissed him again.

Not that Scott didn't trust Nella, but he understood how hard it was for her to make this decision, since one way appeared to put people she cared about in danger and the other only her—maybe. Fortunately, she recognized there were no guarantees either way.

He hoped she was serious about staying and would remain that way. And so he couldn't have been happier, or prouder, at breakfast after that morning's dog walking, to hear her say to the staff members and other managers as they sat at the tables, with Spike now, as usual, at her feet, "Everyone, I've been told some of you heard my conversation with my prior associates yesterday. I've been thinking hard about this. I just don't know what's real and what isn't, but I'm worried for all of us…and don't think my leaving to go back to my previous home is necessarily going to stop anything from happening. And so—well, I may change my mind again, but for now I'll stay here and do all I can to bring this situation to a safe end. But I want each of you to be alert, too. The Chance PD is keeping an eye on us, but if you hear or see anything out of the norm, please be sure to tell one of the managers, including me." She paused and look around.

So did Scott. He didn't hear what anyone was saying, but a lot of people talked to one another. Telma, across the table, only looked at them, her expression hard as if she didn't particularly agree, but she fortunately didn't say anything. Alice sat beside Telma, and after talking to Bibi, at her other side, and Warren, beyond Bibi, she stood and clapped and said, "We're glad you're staying, Nella. And we'll all be fine." Then she glanced at Scott and asked, "Right?"

"Look, everyone," he said. "None of us knows who this person is or what his intention really is, so as Nella said, please be careful and let us know if you see anything unusual. No matter what's out in public, you're all still under our protective custody. So let's all protect each other."

Later, as everyone left, each stopped briefly by Nella and sounded supportive, although Scott would have liked to know what each of them was actually thinking.

Nella made a phone call outside the dining area to her visiting friends Dan and Jon, then let Scott know the two LAPD cops would be at the shelter again that morning. They arrived, as they told her, only half an hour later since their hotel was nearby. Scott didn't hang around while they talked to Nella as they all wandered around the shelter again for a couple of hours. Nella, Spike beside her, apparently pointed out more details regarding the animal—and people—care.

Scott was in the central court of the shelter when the two men got ready to leave a while later. They came over to say goodbye.

"Like we said before, this place is really something," Dan told him. "And though we'd really like Nella's physical presence while helping us, she's promised to advise us via phone and internet as much as possible—and said you would, too."

That wasn't really a question, but Scott figured that acknowledging he'd be happy to provide what guidance he could would help them leave without attempting to twist Nella's arm any further. "Absolutely," he agreed.

He joined Nella, who had put Spike into an enclosure, in walking them back to the reception area. They all shook hands and said goodbye. Scott noticed Jon's doleful look as he told Nella they'd be in touch soon. Apparently he had really hoped Nella would go with them and help in their planning, but though both these guys had apparently had some role in the gang task force Nella had been involved with, he didn't fully trust them to take care of her—at least not the way he would. After all, they hadn't saved her partner.

Of course, not trusting them was also his unvoiced excuse for urging her to stay, he recognized. But, though she could still change her mind, he was relieved to see Nella send them on their way without joining them.

Then she turned to him. "I just hope I did the right thing, especially for everyone here. But those damn threats, especially the last one—if I was certain it was completely true, I'd have gone with them."

"I know you would," he said, then, since they were alone in the reception area, he took her into his arms. "I wish we could predict the future—and, most of all, lay our hands on that damn menace and end this once and for all."

Then he kissed her.

Despite wanting it to go on forever, he soon pulled away. "Let's go upstairs to my office. I want to call Vince again and see what's going on from the Chance PD's perspective now—since you didn't comply with the terms of the latest threat. Not that they wanted, or expected you to."

"I get it," Nella said. "And let's also push Vince to tell us what we should do now to help them find that horrible jerk."

Nella couldn't know whether she had made the right decision, at least not yet.

And if it turned out to be the wrong one? Well, there was no way she could guarantee she would be the only person to get hurt.

Not that she could have been certain all would be well if she'd gone with Dan and Jon back to L.A., either.

For the moment, she walked through the cat house alone. Not even Spike was with her, though she figured she would go get him out of his enclosure when she left this building. She appreciated his K-9 company—plus the idea that he would protect her, if he could.

As would Scott.

But could she adequately protect both of them?

She heard some fierce meows from behind the chain-link fencing of the nearest enclosure and reached inside to stroke the two cats, one gray and the other sable. Both cute. Both needing real forever homes, rather than having to stay here for such a long time.

At least some staff members took them out of their enclosures for a while every day and let them explore the small indoor garden at the back of the place. But that wasn't enough.

They needed freedom.

So did Nella—even though she had asserted her own ability to make decisions. But with those threats looming over her—and others—she didn't feel free.

While she stroked the kitties, Denise and Leonard came in. Denise seemed quite relaxed these days despite knowing about the threats, and even wore her long, dark hair loose, unbound like the rest of her. Nella had seen young Leonard playing with cats before, so she wasn't surprised.

Knowing the cats would now have company, Nella left to go get Spike and walk him around a bit more. When she had put him on his leash, her phone rang.

It was Jon. "Hi, Nella. We were just about to leave town but came up with another question, something else we'd like to see at the shelter before we go. We're in the reception area now. Could you come out and get us?"

"Sure." Nella would of course do all she could to respond to their latest questions—but hoped they wouldn't try to get her to change her mind and leave with them. As she headed toward the front building with Spike, she didn't see a lot of staffers outside with dogs, but some of those who were out appeared to be working with them, training them the way she'd demonstrated. She smiled and waved, and continued on. Of course Jon was one of those she could take through the shelter with staff members out and about, but she'd have to decide if that was appropriate now.

Inside the building, Spike and she passed the interior enclosures and the few dogs within them, which today included Jack and Cheesecake. Spike and she soon reached the front, where Nella used her keycard to open the door into the main reception room. Then, she locked it behind them.

Inside, she only saw Jon, dressed as casually as before, his short blond hair somewhat messy. Assuming Dan was still outside, she asked, "What do both of you want to see? And where's—"

"Dan? My buddy, fellow cop and boss on this shelter project?" There was a nasty tone to Jon's voice and a sneer on his face. "Like we told you, we drove here separately. He's already on his way to L.A. And I'm here to pick you up and bring you along."

"But I told you before—" Nella began, then saw him draw a gun from his pocket and aim it at her. She blinked, looked him in the eyes and asked, "What's this about?"

"Oh, I think you know. I've been interested in you for a while now, and you ignored me. Even worse, you were one of those designated to run that special anti-gang task force, even though I'd requested the post and I'd been with the LAPD a lot longer than you. Even my assistance to you was hardly recognized. And now, with our dear Deputy Chief Dan's stupid shelter idea. I wanted you to at least notice me as more than a fellow cop. To care for me. And to be there to support me if there was another task force formed or something similar where I could be in charge. Be my backup this time. But you didn't even promise to come back to our department, let alone show that you liked me or would do anything to help my career. I even sent those damn text messages, to get you back to L.A. But you've been stupidly stubborn, and now I'm going to smarten you up. Now, tie up that damned dog, and let's get going."

Jon. He had been the one to send all those threatening texts and undoubtedly drove the car at her, too. Had he intended to follow through and kill her, and reveal everything about this shelter, if she didn't go back to L.A. today? And pay attention to him? And—what? Engage in a romantic relationship with him? Get her support somehow for bettering his career? Both?

No matter what, that wasn't going to happen.

And now—Spike was sitting beside her as she still held his leash. He was quivering, the wonderful K-9 aware something was wrong.

At least he wasn't growling. But if he did, if he leaped on Jon or did anything else, would Jon shoot him?

She couldn't let that happen.

But she wasn't armed.

All she could do was hope that Scott was on alert, was—

She heard a keycard scrape against the door behind her and turned slightly. The door opened, but it wasn't Scott who stood there.

No, it was Warren.

"Go back!" she yelled, unsure why he was there but not wanting him to get hurt. "Tell Scott what you see here." Like, this man holding a gun on her.

"Oh, I don't think so." Gray-haired Warren grinned maliciously, then closed the door as he came into the room. What was going on?

Who was he?

Nella stared at him. "But—you're one of our staff members. You need to leave here for your own safety."

"Nah. I'm fine. Should I tell her what's going on?" Warren was looking at Jon now. And Jon hadn't moved the gun toward Warren. It was still aimed at Nella.

"Sure." Jon shrugged as if he didn't give a damn.

Warren explained he'd only become a staff member a short while before Nella's arrival. "My partner was after me, so I didn't lie. I was just lucky to learn about this place when I did, got here not long before you did. What I didn't say—but had been able to hide—was that while my partner and me were both in the car business—not real estate—we provided cars to the gang members you were after." He giggled. "Now, thanks to Jon, I can stay here, out of sight. I'll help the new LAPD task force catch my former partner and the rest of the gang, then still stay here and let Jon know who to send to the shelter as a staffer and why. I'm fine hanging out at this *wonderful*—" he exaggerated the word "—shelter." Nella shuddered as he winked at her. "Or maybe I'll go back to L.A. and join what's left of the gang after my former partner is in jail, although if Jon winds up in charge that might not work. Still, lots of choices. And they're partly thanks to you, since I got in touch with Jon after he came to see you. I told him who I was. And I even helped him already. Guess who stole and drove that car at you at his request, at a time I knew you'd be returning to the shelter. Plus, that little dog, Jack, just happened to be wandering the street at the right time. It was fate, right? Of course I had to aim him in the right direction. But it worked, though I wished I'd been able to run you down. Even so, Jon said he'd honor his promise if I helped again now, that he'd lead his fellow officers to my partner and bring him down, so I can finally return to my car business if I want."

Nella moaned inside. She should have thought about the fact that Warren had claimed his business partner had driven a car at him when she'd had the same thing happen to her. It should have been a clue—even though she had no idea how this staff member had gotten outside the shelter. But seeing what he was like, he had probably stolen a key and somehow gotten away with it.

And she hadn't thought that was who Warren was. He'd seemed to be a good guy, a staffer who liked animals, had a fun attitude sometimes and needed protection.

He wasn't what he seemed.

Neither was Jon. She might not have seen him as dating material, but she hadn't thought he would resort to something like this to get her attention. But more important, and she hadn't realized it before, he'd been jealous about her running the task force despite his apparent attempts to help her. He certainly couldn't think she would ever give him positive attention after this, or that she'd ever support him as head of a task force or anything else. But he'd certainly seemed to want her back in L.A. Why? So he could dispose of her there? But rather than insist she get in his car with him, it looked like he might kill her now. Then, despite his apparent promises to Warren to ensure his safety here, would he reveal the shelter's purpose to the world?

Whatever he planned, she had to stop him.

And now Warren, too, aimed a gun at her. Where had he gotten that? She figured it had to be one of the weapons hidden for the managers at the shelter. This man had certainly found ways around a lot of the safeguards here.

"What, you're going to shoot me, too, Warren?"

Nella knew she sounded not only skeptical but furious. And she was angry. With both of them.

If only she'd realized before who her threatening foes were.

"Sure," the senior said, smiling. He looked ready to shoot—so Nella did the only thing she could.

"Spike, attack!" she shouted, letting go of her dog's leash as she leaped toward Jon, knocking his arm aside and then making sure Spike had Warren's wrist in his mouth. He did.

And now Nella hoped that her belief in this shelter, her belief in Scott, would all be realized. Fast.

But she couldn't count on anything. She had to act.

"You damn—" Jon began, but Nella got hold of his arm and attempted to wrest the gun away. But he was a cop, too, and wasn't about to let go.

Only—the door into the shelter opened again. This time, Scott came through it holding a gun, followed by Telma and Camp, also armed.

Scott got control of Jon and handcuffed him, and Nella told Spike, "Drop it." The wonderful K-9 let go of Warren, and Camp then handcuffed him, too.

"How the hell did you know I was here?" demanded Jon.

"You forgot, this is a very special shelter," Scott said with a large smile that Nella ached to kiss. "We've got lots and lots of hidden security cameras." He motioned toward a couple of them, one hidden at the side of the floor and more in the upper corners of the room. "They also provide alarms if they're filming anything. So— Jon whatever your name is, I'm still a member of the Chance Police Department—and you're under arrest. Warren, too."

Chapter 25

Scott couldn't have felt more relieved. It was over.

He had Nella in his car beside him now, with Spike in the back seat, and he was driving them all to the Chance PD.

Immediately after subduing the suspects, he had called Vince, who'd had cops in a couple of the cars already patrolling the area come in and take Jon and Warren into custody.

Now Nella kept looking over and smiling at him. She'd already thanked him, several times.

"I can't believe it's actually over," she said to him, not for the first time and echoing his own continuing thoughts.

"Believe it," he said. "Although we'll all still have to stay on guard. I figure Jon was telling the truth, but we'll need to remain careful in case there's more to it than that. We'll need to continue to both protect our staff members and to watch for any indication that someone else is making the purpose of our shelter public."

"Our shelter… I wonder if Dan will continue to try to start one in L.A."

They'd already called him from Scott's car to let him know what had happened.

"What?" he'd blasted. "Damn! I'm turning around. Will be back there soon."

After further conversation, it didn't sound as if he was going to stick up for his fellow LAPD officer Jon.

In addition, Dan let them know that he'd already increased the number of officers tracking down the remaining gang members, formed another, experienced, task force, but now he'd make sure they focused on their assignment even more. "It's way past time to bring that whole thing to an end," he said before they hung up.

Scott soon parked along the street near the police station. Nella didn't seem quite ready to run inside.

"I can guess how you happened to walk into the reception area right at the critical moment," she'd already told him.

"Like I said, security cameras."

Now she apparently wanted to talk more about it as she continued to sit beside him. "The shelter you started is so wonderful in so many ways," she said. "I was happy before about those security cameras you'd installed, and now I'm thrilled. They're all over the place, as they should be."

"Not in the rooms where people sleep." He winked at her, and she flushed a little—appearing even prettier than usual, if that was possible. Yes, she wore a Chance Animal Shelter manager's T-shirt, as he did. But the fact she'd put hers on early that morning when she'd still been considering leaving made him recognize even more the turmoil she'd been going through.

Before she made the right decision.

And dealt with the consequences.

"Of course not," she said. "So I gather you were checking the videos they were taking—but why right then?"

"I think you know. I've been keeping an eye on you while I could."

"Because?"

"Because I've been worried about you. I'm always worried about you, and when you made public this morning the fact you were staying—" and he was definitely glad she was staying "—I was concerned that the person issuing the threats would finally act. Not that I knew who it was or how they'd find out, but I didn't want to take any more chances than I had to."

"Got it."

So he'd kept watch not only in his office but also on his phone screen. And saw what he feared—Nella in trouble.

He'd rounded up Telma and Camp immediately and rushed to the reception room, scared he would be too late.

But he couldn't be prouder. Nella had come through herself. She had sicced Spike on Warren and gone after Jon—and could have gotten shot much too easily.

But her way of doing it with the dog, and her own police training as she attacked... Well, it was still a good thing that he and the other managers arrived when they did.

And yes, it had all worked out.

Nella was fine. Thanks to the confessions of Jon

and Warren, Scott felt nearly certain there would be no more threats.

And Nella could now stay at the shelter and feel comfortable about it. She would be safe.

And he would be glad.

They went inside the station, where they first met with Vince. Yes, the two suspects were in custody. They would remain in solitary confinement so they couldn't announce to the world or anyone else, except their lawyers, the real purpose of the Chance Animal Shelter.

More meetings after that, where other police department members, including Chief Sherm, Assistant Chief Kara, K-9 Officers Maisie and Doug, and others, congratulated them both on a job well done.

Nella and he were, after all, still cops at heart.

Dan had arrived before they left and began talking with the officers in charge about his role and Jon's with the LAPD—and how he would cooperate in any way he could to ensure justice was done. He also swore, while looking straight at Nella, that he would ensure that the remaining gang members would be caught fast.

Which proved to Scott that Nella had a good friend in Dan.

Dan told her that he still hoped, someday, to open a shelter like the one in Chance—but without anyone to help, it would remain a dream for the moment.

Dan talked for a while longer with those in charge at the Chance PD.

Before too long, Scott, Nella and Spike were on their way back to the shelter.

It was as if someone had planned a welcome home party. Nella was thrilled to see all the staff members with leashed dogs in the central area when Scott and she got back to the shelter, and Telma and Camp were with them.

So was a woman Nella didn't know but believed to be Dr. Brenda Moran, the therapist. She'd glimpsed her that one time between patients outside the room she used for her sessions—in her thirties, blonde, nice-looking and grinning now as if she meant it. Nella had considered scheduling a time with her, but now didn't think she'd need it. Any PTSD she'd had was surely under control.

The whole crowd cheered when Scott and she and Spike joined them.

They also, Bibi at the helm, demanded to hear what had happened—and how Warren had been involved.

No need to hold anything back. A lot of it was captured on the security cameras' footage anyway.

Everyone seemed impressed—and grateful. Their positions here, in protective custody, had been saved.

Eventually, the crowd dispersed. Nella determined to turn the scant rest of the day into something ordinary—but she didn't really want to leave Scott's company. And so she worked upstairs for a while on her computer, researching to see when and if any site picked up on what had happened here and the arrests that were made.

Or anything new about the shelter.

Fortunately, she found nothing. And, checking with Scott a little later, he confirmed that the techs at the Chance PD hadn't located anything worrisome either but were ready to do counterposts if necessary.

After working a while longer in his office, Scott popped into hers and told her some good news. It wasn't a done deal yet, but he had found a veterinarian he thought would be a great fit for the shelter—working with both animals and people. They'd talked on the phone, but there was more to come before a decision was made.

For a short while, since it was very late in the afternoon, Nella did some initial vetting of a few potential adopters Scott told her about. Then she went out to walk Spike, who'd remained with her, and do some more training demonstrations.

Yes, she had rewarded Spike handsomely with treats for his wonderful K-9 help earlier, though she doubted he understood that he had done anything but what he should have—obeyed her commands.

Camp had apparently gone out to buy some wine that afternoon, so at dinner there were a lot of happy toasts.

Then it was evening.

Nella put Spike in his enclosure near other dogs for the night. She enjoyed having him around, but he was here not for her, but for helping out at the shelter—and, as much as she adored him, someday even getting his own perfect forever home, though he was a senior. Still, she gave him a big hug before leaving him—and realized she'd most likely keep him close on other nights, as she had before.

Nella assumed Scott would at last return to his own home that night. He didn't need to stay here with the excuse of protecting her.

After checking on all the animals one last time, Scott did hang out with her and others in the upstairs community room in the apartment building and watched a little TV. The staffers began to say good-night and leave.

"Guess it's time to head to my apartment, too," Nella finally said when they were the last ones remaining. "Are you staying here?"

"No, I thought I'd go home tonight. It's been a while."

"Good idea," Nella said, even as her heart plummeted.

Taking care of her had been a good excuse, but the need for that was over.

Spending this night alone—well, it made sense, though the idea made her sad.

"But you're coming with me, I hope," he said, surprising her, making her smile, reaching out his hand to clasp hers. "I think we made it clear to everyone that things are returning to normal, and that they need to immediately call one of the managers if anything happens in the middle of the night that needs attention. But I at least implied that though we remain on duty 24-7, we don't need to hang out here all the time, don't you agree?"

"I...maybe." Nella knew her voice was hoarse, and she was highly conscious of the feeling of Scott's large, warm hand holding hers. She grasped his, as well.

His beautiful blue eyes stared into her face, and his smile caused her to feel all hot and sensual and emotional.

"Then, if all goes as I hope it will," Scott said, "we can bring the supplies I brought to you at your place to mine soon. And we've hopefully learned some things about managing this place in the future."

"Yes, and I think I've got some further ideas about improving the way we handle things, including both our staff members' duties and the animals, and keeping things even more secure, and—" Nella hoped she didn't sound critical, because she wasn't. She loved this place as it was, and wanted to help it become even better.

"And it sounds as if you plan to stay here for a long time," Scott said.

Nella nodded, looking up at him. "Forever." Meaning it. She loved this place, and her career as a cop had come to an end—unless, of course, she could get hired by the Chance PD while she worked at the shelter, as Scott and the other managers did.

"Good. Forever." He bent down, and their kiss suggested… Yes, forever. "So hopefully you will also wind up staying soon in my house, too…forever."

"Let's start with tonight," she said hoarsely. "And then we'll see."

"Sounds good," he said, and, hand in hand, they headed toward the stairway that would take them downstairs—and, Nella hoped, toward forever.

* * * * *

Look for the next book in
Linda O. Johnston's Shelter of Secrets miniseries
coming soon from Harlequin Romantic Suspense!

WE HOPE YOU ENJOYED
THIS BOOK FROM

HARLEQUIN
ROMANTIC
SUSPENSE

Danger. Passion. Drama.

These heart-racing page-turners will keep you guessing to the very end. Experience the thrill of unexpected plot twists and irresistible chemistry.

4 NEW BOOKS AVAILABLE EVERY MONTH!

HRSHALO2020

HARLEQUIN

*Uplifting or passionate,
heartfelt or thrilling—
Harlequin has your
happily-ever-after.*

With a wide range of romance series that each
offer new books every month, you are sure to
find the satisfying escape you deserve.

**Look for all Harlequin series
new releases on the
last Tuesday of each month
in stores and online!**

Harlequin.com

HONSALE052

COMING NEXT MONTH FROM

ROMANTIC SUSPENSE

#2147 COLTON 911: TEMPTATION UNDERCOVER
Colton 911: Chicago • by Jennifer Morey

Ruby Duarte and her daughter are finally free of her ex—but his followers are still a threat. Damon Jones seems like a friendly local bartender, but he's secretly undercover and determined to take down a dangerous ring while keeping Ruby safe. But will his lies ruin any chance they have at a future?

#2148 COLTON K-9 TARGET
The Coltons of Grave Gulch • by Justine Davis

When he came to Grave Gulch PD, K-9 handler Brett Shea never expected to land in the middle of a criminal catfishing case. Annalise Colton may be a part of the family that seems far too entwined in Grave Gulch's police department, but she's also at the center of his current case—and Brett finds himself falling for her even if he's not sure the Colton family can be trusted.

#2149 FIRST RESPONDERS ON DEADLY GROUND
by Colleen Thompson

Determined to expose the powerful family that destroyed his mother's life, paramedic Jude Castleman knows he stands little chance of success. Then widowed flight nurse Callie Fielding comes up with a high-risk plan to find the justice they crave...if their own unstoppable attraction doesn't lead them into danger.

#2150 A FIREFIGHTER'S ULTIMATE DUTY
Heroes of the Pacific Northwest • by Beverly Long

Daisy Rambler's new job in small coastal Knoware, Washington, is a new start for her and her sixteen-year-old daughter, away from an abusive ex. When her daughter goes missing, local hero and paramedic Blade Savick comes to the rescue—but more danger lurks around the corner...

YOU CAN FIND MORE INFORMATION ON UPCOMING HARLEQUIN TITLES, FREE EXCERPTS AND MORE AT HARLEQUIN.COM.

HRSCNM0821

Get 4 FREE REWARDS!

We'll send you 2 FREE Books plus 2 FREE Mystery Gifts.

Harlequin Romantic Suspense books are heart-racing page-turners with unexpected plot twists and irresistible chemistry that will keep you guessing to the very end.

FREE Value Over $20

YES! Please send me 2 FREE Harlequin Romantic Suspense novels and my 2 FREE gifts (gifts are worth about $10 retail). After receiving them, if I don't wish to receive any more books, I can return the shipping statement marked "cancel." If I don't cancel, I will receive 4 brand-new novels every month and be billed just $4.99 per book in the U.S. or $5.74 per book in Canada. That's a savings of at least 13% off the cover price! It's quite a bargain! Shipping and handling is just 50¢ per book in the U.S. and $1.25 per book in Canada.* I understand that accepting the 2 free books and gifts places me under no obligation to buy anything. I can always return a shipment and cancel at any time. The free books and gifts are mine to keep no matter what I decide.

240/340 HDN GNMZ

Name (please print)

Address   Apt. #

City   State/Province   Zip/Postal Code

Email: Please check this box ☐ if you would like to receive newsletters and promotional emails from Harlequin Enterprises ULC and its affiliates. You can unsubscribe anytime.

Mail to the Harlequin Reader Service:
IN U.S.A.: P.O. Box 1341, Buffalo, NY 14240-8531
IN CANADA: P.O. Box 603, Fort Erie, Ontario L2A 5X3

Want to try 2 free books from another series! Call 1-800-873-8635 or visit www.ReaderService.com.

---

*Terms and prices subject to change without notice. Prices do not include sales taxes, which will be charged (if applicable) based on your state or country of residence. Canadian residents will be charged applicable taxes. Offer not valid in Quebec. This offer is limited to one order per household. Books received may not be as shown. Not valid for current subscribers to Harlequin Romantic Suspense books. All orders subject to approval. Credit or debit balances in a customer's account(s) may be offset by any other outstanding balance owed by or to the customer. Please allow 4 to 6 weeks for delivery. Offer available while quantities last.

Your Privacy—Your information is being collected by Harlequin Enterprises ULC, operating as Harlequin Reader Service. For a complete summary of the information we collect, how we use this information and to whom it is disclosed, please visit our privacy notice located at corporate.harlequin.com/privacy-notice. From time to time we may also exchange your personal information with reputable third parties. If you wish to opt out of this sharing of your personal information, please visit readerservice.com/consumerschoice or call 1-800-873-8635. **Notice to California Residents**—Under California law, you have specific rights to control and access your data. For more information on these rights and how to exercise them, visit corporate.harlequin.com/california-privacy.

HRS21R

Love Harlequin romance?

DISCOVER.
Be the first to find out about promotions,
news and exclusive content!

Facebook.com/HarlequinBooks

Twitter.com/HarlequinBooks

Instagram.com/HarlequinBooks

Pinterest.com/HarlequinBooks

YouTube.com/HarlequinBooks

ReaderService.com

EXPLORE.
Sign up for the Harlequin e-newsletter and
download a free book from any series at
TryHarlequin.com

CONNECT.
Join our Harlequin community to
share your thoughts and connect
with other romance readers!
Facebook.com/groups/HarlequinConnection

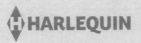

HSOCIAL2021